A FIRE
IN THE
NIGHT

A FIRE IN THE NIGHT

A NOVEL

CHRISTOPHER SWANN

CROOKED
LANE

NEW YORK

Published in the United States by Crooked Lane Books, an imprint of The Quick Brown Fox & Company LLC.

Crooked Lane Books and its logo are trademarks of The Quick Brown Fox & Company LLC.

Library of Congress Catalog-in-Publication data available upon request.

ISBN (hardcover): 978-1-64385-756-5
ISBN (ebook): 978-1-64385-757-2

Cover design by Melanie Sun

Printed in the United States.

www.crookedlanebooks.com

Crooked Lane Books
34 West 27th St., 10th Floor
New York, NY 10001

First Edition: September 2021

10 9 8 7 6 5 4 3 2 1

To Mom.

The gap of danger where the demon waits
is still unknown to you. Seek it if you dare.

—Beowulf, translated by Seamus Heaney

CHAPTER ONE

THE CABIN SAT AT THE ARROWPOINT OF A NARROW LAKE, MOSS carpeting the shingled roof in patches of juniper and verdant green. Beneath the moss the shingles were gray and weathered, some bleached nearly white. But the roof still held. A stacked-stone chimney jutted up from the back. The cabin's windows were dark but clean. The solid front door would not have looked out of place at the entrance to a stone tower. To the left, a covered porch held a cord of split wood, stacked and seasoned; at the other end of the house, a dusty SUV was parked under a carport. A short stretch of grass sloped from the back of the cabin to the lake, where the lawn curled sharply down to the dark water's edge, leaving no shore or beach. Rhododendron bloomed at the edges of the lawn and stretched up the rutted, unpaved drive, tall oaks and beech and maple rising full and green above the rhododendron, the entire scene—cabin, lake, trees—sitting in the cradle of three mountains as if in the palm of a gigantic hand.

The kitchen door opened and Nick stepped out into the carport, holding a bag of garbage. With his free hand he took a machete from a shelf by the kitchen door, then scanned the ground around his SUV. Satisfied, he walked to a trash bin at the back of the carport and dropped the bag of garbage in. He cocked his head, then headed to the front of the carport and looked up the gravel drive that ran into the trees. The low-gear whine of an approaching vehicle sent two squirrels scampering up a red oak. Presently a white Ford Explorer nosed its way down the drive between banks of dark-green rhododendron. Stenciled on each door of the Explorer was a gold star and the word SHERIFF, underneath which in smaller letters was JACKSON COUNTY. The Explorer emerged from the drive into a small gravel turnaround at the front of the cabin and came to a stop. The engine cut off, giving the illusion that the afternoon quiet had returned. Nick remained under the roof of the carport.

A man in the brown-and-khaki uniform of a sheriff's deputy stepped out of the Explorer, closing the door behind him with a solid *thunk*. He was tall and stick straight, his hands large and knobby. He sized up the front of the cabin, then walked up to the front door and rapped on it. He closed his hands into loose fists as if bothered by their size.

Nick stepped out from the carport. "Can I help you, Deputy?"

The deputy, startled, took half a step back. His right hand dropped to his holster, although his fingers didn't touch the butt of his revolver. Nick saw the deputy sizing him up: faded jeans, gray long-sleeved Henley, dark shaggy hair with threads of silver, the iron-colored blade in his hand.

"Professor Anthony?" the deputy said.

"Retired," Nick said.

The deputy frowned. "Sorry?"

"I don't teach anymore," Nick said. "So you don't need to call me Professor. But yes, I'm Nick Anthony."

The deputy glanced at the machete in Nick's hand. Nick lowered the point of his blade to the ground, then leaned it against the wall of the house. "There's a rattlesnake out here somewhere," Nick said. "Heard it this past week. Just being careful, is all. What can I do for you?"

The deputy took a moment to reorient himself, then took a step toward Nick. "My name's Joshua Sams," he said. "I think it would be better if we spoke inside, Professor." He clasped both hands in front of him at his waist, like a penitent.

Nick said nothing for a long moment. The deputy seemed content to wait. A blue jay gave a harsh cry from a nearby pine.

Finally Nick turned to the house. "In that case, I'll make tea."

INSIDE, NICK'S CABIN wasn't terribly unlike any other cabin built by newcomers. A small foyer off the front door, a dining room opening on the right, a hall bathroom and then a bedroom to the left. Passing through the foyer to the back of the house, Nick and Sams entered a great room that included a den, breakfast table, and kitchen. A set of stairs against the central wall shared with the dining room led up to storage and a guest bedroom. A stone fireplace rose in the middle of the back wall; behind that was a porch that stretched the length of the house and looked out at the lake. The house was clean and well maintained but somewhat plain. The only personal touches were a crimson-and-blue oriental carpet in the den, a little tin statue of a knight on horseback on the fireplace mantel, and the books in piles on side tables, stacked on the floor next to the sofa, lined on a low bookshelf backed against the stairs, displaying their spines. These weren't thrillers or coffee table picture books but hardcovers or trade paperback tomes: *The Canterbury Tales, The Civilization of the Middle Ages, A Distant Mirror.* Scholarly books, appropriate for a college professor of medieval studies. Aside from the books, the cabin almost looked like it could belong to a family from Atlanta or Charlotte driving up here in their SUV, kids tumbling through the rooms, maybe a dog.

Almost, but not quite. It wasn't because of the books, or how spartan the decor was, the furniture functional rather than elegant, the walls mostly bare of paintings or pictures. It had more to do with how quiet and still the cabin seemed, as if by simply walking into it Nick and Sams had disturbed something.

In his kitchen, a long island between him and the deputy, Nick saw the man taking in the house, then looking through an entryway into

Nick's office, tucked into the back corner of the cabin. Several more books on built-in shelves lined the walls. Sitting on a desk in the office was a photograph of a woman, fair-haired and smiling at the camera, a happy moment captured. Nick could tell by the deputy's expression that the man recognized the woman in the picture. Nick filled a teakettle with tap water and put it on the stove top, then rattled some mugs in a cabinet. "You like sugar, Deputy Sams? Honey?"

"Honey and lemon, if you have them," Sams said.

"Lemon's in the fridge," Nick said. "Fruit drawer, one down."

Sams dutifully walked over and opened the fridge, darting another glance at the photograph on the office desk. The inside of the fridge was about as spare as the cabin—a carton of milk, a package of ground beef, a half-empty jar of marinara, a stick of butter, ketchup and mustard in the fridge door. Sams dug around in the fruit drawer, found a lemon that wasn't yet soft. Nick placed a jar of honey on the counter next to a pair of mugs, a paper tag from a tea bag trailing from each.

"Got a knife?" Sams said, holding up the lemon.

With a nod, Nick indicated a block of knives next to the sink. Sams pulled a paring knife out of the wooden block and, with a clean cutting board, chunked the lemon into wedges. The counter top was wood, but the sink was a massive thing that looked like it had been carved out of a block of dark-gray stone.

"Soapstone," Nick said.

"What?"

"The sink. My wife liked soapstone, so we put in a farmhouse sink. Took four guys just to carry it into the house."

"Well," Sams said, wiping his lemony hands on a dish towel, "happy wife, happy life." As soon as he had spoken the words, he froze, his face blooming with shame. "I'm sorry," he said. "That was thoughtless."

Nick shook his head. "No worries," he said. "And the saying is true. Generally."

They looked at one another for a moment, the silence broken by the teakettle's whistle.

WHEN THEY HAD finished preparing their mugs of tea, Nick led Sams to the breakfast table and sat at one end, his back to the office area. Sams sat next to him, facing the window that looked out on the lake. Beyond, Whiteside Mountain rose into the blue sky, a tiered shelf of stone cliffs. "Beautiful view," Sams said. He sipped from his mug. "Thank you for the tea."

Nick's mug sat to one side, untouched. "What can I do for you?" he asked.

Sams nodded as if Nick had brought up a difficult point. "I'm afraid I'm the bearer of bad news," he said. "I would have called first, before coming out here, but—"

"I don't have a phone line," Nick said, finishing Sams's thought.

Sams nodded again, then put his mug down on the table and gazed steadily at Nick. "It's about your brother, Jay."

Nick gazed back, unblinking. "Is he in trouble?" he asked.

"No," Sams said. "I'm sorry to have to tell you. He died."

That hit home. Confusion, shock, and anguish played over Nick's face. His gaze was unfocused for a moment, and then his eyes locked on Sams. The tone of his voice changed from polite to somewhere just shy of a command. "What happened?"

"There was a house fire," Sams said. "In the middle of the night. Your brother was doing some remodeling, putting in wood floors in his house. Had some cans of polyurethane, a couple of rags. Looks like there was a bad electrical outlet. Spark caught those rags on fire, pretty soon the whole house went up. That's the initial assessment, anyway." Sams said this last part lightly.

Nick's eyes bored in on Sams as if tunneling through him. "You said 'initial assessment,' " he said. "Is there any reason to suspect something other than an accident?"

"Can you tell me where you were yesterday?" Sams asked.

Nick stared at Sams for a moment, then sat back and cleared his throat, disgusted. "I was here," he said. "Lex Matthews came by to replace a gutter. He saw me. Made sure to show me the new gutter was working. I can get you the receipt if you like."

Sams shook his head. "That's not necessary."

Nick tilted his head as if to look at Sams from a new perspective. "You already spoke to Lex," he said. "You think someone set fire to Jay's house?"

"The police in Tampa said—"

"Tampa?" Nick said. "Jay was in Tampa?"

Sams frowned. "Where did you think he was?"

"Last I heard he was in San Diego."

Slowly, Sams asked, "When's the last time you saw your brother?"

Nick leaned back in his chair. He was exhausted, worn. "It's been a long time," Nick said finally. "How did you find me, anyway?" When Sams said nothing, Nick continued, "Like I said, I haven't seen my brother in a very long time. We weren't . . . close. We have different last names. And if there was a fire, I'm guessing any records or address books burned up."

Sams considered him for a few more seconds. "Your brother's lawyer," he said. "In Tampa. He called the police after the fire, said your brother had listed you as his next of kin. Had your address too. Tampa PD called us, we said we'd touch base with you. They may have some questions for you."

Nick nodded absently, and then a thought struck him. "Was he alone? My brother? He's married—"

"I'm sorry," Sams said. "His wife Carol died in the fire as well."

Nick turned his head to look out the back window, but all he saw was a blank emptiness beyond the glass. He heard Sams sipping from his mug.

"How did they die?" Nick asked.

The question caught Sams off guard. He coughed, then cleared his throat. "Sorry," he said. "Went down the wrong pipe. Like I said, there was a fire. The whole house—"

"Were they burned or did they asphyxiate?" Nick asked.

Sams paused, his enormous hands now clasped together on the table. "They haven't completed the autopsies yet," he said.

Nick nodded and closed his eyes briefly. "Can you let me know if you learn anything else?" he asked. He opened his eyes, and he knew Sams could see the pain in them.

To his credit, the deputy didn't flinch. "Absolutely," he said. Sams stood, and after a moment so did Nick, their chairs scraping across the wooden floor. "I'm very sorry for your loss," Sams said.

Which one? Nick thought about saying in a burst of fury. Then, quick as a heartbeat, the thought was gone. He held out a hand, and Sams took it and shook.

"There is one more thing," Sams said. "The Tampa police only found your brother and his wife in the house."

Nick looked at him blankly. "I'm not following," he said.

Carefully, Sams said, "They didn't find your niece."

Nick swayed for a moment as if physically buffeted by the news. "My niece?" he repeated.

Sams considered him. "Annalise. Just turned sixteen. You didn't know?"

CHAPTER TWO

Nick shut the door behind the deputy and then stood in the foyer, head bowed, eyes closed. After several moments he heard the deputy's SUV start up, then the crunch of gravel as Sams drove off, the sounds of the vehicle fading away into the trees. Nick thought about sitting down right there on the floor, maybe lying on the cool wooden boards. Instead he went back to the table, gathered the mugs, and washed them out in the kitchen sink.

A niece. He was an uncle. Had been, apparently, for sixteen years. *Goddamn it, Jay,* he thought. He was too weary to cry. Over the past year he had cried enough for a lifetime. He wondered distantly if perhaps he was no longer capable of tears.

Something shifted in his heart, rode beneath his skin. He stood in his kitchen for a moment, trying to understand what he was feeling. Sometimes his own emotions were a foreign language he had to decipher. Then the answer came: anger. He was angry. At Sams, for disturbing his morning. At Jay, for not telling him about his niece. For dying.

He wasn't sure if the mug slipped out of his hands or if he dropped it. The mug shattered in the soapstone sink. A piece flew up and stung his cheek. When he put a hand up to his face, his fingertips came away red.

Oh, for fuck's sake, he heard Ellie say in his memory. She would say it in an exasperated way at certain mishaps, even though she was usually smiling when she said it.

That's what I'm going to name your canoe, he would say. *The* FFS Ellie.

She had always talked about getting a canoe, letting Nick paddle her around the lake while she trailed her fingers in the water. It was one of the few things he had not gotten for her, toward the end.

I am not going to cry, he thought. *I am not going to cry in my kitchen over a broken mug and another reminder of my dead wife.* But it was too late, and he gave in to the tears, weeping over the sink, his palms flat on the counter, shoulders shaking almost gently.

ACROSS THE LAKE, the mountain cliffs had cooled to gray as the sun slipped behind them into the west, and when the sun set the cliffs vanished. Moonlight and starglow would often coax them out of the darkness, but it was a new moon and a front had moved in from Tennessee, bringing a cool breeze underneath a heavy mantle of clouds.

Nick dropped another log onto the fire and watched the wood kindle, heard the water in the log squeak and hiss from the heat. Although it was June, the evenings could still be cool, and he preferred a fire. His laptop sat on a nearby ottoman, ostensibly so he could continue work on his newest project, a book on the Crusades that had stalled and proven difficult to revive. Instead, Nick poured a tumbler of whiskey, inhaled the scent of smoke and vanilla and sharp apple, and set the glass on a coaster next to his armchair. He gazed at the glass. It was a long-running contest—the idea was to try to convince himself that tonight would be the night he would take a sip. He wasn't an alcoholic, didn't have a drinking problem. It was more a kind of practiced asceticism, an active resistance to temptation. After a while, Nick picked up the glass and carried it to the sink. Not tonight.

He poured the whiskey down the drain, and as he did so an image flashed in his memory: a spilled canteen, water gurgling out into the dirt. With an effort he willed the image away, focused on the problem at hand.

One day. It had taken one day for the police to reach him. He knew part of that delay would be because he didn't have a phone—he'd had the landline disconnected after Ellie died. He felt a swirling sense of guilt. He hadn't been completely honest with Deputy Sams. He had not seen Jay in almost twenty years. But he had spoken to him by phone. Nick shut the door firmly on that memory; he didn't need any more ghosts. But he wondered why Jay had listed him as his next of kin, and why Jay's lawyer had felt compelled to call the police. With Jay and Carol's daughter—Annalise—missing, maybe the police had made a bigger effort to find relatives.

Something circled at the back of Nick's mind, like an errant bat. He sat patiently until it revealed itself.

His brother's teenage daughter was missing, yet Sams had not said anything about an Amber Alert or shared any theories about her disappearance—if she had run away, for instance, or even been abducted. Sams had mentioned her to gauge his reaction.

If the police were looking for her, it was because she was a suspect.

NICK MUST HAVE dozed, because when he opened his eyes, the fire was a glowing bed of coals. That and the single lamp were the only sources of light—the windows were black mirrors. Something had woken him up. He was making to get out of his chair when he heard it again: a scratching sound from outside, like a squirrel tentatively pawing at a porch screen. Except squirrels were like woodland ninjas and his porch was now open-air. Nick had discovered a nest of squirrels on the porch last winter by accident, stepping outside and seeing two of them on a rafter tucked up against the roof. After a short search he had found a squirrel-shaped hole chewed through a screen in a far corner of the porch, behind a chair. Nick had evicted the squirrels and removed the screens, which meant that right now he definitely wasn't hearing a squirrel chewing through mesh. And raccoons and possums were just as stealthy, unless they got into a trash can.

Nick stood, his senses reaching out, trying to locate the noise. There—a low scrape, definitely on the back porch, on the far side of the back door. For a moment Nick thought about the drawer in his office desk. Then he quietly walked out of the den into the foyer, opened the front door, and shut it carefully behind him. The air outside was brisk, his pores closing against the chill. He waited a few moments for his eyes to adjust to the darkness, and then he picked up the machete from where he'd left it leaning against the house when Deputy Sams had come to visit.

Nick crept around the near side of the cabin, past the stacked firewood, holding the machete with the blade down. Could be that rattler, slithering across the porch, but Nick didn't think so. Burglary wasn't unheard of here, although usually thieves stole from empty cabins after the summer folk and other tourists had gone home.

When he reached the back corner of the cabin, Nick crouched so his head was below the porch level, and then ever so slowly he raised his head until his eyes could peer over the floorboards. Faint light from the lamp inside the house shone through the back window, revealing a figure crouched on the porch. The figure was between the back door and the window over the breakfast table. His face was hooded. As Nick watched, the man raised his head and tried to peer through the window into the cabin. The man was slight—all the easier to wriggle into houses, Nick thought.

In a dozen silent steps, Nick made his way around the corner of the house and to the bottom of the porch steps. He raised the machete. "That's enough," he said, not shouting but speaking loudly enough to startle the man. It worked—the man whirled around, hands half raised. He held a long blade in one hand. At least it wasn't a gun. The last thing Nick wanted was to be shot in his own backyard. "I think you're out-knifed," Nick said, waggling the machete to make his point. "Put it down on the porch, slowly."

The man threw the knife. Nick ducked, and the knife hit a post and bounced off, skittering across the wooden steps. The man was already running for the far end of the porch. Nick took the steps in a single leap-ing stride, but he barked his shin on an Adirondack chair and stumbled, nearly falling onto his machete. He dropped the machete and ran, his steps thundering across the porch. The man was so fast—he was already sprinting across the side lawn for the trees. By the time Nick reached the trees, he could see about as well as a man in a box. He stopped, his breath like steam in the cold, and tried to listen over the pulse thudding in his ears. Footfalls, a cracking branch, but the sounds were muted, and reced-ing. If he ran into the woods after the man, he'd likely run into a tree or poke his eye out on a branch. By the time he could retrieve a flashlight from the kitchen, the man would be long gone. And a light would only reveal his own location.

Nick went back to the porch and picked up his machete, then looked at the window the man had been peering through. No sign of tampering on the window or the sill. He found the knife the man had thrown at him at the foot of the porch steps. It was a kitchen knife, long and curved, the kind of thing you'd use to carve a roast. A lousy handheld weapon. For a moment he thought about evidence, fingerprints. Then he picked up the knife and carried it and the machete inside, going through the back door, which was unlocked as usual, the screen door squalling as loud as any alarm system. He left the knife on the kitchen counter, locked both the back and front doors, put the fire screen up to cover the hearth, and then went to bed, the machete propped in a corner of the bedroom.

WHEN NICK WOKE, his first thought was of Ellie. She had been in his dreams again, this time dancing away through the trees at night. There was a fire on a mountain peak ahead, and Ellie was leading him there, winding up a path of twisting tree roots, a granite cliff rising on his right. He couldn't see Ellie. He called to her, and her laughter floated back to him. Then he opened his eyes, the dream gone.

He sat up in bed. The light through the bedroom windows was color-less. He saw the machete leaning in the corner and recalled last night: the man on the porch, the short chase. He rubbed his face with his hands. He needed a shave, a good night's sleep, a week of such nights. What he really needed was Ellie. He would have to settle for coffee.

In the den his laptop remained open, balanced on the ottoman, the screen blank. A postmodern mirror reflecting his own blank life. He shook his head. It was too early for such bleak thoughts. He'd just forgotten to plug the laptop in last night to recharge. *Look outside*, he thought—the sun was coming up. Mist curled up off the lake; the mountain cliffs shone in the dawn. Another day of beauty, of possibility. But what was another day when the world had stopped?

On his way to the kitchen, Nick paused by the back door, then looked out the door's window at the porch. After several moments he returned to his bedroom and retrieved the machete. Slowly he unlocked and opened the back door, then pushed the screen door open with the point of the machete. The screen door protested with a rusty squeal, but the figure lying on the porch barely moved. The man wore jeans and a thin gray sweat shirt with the hood up, the same clothes he'd worn last night.

"You come back to apologize?" Nick said.

"No," the man said. A boy—the voice was high, young. He was still curled up on the porch, knees tucked into his chest, facing away from Nick.

"Polite people knock," Nick said.

"Sorry," the boy said. His voice had a croak in it.

Nick laid the machete on the floor inside the doorway and then reached for the boy's shoulder. When he touched it, the boy shot up into a sitting position, trying to scramble away from him. Nick stared at the dark hair framing the bronzed face, the eyes wide and glittering, mouth open in protest, cheeks smooth and flushed, red as raspberries. A girl.

"Please," the girl began, then swallowed. It looked like it pained her. Her hair was matted, and her eyes weren't shining from fear but from fever. "Please tell me you're Nick Anthony." Then she slumped to the porch floor, as if all the screen doors in the world wouldn't wake her up.

CHAPTER THREE

Annalise hated whenever she got sick. She always caught a bug from someone at school who had a snotty nose, or coughed on everyone, or puked like Sally Maybank in eighth grade who had just walked up to Mrs. Honeycutt's desk at the front of the room to say she didn't feel well and then leaned over and barfed right into the trash can. All the air freshener in the world couldn't cover up the sour reek, but Mrs. Honeycutt had just sprayed Lysol and then continued teaching them algebra.

Annalise didn't smell vomit now, but she knew she was sick. She was shivering and burning up all at once, like she was being roasted over a fire in the Arctic. That wasn't a bad description. A little graphic, maybe, but her English teacher Mrs. Rivera would have liked it. But Annalise wasn't going back to Mrs. Rivera's class, wouldn't finish the Neil Gaiman novel she had started for summer reading, wouldn't see Eric or any of her friends again, because her house had burned to the ground and her parents were dead and she had run all the way to the mountains, and my God the hot and cold shivering, maybe this was what her mother meant by hot flashes. It was like the menopause of the damned, ha that was funny, Mrs. Rivera would like that too wouldn't she, stop it how could she be making jokes, her parents were dead they were dead they were dead.

She was tangled in bedsheets, her head sweaty against a pillow. A man was trying to give her a drink of water. He reminded her a little of her father and yet was not her father at all. She started crying. "Shh," the man said. "It's okay. It's just water. You have to drink something." He put the glass to her mouth. Ice cubes bumped against her lips as she sipped. The cold water stung her throat, but she sipped as much as she could. "Okay," the man said, and he said something else, but she had already slipped under, borne away by the current of her fever.

WHEN SHE NEXT woke up, she was in a bed in a room she didn't recognize. The shutters over the windows were closed, but the sunlight around the edges was bright. Wooden rafters crossed overhead, and there was a dresser across from the foot of the bed, with a long mirror on the wall above it. She saw herself in the mirror and stared. She looked like Medusa. Could Medusa turn herself to stone if she looked in a mirror? Maybe that would be a good thing, being turned to stone, everything grinding to a stop that would last for an eternal petrified moment. But what if her body was turned to stone and her *mind* kept spinning, like one of those magnetic top toys?

"Shut up," she said aloud. Her own thoughts exhausted her.

"You're awake," someone said. A man's voice. Annalise tried to sit up, but the best she could manage—she was so tired—was to turn her head to the left. A man sat in an armchair between the two casement windows. He looked a bit like a shaggy lion, dark hair shot through with silver, dark eyebrows over amber-colored eyes.

"You've got a fever," the man said. "Peaked at a hundred and four. One more degree and I was going to call a doctor."

There was a plastic bottle of water on a side table next to the man. Annalise looked at it. Her lips were so dry. When she licked her lips, the man stood and picked up the bottle and brought it to her.

"Don't have any straws," he said, as if apologizing. He managed to tip some of the water into her mouth without spilling it all over her chin.

"Thank you," Annalise said. Her voice sounded like she was speaking through broken glass in her throat.

The man nodded and put the bottle down, then sat on the edge of the bed, not too close. "You're Annalise," he said.

She nodded. How could nodding her head be so damn difficult? *You're my Uncle Nick*, she tried to say, but the words felt strange in her mouth. She had known her father had a brother, but when she was growing up her father had hardly ever spoken about him or told her anything about him. Until just a few days ago—two? Three? Then the fact of her parents' deaths flattened her and she couldn't move, couldn't think beyond the enormity of that single awful truth. She must have started crying, because her uncle pulled two tissues out of a box and held them out to her. She shook her head, even though she felt the tears slide down the side of her face. She turned away from him and wept quietly, and mercifully fell back asleep.

ANNALISE WOKE WITH a start. The light around the window shutters was dimmer, her reflection in the mirror above the dresser barely more than a shadow. Still she could see the handwritten note taped to the mirror: *Gone to store for meds. Please don't leave.* It was the "please" that got her, as if her uncle knew that just writing "Don't leave" would be creepy. She wondered what meds he needed to get. She wondered if she could stand up, and if so if she could then find a bathroom. She could make out two doors to her right. The one farther away was closed. Probably the bedroom door. The closest door was open onto what looked like a tile floor. Okay, bathroom located.

Getting out of bed felt like facing the last stretch of a marathon, but she managed to swing her legs out to one side and sit up. Her head spun and she gripped the headboard, taking deep breaths. There was a tall plastic trash can next to the bed. She had a vague memory of throwing up in it sometime earlier. Fantastic. Someone had washed it out, and while her stomach didn't feel too hot, she didn't think she was going to be sick now. Her jeans were gone and she was wearing just a T-shirt and underwear. Had she taken off her hoodie when she came into the house? She didn't want to think about how her jeans had been removed. And then she remembered what she had in her pocket, what she had to give to her uncle. Shit. Had he found it? And was she certain this was her uncle?

First things first. Annalise put her bare feet to the cool wooden floor, paused for a breath, and then, one hand still on the headboard, stood up. A wave of light-headedness hit, and the room swam before her. When it stopped moving, she took a tentative step forward, then another. The tile-floored room beckoned through the open doorway. Her limbs felt like they were filled with wet sand. When she made it to the doorway, she sagged against it. Somewhere in the back of her mind, the thought of her dead mother and father circled like a vulture. But she wasn't dead. Just hanging on to a doorway. She just needed a minute.

The bathroom was like a hallway leading away from the door—a built-in counter with two sinks on the left, a glassed-in shower on the right. She saw the bright-yellow container of bleach wipes on the counter at the same time she registered the faint astringent scent of disinfectant. At least her uncle, or whoever he was, had apparently wiped down the bathroom. Beyond the shower was a water closet with a toilet, and beyond that at the end of the bathroom was what looked like a walk-in closet. Annalise didn't see her jeans or hoodie anywhere. She made her way past the sinks and shower to the water closet, then sat down on the toilet to pee. And, honestly, to rest her shaky legs. Was this what it would be like to get old?

She flushed and then stood back up, almost proud when she didn't feel immediately dizzy. Baby steps. Still, she wanted to go back to bed. There was a bar of soap by one sink, though, so first she washed her hands, then dried them on the hand towel dangling from a ring in the wall. As she did so, she looked at the counter. The sink she was using, the one farthest from the door, had a little plastic caddy holding a toothbrush and a tube of toothpaste, plus the bar of soap. Except for the container of bleach wipes, the other sink was bare. Annalise looked at the glassed-in shower, saw soap and shampoo and a shaving mirror suction-cupped to the glass, a razor hanging from the bottom. A man's razor. No pink plastic disposables like her mother had. *Used to have*, a voice in her head corrected, but she ignored it. She opened a drawer and found a stick of deodorant, shaving cream, aftershave, Q-tips, a hairbrush, and an electric razor. Another drawer had mouthwash, more toothpaste, floss, and more shampoo. Two cabinets contained towels and toilet paper and an old hair drier. No hair products, no flat iron, no makeup. There was nothing feminine at all, in fact, in the whole bathroom.

Annalise looked at the walk-in closet at the back of the bathroom. The bed called for her. Instead she walked, steadily for the most part, to the closet. It was carpeted and held built-in shelves and drawers and rods. A window in the closet let in a little light—it was late afternoon, almost dusk, she guessed. She stood on tiptoe and looked out the window and saw the front yard and the gravel drive that led away to the trees. There was a light switch inside the closet door, and she turned on the light and looked at the hanging clothes, men's shirts and pants and jackets. Sweaters and shorts and socks and underwear were stacked neatly on shelves. There were a couple of pairs of jeans, but they weren't hers. Nothing had a name on it. On the far side of the closet, almost all the shelves were bare, but a single red garment bag hung from the rod.

She was reaching for the zipper on the garment bag when she heard the sound of a car engine. She got back on tiptoe and looked out the window again, just in time to see a dark-green SUV exit the trees and approach the house. Annalise turned and hurried out of the closet, remembering to turn the light off. She crossed the bathroom and reached the bed, sliding beneath the comforter at the same time she heard a car door slam. A few moments later, she heard a door into the house open. She closed her eyes, pretending to sleep.

She must have really fallen asleep, because when there was a tentative knock on the bedroom door, she jerked awake. "Are you up?" her uncle—the man she thought was her uncle—called from the other side.

Her heart beat like a caged bird in her chest. "Yes," she called out.

"Okay, I'm coming in," he said. The door opened, and he stood there in a plaid flannel shirt and jeans and tall boots. He had some folded clothes under one arm. "How are you feeling?"

"Tired," she said truthfully. "But better."

He smiled, clearly relieved. "Good," he said. "I got you some Theraflu," he said.

"I've got the flu?" she asked, surprised.

He shrugged. "Fever, chills, exhaustion, sore throat. Figured we'd hit all the symptoms. You don't seem to be having any trouble breathing." He paused, and Annalise realized he was waiting for her to confirm. She shook her head and he continued. "If you get worse, I'll take you to the doctor. There's a decent ER nearby." He glanced around the room, saw the note he had left for her and took it off the mirror. He held the note up. "Thanks for not leaving," he said.

Annalise wasn't sure why he thought she might have left. She had come all the way up here, after all. Plus, she was sick. "Sure," she said.

He laid the note on the dresser, then put the folded clothes on the foot of the bed. She saw it was her jeans and hoodie.

"I washed your sweat shirt," he said. "And your jeans." He looked out the window, then back toward her, but not directly at her. "You kicked your jeans off when you were trying to sleep."

Annalise felt her cheeks blush a little, not from her fever. "Thanks," she said. And then she remembered. Fear stabbed her. "Did you find anything in my jeans?" she asked. "Before you washed them?"

He paused, then turned to her and nodded. "Some cash," he said. "And a smartphone. They're under the hoodie there."

Relief washed over her like a warm bath. Her phone wasn't lost. And hopefully neither was what her father had told her to give her uncle. But she had to make sure this was Uncle Nick, and that she could trust him. "Thank you," she said. "Could . . . I have my phone, please?"

He retrieved the phone from under the hoodie and handed it to her. "Looks like it's dead," he said.

"Didn't have a charger," she said. It was stupid, but she felt better once she had her phone in her hand. She couldn't look at it, or at the sleeve on the back of the phone, while he was watching her. First she had to make sure. "So you're my uncle," she said.

"Looks like it," he said.

"Can you prove it?"

He raised his eyebrows. "You want to see my ID?"

She shook her head. Her dad had told her what to ask him, but she was so tired, and the thought of her father about did her in. But she had promised him. "How old were you when my father fell off the roof?" she asked.

He stared, those amber eyes locked on her. "He didn't fall off the roof," he said. "I did. I was ten."

She closed her eyes. Her father had told her only her uncle would know that. This was her Uncle Nick. *Mission accomplished, Dad,* she thought, and while she wanted to weep, she felt herself smiling. She had made it, all the way to her uncle.

She felt the mattress sag as he sat on the end of the bed, like last time, not too close. "Why did you come up here?" he asked.

She so wanted to keep her eyes closed, to drift off to sleep, to not think about any of this. Instead she opened her eyes to see him looking at her, his forehead quirked with concern. God, she hoped he could help her.

"Because," she said, "someone killed my parents."

CHAPTER FOUR

COLE WIPED OFF HIS KNIFE ON THE BOY'S SLEEVE—HE WOULD CLEAN IT more thoroughly later—and then slid it back into the sheath in his boot. *A place for every thing and every thing in its place,* he thought. He liked the saying, the mirrored structure of the sentence, how it underscored an irrefutable fact: there was order in the universe. Man just tended to fuck it up. Exhibit A lay in a heap at his feet.

"What do you want me to do with this?" Hicks said, toeing the heap.

Cole longed for a cigarette, a hand-rolled one, preferably filled with hash, but he refrained. He didn't want to ruin his night vision—old habits died hard. And there was still Winslow to deal with. "Leave it for now," he said. "And get Winslow out here."

Hicks nodded, shifting his jaw. Cole could smell the pungent wintergreen scent of the man's dip, a generous pinch already between Hicks's lower lip and gums. Hicks rarely dipped during a job but always dipped after one, and so Cole associated the scent with downtime. But this wasn't downtime. The scent seemed a violation. A flare of anger spurted in Cole, and just as quickly he quenched it. It wasn't Hicks he was mad at.

Hicks crossed the yard to the house and went in through the sliding glass door. Cole whistled tunelessly and looked up at the stars which shone like wet diamonds in the night sky. Cole's right ear itched, but he refrained from scratching the gnarled scar tissue there. He caught a whiff of the bayou that led to the sound and the Intracoastal Waterway, and he tilted his head back and breathed in through his nose. The air was rank and salty. Like life.

The sliding glass door opened and Hicks returned with Winslow, followed by both Dawes and Zhang. Winslow was thickset with a perpetual scowl, and he walked ahead of the other three with the rapid steps of an angry man. Before he reached Cole, he pointed at him and said, "This is bullshit. The fuck you mean sitting me in the house like I'm in time-out?"

"I needed a minute to clear my head," Cole said. "Figure out what to do here."

Winslow looked at the heap lying at Cole's feet. "Take it out to the bayou and dump it," he said. "If the gators don't take care of it, the sharks will."

Cole gave him a hint of a smile. "My thoughts exactly. But that's not the problem."

Like watching the moon rise, Cole saw realization slowly dawn on Winslow's face, and then Winslow glanced around to confirm that he and Cole were now flanked by the other three men, who had formed a loose arc at the perimeter of the yard. Winslow hesitated, then forged ahead, as Cole had known he would. "He tell you where the girl went?"

Cole considered his own boots, then raised his gaze to Winslow's. His smile was gone. "And why would I need to find that out from him?"

Winslow didn't flinch but met Cole's gaze. Cole gave him credit—the man had balls. "Because I fucked up, I know," Winslow said. "Did he—"

"Sun Tzu said, 'He wins his battles by making no mistakes.' " Cole continued to look straight at Winslow. " 'Making no mistakes is what establishes the certainty of victory, for it means conquering an enemy that is already defeated.' Pretty good, right?"

Winslow clenched his fists, then relaxed them. "Look, Cole, I'm sorry, okay? I am. I shouldn't have let the girl get away. But I didn't know she'd sneak out the back window. I couldn't watch the front and back of the house at the same time. Maybe if I'd had Hicks with me, I—"

Cole waved a hand in a cutoff gesture. "You had one job. I trusted you to handle it. And you fucked up."

Winslow stabbed a finger at the heap on the ground. "That's why I got the kid! I figured she must've gone to see her boyfriend. It was an easy snatch, no one saw a thing—"

"Like you didn't see the girl sneak out of the house?" Cole said.

One of the men standing at the edge of the yard started to chuckle, then turned it into a throat clearing when Winslow glared. After a beat Winslow returned his attention to Cole. "I know I fucked up, and that's why I got him. We needed a lead."

Cole considered this. "So you kidnapped a kid and brought him back here," he said. "Without calling me first."

Winslow's face flushed with anger. "I didn't have *time*! The kid was alone in his backyard, staring at his phone. There wasn't time to call you. I grabbed him and threw him in the truck. No one was home, no one was around to see. And I left his phone there so no one could trace him."

Cole sighed. Maybe smoking some hash beforehand would have been a better idea. "Did you look at the phone first?" he said. "See if he was texting someone? Maybe the girl? Maybe that would have been easier? Told us something about where she is?" He pointed at his damaged ear. "See this? Happened on my last job working for somebody else. The team I was on got hired by the cousins for a security gig." Winslow made a sour face; the cousins—slang for the CIA—liked their paramilitaries, but the sentiment was not always reciprocated by those who fought dirty, secret wars for the analysts back at Langley. "We were meeting somebody at the Syrian border," Cole continued. "In and out, they said. We walked into a fucking ambush. Lost three men plus one of the cousins. Had to drag the bodies out. And my ear got chewed up by shrapnel. An inch to the left and I'd be dead. When we got out of there, I made a vow I'd set up my own team and run it right." He fixed Winslow with a hard look. "I could get the ear fixed. But I keep it to remind me that this isn't a game, that if you're on a job and you fuck up or get distracted—" Cole snapped his fingers. "Lights out. And you fucked up, Winslow. And that's not acceptable."

Winslow threw his hands up in frustration. "I saw an opportunity and I took it. How many times have I done that right? Remember Mexico?

Uganda? Yemen?" Winslow took a breath, visibly controlling himself, then spoke in the low tones of a man pledging an oath. "I promise you, Cole, I'll get her."

Cole locked eyes with Winslow. He sensed the three men around them shift almost imperceptibly, but he kept staring at Winslow. Winslow maintained eye contact for several long seconds. Then he lowered his head a fraction, a sign of submission.

Cole nodded. "Okay," he said.

Winslow visibly relaxed. "Okay," he said. "Thank you. I won't let you down."

Cole slapped Winslow's shoulder. "I know you won't," he said. He stepped back and smiled. "I know I bore you all quoting Sun Tzu, but the man said some wise shit. You know what he said about being a leader?"

Winslow assumed the air of a student patiently awaiting a lecture. "I don't."

"He said if you regard your soldiers like your own sons, they will stand by you, even unto death." Cole kept his eyes trained on Winslow. "And you know how I feel about my men."

Winslow shifted his feet. "Cole," he said. "You know I would . . . that *we* would do anything—"

Cole raised a hand, silencing him. "But," he continued, "if you are indulgent, and cannot make your authority felt, then your soldiers are like spoiled children, and useless for any practical purpose."

Winslow frowned and opened his mouth to speak. Before he could, Cole drew his pistol and shot him in the forehead, a flat *crack* that rolled over the night marsh. Winslow fell backward, still frowning. None of the men around Cole jumped. Cole stepped forward and shot Winslow in the head one more time. He stood there for a moment, gazing down at the body, then holstered his pistol. To Hicks he said, "Take them both out into the sound."

Hicks waited a beat, then spit a short stream of dip juice and nodded at Dawes. Zhang produced a pair of tarps, and the other two men started wrapping the heap in one of them. They paused as Cole unfolded the other tarp and laid it on the ground next to Winslow, then rolled Winslow onto it. Cole stopped and looked back at his men. "My mess, my responsibility," he said. He continued wrapping the tarp around Winslow, and the other two went back to their work. When both bodies were secure, Hicks and Dawes carried them one at a time off into the dark.

Cole turned to Zhang, the one remaining man in the yard. "You find anything?"

"Emergency contact number in the girl's school file," Zhang said. "Grandparents. It's an 843 area code, South Carolina. I'll narrow it down."

"Do it," Cole said. "Check in with Poncho, see if he's seen anything. And tell him what happened with Winslow." Poncho was on lookout near the bridge, watching the one road leading on and off the island. Cole wasn't worried about the gunshots—the rednecks around here shot off bottle rockets and rifles like every weekend was the Fourth of July— but he didn't want Poncho getting nervous.

Zhang nodded and stepped away, pulling out a cell phone. From the darkness, an outboard motor kicked up, a sound that faded as the boat with the two bodies headed out into the shallow bayou. Cole took in a deep breath, then exhaled. His men had reacted as he had thought they would—hoped they would. Winslow had fucked up; everyone knew it. An example had to be made. It wasn't the first time he'd lost a man, but it was the first time he'd had to shoot one of his own. Still, Cole was glad it had gone smoothly. Now he had an hour, maybe two, before the boy Winslow had taken would be truly missed. The boy hadn't known much except that the girl was scared and on the run, with a backpack of her daddy's. And the boy had dropped her off at the Tampa airport. For that information, the boy had traded his life—no way they could let him go once he'd seen their faces. A fucking waste. Cole's ear itched savagely. He ignored it.

Cole walked back to the house and went in through the sliding glass door. Inside, Jonas was scrubbing plates at the kitchen sink while Waco played *Call of Duty* on the flat-screen in the living room. "What up, boss?" Waco called, his eyes on the screen. "Come on, come *on*, motherfucker, don't you—*yes*, that's what I'm talking 'bout, you bitch!"

In his bass rumble, Jonas said, "That's all he's been doing since we got here." He squeezed a sponge out. "Playing games like a little boy."

A month shy of being able to drink legally, Waco was the youngest of Cole's men, and it was easy enough to think of him as a kid. But in his three missions so far, Waco had already made four kills, and he followed orders eagerly, so Cole was willing to cut him some slack.

"You doing a little housecleaning?" Cole said to Jonas, a grin drifting across his face. "All you need's a hoop earring and you'd be the black Mr. Clean."

Jonas rinsed off a dish and put it in a drying rack next to the sink. "Just taking care of business, is all," he said. He glanced out the window, then at Cole. "Winslow?"

Waco's video game was loud, maybe loud enough to cover the pistol shots earlier, but Jonas had a clear view of the backyard through the window over the sink. Of all the men, Jonas was the one whose reaction Cole was most curious about in regard to Winslow's death. "We had a parting of the ways," Cole said.

Jonas said nothing at first, just dried his hands on a towel, then hung it on the stove door. "How you want to handle his next of kin?" He meant Winslow's. He had a sister and nephew in Kansas City.

"Full payment," Cole said. Whatever Winslow would have earned on this job, his sister and her kid would get, plus five K for bereavement.

Jonas raised his eyebrows.

"He fucked up, but he was one of us," Cole said. "And I take care of us."

Jonas nodded. "I'll handle it," he said. "We heading out?"

Cole reached down and pulled his knife from his boot and laid it on the counter. "Soon as the others get back," he said. "Got to go find that girl." He picked up the sponge Jonas had been using, squirted a bit of liquid dish soap on it, ran it under the faucet, and started cleaning his knife. The action calmed him. He hadn't realized he needed calming. He would need to watch that.

CHAPTER FIVE

NICK LOOKED AT HIS NIECE LYING IN THE BED, PALE AND STILL FEVERISH but clearly not ranting. She knew what she had said, about someone killing her parents. And she was remarkably calm.

"What do you mean?" he asked.

"They *killed* them," Annalise said. "They went into my house and burned it to the ground with my parents . . ." She closed her eyes and her breath hitched—she was holding back a sob. Then she took a deep breath and opened her eyes again. They were wet but clear. "I was at my boyfriend's house and saw the fire. I saw the men who did it. I saw them leave. My house was burning, I tried to go inside to see if my parents . . . but it was so *hot*. I couldn't—" She took another breath. "I ran away, but I read the news reports after on my phone, before it died. My parents were still inside."

Nick had spoken with many people who were lying. There were generally signs, what a professional poker player would call tells, physiological reactions to a spike in anxiety. Annalise wasn't unconsciously touching her face, or becoming very still, or adjusting the bedsheet or her T-shirt or her hair. But Nick hadn't watched her long enough to establish a baseline, and she was recounting a traumatic experience. That made reading her reactions trickier. In his gut, though, Nick felt a kind of certainty stirring. She wasn't lying.

"Okay," he said. "Where did this happen? In Tampa?"

She nodded.

"When?" Nick asked.

"Two days ago," Annalise said. She frowned. "Or three? What day is it?"

"Thursday."

"It was Tuesday night. Or really early Wednesday morning. I guess that's two days. I'm sorry, but . . . could I have some water?"

Nick made himself smile gently and nod. "Sure," he said. "I'll make some soup later too."

Annalise's expression didn't relax, but her voice did. She sounded smaller. "Mom always made me chicken-and-rice soup when I was sick," she said.

Now Nick gave her a genuine smile. "My mom did the same," he said. "And my father would always give me ginger tea. I can make that, too, if you want to try it." She shrugged. Nick got a clean plastic cup from the bathroom and filled it with water from the sink, then brought it to Annalise. "I'll go get you that tea," he said.

He left the bedroom, closing the door. Immediately he felt a weight descend on him, his heart a heavy stone in the cage of his chest. Why was he suddenly responsible for this girl? He had constructed his life in a way that minimized disruption, kept the outside world at bay, and then this sick, lost teenager had blown it wide open. Of course he wasn't going to kick her out of his house—even if she weren't his niece, he wouldn't do that. What he ought to do was call the sheriff, get Deputy Sams back up here, turn this over to the authorities. If he still had a landline, he would probably do just that, call him right now. But he could drive into town and call from any of half a dozen stores. Later. First, he'd find out as much as he could from his niece.

He could almost hear Ellie. *She's not lying.*

I don't think she is either, he said. *But that doesn't mean she's telling the whole truth.*

He poured water into a saucepan and put it on the stove, then sliced up some ginger and dropped it into the pan. He added a cinnamon stick and cloves and turmeric and a dash of cayenne pepper, then squeezed half a lemon into the pan as the mixture heated.

The mingled scents opened a door in his mind, a door that had long been closed and locked.

NICK'S MOTHER WAS having one of her bad spells again, and his father told him to watch his little brother. Dad had his hands full taking care of their mother, who was alternating between anger and listlessness. The anniversary of his parents' departure from Afghanistan was approaching, which always brought out the worst in his mother. She had not wanted to leave her parents, Nick and Jay's grandparents, who were buried in the Kart-e-Sakhi cemetery in Kabul. But their father, an American who had worked for USAID in Afghanistan, had said they had no choice once the Communists supported a coup against King Zahir Shah. Dad had always respected Mâmân's heritage, had been married to her by an imam even though he was agnostic. He knew that asking Mâmân to leave Afghanistan was like asking her to learn how to breathe water. But with the Soviet Union backing the new regime in Kabul, Afghanistan was a tinderbox waiting for a lit match, especially for an American. Nick's father knew they had no future there, and they had left when Mâmân was pregnant with Nick, a move that might have saved their lives and for which his mother had never forgiven his father. So when his father told him to watch his brother, Nick went to find Jay without complaint.

Jay, of course, had decided, at that moment, to climb up onto their roof. Nick knew Jay wanted to watch for Soviet tanks. Everyone knew the tanks were coming, that Soviet paratroopers were going to parachute out of the sky like in the new movie *Red Dawn*—just like they had in Afghanistan. When Nick was six years old, his mother had woken him up Christmas morning to tell him her homeland had been attacked. "You were born here, but you were first in Mâmân's belly in Afghanistan," she had said to Nick. "That is your homeland too."

This had confused Nick, because he had been born in America, and while he liked Mâmân's lamb kofta and all his various "uncles" from the Afghan community in San Diego, each of whom had told Nick how beautiful a bride his mother had been and how fortunate his father was to have married her, Nick had never been to Afghanistan, so how could that be home? He hadn't understood why his mother insisted he and Jay go to a nearby mosque for religious instruction, or why they call her Mâmân instead of Mommy, or why he should feel any connection to a country he had never seen.

Now that he was a few years older, Nick saw things more simply—Dad had to take care of Mâmân, and Nick had to take care of Jay.

And now Jay was on the roof when Nick was supposed to be keeping him safe.

"Jay!" Nick hissed from the backyard patio, staring up at the roof. It was dark that night, with no moon, but he had seen Jay climbing over the lip of the roof before vanishing. "Jay!" he called again.

Jay's voice floated down from the dark. "Go away."

"Mâmân will kill you," Nick hissed.

Nothing.

Cursing under his breath, Nick climbed up the downspout and grasped the edge of the roof with one hand, then another, until he was dangling with his feet over the stones of the patio. It was only a single story high, but Nick knew a fall could be bad. Then he hauled himself up, getting one leg over the gutter and onto the shingles, which gave him enough leverage to finally clamber onto the roof and crouch there, catching his breath.

Something small and hard struck his chest, then his head. "Ouch!" He glared into the dark, and then he saw Jay above him on the ridge of the roof, arm back, ready to throw another pebble. "Stop it!"

"Go away," Jay said.

"You need to come down here right now," Nick said. "You could fall. Mâmân will be so mad."

"Don't tell me what to do."

Then their father's voice, like a lash in the night. "Boys!"

Nick heard Jay's startled gasp, and as he tried to turn around on the roof to look for his father, his foot slipped. He fell hard onto his hip and slid down the tiles, barely having time to scrabble for a handhold before he rolled off the edge and dropped onto the patio. When he hit the stones, something exploded in his left elbow, and he shrieked from the pain, a bright yellow universe of it.

He had broken his arm just above the elbow. His parents had to take him to the hospital that night, and the pain of his broken arm was almost worth the concern and attention his mother lavished on him, bringing him bowls of warm *aush* in bed and calling him her brave *moosh*, never mind that being called a brave mouse made no sense. And in all the commotion, Jay escaped punishment for climbing on the roof, which annoyed Nick.

"Cheer up, brother," Jay had told him, grinning. "Mâmân is happy now."

WHEN THE GINGER tea on the stove came to a boil, Nick turned the heat down and got an old breakfast tray and set the box of Theraflu on it. After the tea had brewed, he poured it through a strainer into a mug, stirred in some honey, tasted it, and stirred in more honey. He carried the mug on the tray to the bedroom, tapped the door with his toe to give Annalise a heads-up, then used his forearm to push the lever down and open the door. Annalise was sitting up in bed, the lamp on the side table on. She was on Ellie's side of the bed, closest to the bathroom. Nick walked over to the far side. "Here you go," he said, placing the tray on top of the comforter.

"Thanks," Annalise said. "What's in this?"

"Ginger, honey, other things," Nick said. "Old family recipe."

She eyed the mug. "No eye of newt or toe of frog?"

"You know *Macbeth*?"

"Read it last year in English." She picked up the mug, sniffed it, took a tentative sip. She made a face.

Nick smiled. "It'll help with your throat. Settle your stomach too."

She looked doubtful but took another sip, then carefully put the mug down on the bedside table. "So, are you going to help me?"

It was as if they were sailing on a lake and their boat had suddenly veered in a new direction. He went back around to her side of the bed and sat at the foot again. "Help you what?" he said.

She stared at him. "With what happened to my parents." She slid down in the bed a bit. Ellie would do that sometimes, act like a little kid and slide down under the covers, like she was hiding.

Stop it, Nick thought. Gently, he said, "I want to ask you what happened. And then we can figure out what to do. Who to call."

Immediately Annalise sat up, shaking her head. "You can't call the police," she said.

"If someone . . . did what you say they did, we have to."

"No," she said, shaking her head more insistently.

"Why not?"

"Because my father said not to," she said. She was crying now, but she wiped the tears away with her wrists. "And because they're going to think I did it."

He paused, like a man who had found himself stepping across a minefield. "Did what?"

"Killed my parents! Jesus." She was still crying, but she was also furious. "What do you not get? These men just showed up and killed my parents! I'm fucking freaking out here, okay? They came to my house and burned it down! And they're probably looking for me! And I've been like a *fugitive* or something trying to find you, and I'm *sick* and I'm *scared*—"

34

"Okay, okay," he said as she started sobbing, and he reached out a hand and put it on the comforter where he thought her knee was. She hugged a pillow to her and sobbed into it, muffling her cries. He just sat there with her, his hand on her knee, while she cried.

Presently she let go of the pillow and pushed it to the side. "Sorry," she said, wiping her eyes. "I think I got snot all over your pillow."

Nick shook his head. "It's okay. I can wash it." He glanced at it, then looked back at Annalise. "Or throw it away. Might be best."

She stared at him. He smiled gently and pulled out a tissue from a box on the side table and handed it to her. She took it and blew her nose, then folded up the tissue into a tight square and dropped it into the trash can next to the bed. "Okay, so," she said, her voice mostly recovered from crying.

That was when Nick heard the distant drone of an engine. Someone was driving down the road to the cabin.

CHAPTER SIX

Cole and his men were driving to the airport, not Tampa International but a smaller field closer to downtown, frequented by private planes, when Cole's cell phone vibrated in his pocket. Except for Jonas, only clients called on this phone. Jonas and the others were following them in a second Suburban—maybe they needed something. But Cole's gut and scalp tightened in anticipation. He knew it wasn't Jonas. He slid the phone out of his pocket and glanced at the screen. Bingo.

"Phone," he called out. Waco, who was driving, immediately turned the radio off. In the back seat, Zhang opened a laptop. Cole's phone continued to ring. He glanced over his shoulder at Zhang, who was typing.

Without taking his eyes off his laptop screen, Zhang gave a single nod and said, "Go."

Cole held the phone up to his good ear and answered the call. "Hello?"

"Mr. Cole," the voice on the other end said, stirring the hairs on Cole's neck. "This is Mr. Kobayashi."

"And I thought you were a telemarketer," Cole said. "Maybe trying to sell me a condo in Jamaica."

"I take it your mission was not a success," Kobayashi continued. He had the faintest Japanese accent, overlaid with clipped British tones. It was the voice, Cole thought, of a man questioning prisoners in a dungeon while a colleague heated up tongs.

"We took Bashir and his wife," Cole said.

"But not his daughter," Kobayashi said. "And not the information you were sent to retrieve. My employer is quite unhappy."

"As are we," Cole said. "We are tracking the girl now. Anything her father told her will end with her."

"You sound certain for a man whose hands are empty."

Cole realized he was squeezing his cell phone and forced himself to relax his grip. "I am certain," he said. "I know my men, none better. I suspect you know that as well."

"The skill of your men, Mr. Cole, is relevant only with regards to them obtaining the information you were hired to procure. If they cannot accomplish that task, they are worthless to my employer."

"We," Cole said.

"Pardon?"

"Not *they*," Cole said. "*We*. We will accomplish the task. The girl hasn't gone far. As soon as we get in the air, we'll be after her with multiple teams. I'll keep you apprised."

There was a brief pause. "Very well," Kobayashi replied. "Do you require any logistical help?"

"Only if you can tell us whether or not the girl took a flight out of Atlanta in the past ten hours or so," Cole said.

There was another brief pause. "I shall get that information to you by morning," Kobayashi said.

Jesus, Cole thought. Who *was* this guy? He could get access to domestic flight manifests? "Understood," he said. He glanced up at Zhang, who gestured at him to keep talking. "This information we're looking for, you said it was in electronic form, on a flash drive," he continued. "You sure there aren't more copies?"

"It cannot be copied or downloaded or even opened without the correct software," Kobayashi said. "Seeing that I have already told you this before, I assume either your memory is slipping or you are keeping me on the phone while you try to trace this call. Probably Mr. Zhang is doing it. I believe he is the member of your group in charge of intelligence and surveillance. A hacker, yes?"

Cole said nothing but glanced again at Zhang, who continued typing furiously on his laptop.

"While I am certain that Mr. Zhang is more than competent in his craft," Kobayashi continued, "he will not successfully trace this call, or any call I make to you. Focus your energy on finding Annalise Bashir, Mr. Cole." There was a click, and Kobayashi was gone.

Cole hung up. "Anything?" he asked Zhang.

Zhang closed the lid of his laptop. "No," he said. "It's VoIP, but the IP keeps changing. It's like he's calling from eighteen different computers around the world. Call's routed through Bahrain one minute, London the next. Layer that with encryption tech and it's like trying to hack into an NSA mainframe." He blew out a breath in frustration. "Sorry. It's going to be impossible this way."

"I know," Cole said. "We had to try."

Waco, keeping his eyes on the road, said, "Not to question you or anything, but why do we want to try and find out who this guy is? He's paying us enough, right?"

"Waco, shut the fuck up," Zhang said.

"Hey, shove it up—"

"Enough," Cole said, and the other men fell silent. "We're doing it because I don't like not knowing who's pulling the strings. That's why. Let's just get to the plane and find the girl." He sat back in his seat and squeezed the bridge of his nose. He didn't like it. His squad had often not known exactly who the paying client was, although usually it wasn't hard to guess. But this job was different all around. Who paid a thousand a day per person? For information retrieval? Cole didn't really care what the information was or who needed it. He had long ago abandoned any moral qualms about his work, replacing them with a reputation for professionalism and a fierce loyalty to his men. And they *were* his men. All of them, even the ones they'd lost over the years—Deac, Rat, Mikey, and now Winslow. He carried them all with him, including the dead. And now this girl had escaped them. It was a problem. But they would do what Cole had told Kobayashi they would do.

Soon the two Suburbans arrived at the airport, which was surrounded by a chain-link fence and lit by arc sodium lights that sat atop their posts like glaring moons. They drove through a gate in the fence directly onto the tarmac—no TSA check-in here—and pulled up next to a sleek Challenger jet that dwarfed the Suburbans. A man in a white short-sleeved button-down and a clipboard in his hand stood at the bottom of a flight of airstairs that led up to the plane's cabin. Cole noted with pride that as soon as the first Surburban stopped, Jonas and Poncho exited their vehicle and moved to establish a perimeter.

When Cole stepped out of his Suburban, the man with the clipboard stepped forward. "Mr. Simmons?" he said to Cole, using the alias he had been given. "I'm Randy, your pilot. We're fueled up and ready to go when you are."

"Excellent," Cole said. He looked at the length of the plane, then back to the man with the clipboard. He raised an eyebrow. "Nothing like riding in style, huh, Randy?"

"No, sir." Randy smiled briefly, then switched it off, all business. "Do you need any help with luggage?"

"We've got it, thanks," Cole said. As he spoke, his men pulled heavy cases out of the Suburbans and wheeled them over to the cargo door at the rear of the plane. "Wheels up in fifteen," Cole said. Randy nodded and climbed the stairs.

Cole walked up to Jonas and stood for a moment, both of them watching the men load the cargo efficiently. "Girl caught a plane to Atlanta," he said. "At least according to the boyfriend. He held out a while before coughing that up, so I'm willing to bet it's legit."

"He also said the girl had a stack of bills," Jonas said. If she had paid cash for her plane ticket, that would mean no credit card payments to trace.

"Kobayashi says he'll find out if she took a flight out of Atlanta."

Jonas raised an eyebrow. "How the fuck can he do that?"

Cole shrugged. "Said he'd let us know by morning."

Jonas said nothing after that. Cole knew the big man was thinking the same thing he was—who was Kobayashi, and what kind of influence did he have? "Zhang's working on getting to the girl's phone," Cole added. "As long as she keeps her phone on, we'll be able to track her."

Jonas looked skeptical. "My cousin has a twelve-year-old daughter, got her an iPhone for Christmas. She figured out how to turn off location tracking by New Year's."

"Then Zhang'll go through the girl's carrier," Cole said. "Anytime her phone pings a tower—she makes a call, checks her email—we'll see where she is. He's got Hicks checking her social media too. You never know."

Jonas shrugged. "So what's the play? Zhang said the girl's grandparents are in Hilton Head. We heading there?"

"You are," Cole said. "Take Hicks and Waco with you. The rest of us will stay in Atlanta, try to pick up her trail from there."

Jonas squinted at Cole. "You don't think she went to Hilton Head."

"She told her boyfriend Atlanta."

"But you still want us to go to Hilton Head."

"Her grandparents are there. Gotta cover all the bases." Cole stretched his arms over his head, winced.

"Shoulder?" Jonas asked.

"Fuck," Cole said, disgusted. "I'm getting old."

"Better than the alternative."

That was true. But Cole hated the slow accumulation of aches and pains, like grit collecting in his joints. Of course, he'd also been stabbed in that particular shoulder a year ago, so there was that. "Just need a warm shower and some rack time," he said. "Concentrate your energy and hoard your strength." When Jonas looked blankly at him, Cole added, "Sun Tzu."

Jonas grunted. "Thought it was 2Pac."

CHAPTER SEVEN

"WHAT IS IT?" ANNALISE SAID.

Nick held up a hand and half turned toward the bedroom door, his eyes unfocused as he listened. He felt Annalise tense on the bed—she'd heard it too. The whine of a car or truck in low gear as it came out of the trees and into the clearing at the front of the house.

Nick stood and went to the door. "Stay here," he said. "And be quiet." He left the bedroom, closing the door behind him. He saw the machete in the foyer, leaning in a corner by the front door. That would do. Nick stepped to the front door and looked out the sidelight to see Deputy Sams getting out of his Explorer. The deputy clasped his hands as if absently rubbing his knuckles. When Sams looked up toward the house, Nick drew back from the sidelight so he wouldn't be seen. He wasn't sure why, and that bothered him. Ten minutes ago he had been thinking about when to call the sheriff, and now the deputy was conveniently outside his front door.

Maybe it was too convenient.

You can't call the police, Annalise had said.

She's not lying, he could hear Ellie say as if she were standing next to him in the foyer.

Nick opened the front door to find Sams on the top step, hand poised to knock. Sams took a half step back. "Jesus," he said. "Sorry, Professor. Startled me."

"Deputy," Nick said. "What brings you back?"

Sams wrung his hands together briefly, then rested them on his belt buckle. "We got a call from the Tampa police," he said. "They heard from the medical examiner's office."

For a second, Nick looked blankly at the deputy. Then he understood—the autopsy of his brother and sister-in-law.

Sams tilted his head slightly, looked over Nick's shoulder then back at Nick. "Do you mind if I come in?"

"Please." Nick opened the door and stepped aside. Sams entered the foyer, glancing at the machete in the corner. Nick closed the door and walked through to the great room. His boots thunked on the floorboards. "Can I get you some tea or anything?" he called, his voice a bit louder than necessary. He hoped Annalise kept quiet.

"No, thank you," Sams said, following Nick. Then he stopped and looked at the sofa. A pillow and folded blanket lay there where Nick had put them earlier. He was planning to sleep on the sofa while Annalise slept in the master bedroom. There was a guest room upstairs, but Nick wanted to be close to Annalise in case she needed him.

"Got company?" Sams asked.

"Just doing laundry," Nick said. He nodded toward an armchair, then sat in his own chair by the hearth. Sams sat down on the edge of his chair, back straight, arms resting on his thighs, fingers intertwined, a man about to deliver a report.

"What did the autopsy find?" Nick asked.

"The ME said your brother died of hypoxia," Sams said. "There was soot in his respiratory tract, other signs of smoke inhalation. He died before the fire burned him."

Nick nodded. He felt he was reacting in slow motion, like a victim in a horror movie who couldn't escape and was numb with shock. He hoped

Annalise couldn't hear what Sams was saying. Asphyxiation was technically better than burning to death, but he didn't think Annalise would appreciate the difference very much. He barely did himself. Then he realized what Sams had not said. "What about his wife? Carol?"

Sams shifted on the edge of his chair. "That's the thing. She did *not* have any signs of smoke inhalation."

Nick lowered his voice. "She burned to death?"

Sams shook his head. "There were cuts on her arms and torso," he said. "Knife wounds."

"Knife wounds? Someone stabbed her?"

Sams hesitated. "The ME said most of the cuts were shallow, not life threatening. But they would have hurt."

Nick didn't understand. "Defensive wounds?"

Sams looked oddly at him. "No. They were too deliberate. Someone cut her on purpose. The ME found what might have been ligature marks on her wrists. Hard to tell with a fire, but she wasn't wearing any jewelry, so . . ."

"They think her hands were tied," Nick said, finishing the deputy's thought. He felt so tired, as if he were being very slowly crushed under an enormous soft weight. The next words were hard, but he forced himself to ask. "How did she die?"

"Her throat—" Sams began, then grimaced and flexed his enormous hands. "Her throat was sliced open. She was dead before the fire got her."

They sat there in the living room, looking at one another, for a long moment. Nick spoke first, his voice even lower. "Do they have any suspects?"

Sams said nothing for a long moment. "They don't think it was your brother," he said. "I'm sorry to even say that to you, but it's routine to investigate people who are close to the deceased. There was a knife wound on your brother's hand, like someone had stabbed it. The knife went all the way through the back of his hand and through the palm. And there was no knife found on the scene."

Nick understood. Unless Jay had tortured and killed his wife, stabbed himself in the hand, and then magically made the knife vanish before setting the house on fire with both him and his wife in it, someone else had done this. Multiple someones, most likely. Nick's eyes burned with fatigue, and with tears, and he closed them briefly, wiping the tears away with his fingers. And then he remembered the kitchen knife Annalise had thrown at him, the one now in his dishwasher. His blood cooled at the thought.

"What about . . . my niece?" he said. He had hesitated just enough, he thought. "Has anyone seen her?"

Sams shook his head. "Not for lack of looking. They've issued a BOLO for her. It's even more important now that we talk to her. Tampa police have two possible homicides."

"You were a policeman somewhere else," Nick said. "Before here."

Slowly, Sams nodded. "The army," he said. "I was a military police-man before I came back home. How'd you know?"

Nick shrugged. "You seem pretty familiar with ligature marks and homicide. I'd guess most deputies around here aren't."

"You'd be surprised," Sams said. "You notice a lot, don't you?"

"I was a teacher," Nick said. "You get to be pretty observant about your students, if you're any good." Before Sams could continue, Nick stood, and after a moment Sams stood as well. "About my niece," Nick said. "Is she a suspect?"

"A person of interest," Sams said.

Nick shook his head. "Do they really think a sixteen-year-old girl could have done this?"

Sams ran his hands over his knuckles once, twice. "I don't think one person could have done this," he said. "But her boyfriend is missing too." He lowered his head slightly and opened his eyes a bit wider, looking directly at Nick. "If you see her, let us know as soon as possible."

Nick walked out with Sams and watched the deputy drive away. He agreed with what Sams had said, that one person couldn't have done it.

He would guess three, at a minimum. At least one to restrain Jay, and one to do the same with Carol. And the one with the knife, the one who had cut up Carol while making Jay watch.

NICK STIRRED A saucepan of chicken-and-rice soup and tried to process what he had just learned. Jay and Carol had been murdered. Someone had tied Carol's hands and stabbed her repeatedly, not in a frenzy but in a deliberate way. It would have hurt. And then they'd slit her throat. Jay died later, from smoke inhalation. Where had he been while his wife was being tortured? At some point he'd been stabbed through his hand. But after slitting Carol's throat, the killers had left Jay alive in the house and set it on fire.

The knife Annalise had brought with her was still in his dishwasher. If there had been any trace evidence on it, the dishwasher cycle had washed it all away. Nick thought about it, then shook his head. It wasn't his niece. If she had killed her parents, why then run to her father's brother, a virtual stranger who would be far more likely to call the police than to help her? But if she hadn't been involved in her parents' deaths, she might know more than she had shared so far. And now her boyfriend was missing.

He broke it down while heating the soup. Burglars didn't torture their victims and then burn the house down. They did smash-and-grabs, or they held people hostage briefly while they looted a house and then left. More rarely they would shoot their victims. This, however, was calculated. But to what end? Nick continued stirring, his mind setting aside the horror of the situation and analyzing the problem. It could be a warning to others if Jay had upset someone powerful enough to send a team of men to his house. It could be revenge. But this seemed like something else. You might make a man watch his wife being tortured if you were a psychopath. Or if you needed to get information out of him, and quickly. Nick shook his head. Now he was starting to guess, which was always a bad idea. He would give Annalise her soup and listen to her story, and then he would see if things made any more sense.

Unbidden, the memory rose again like a dead fish floating to the surface—the canteen spilling into the dirt, a fire casting shadows against stones. Nick blinked, his focus returning to the soup on the stovetop. It was about to boil. He turned off the heat and moved the saucepan off the burner so it would cool.

He had to put the bowl of soup on a plate to carry it because he had left his one breakfast tray in the bedroom with Annalise. Carefully he navigated around the sofa, trying not to spill the soup. It smelled good. Maybe he'd have some too—lately his meals had been a bit sporadic. He reached the door and called Annalise's name and again used his forearm to push down the lever and open the door. His greeting died on his lips because the bed was empty, the folded jeans and sweat shirt gone. One of the casement windows was open, giving Nick a view of the lawn leading down to the lake, the water black and still in the coming dusk.

Nick put the bowl of soup down on the dresser and went to the window. He hadn't heard it open. She must have overheard him and Sams talking. A faint shoeprint lay across the window sill. Nick poked his head out the window. There was maybe a three-foot drop from the window to the ground. Across the lake, Whiteside Mountain loomed, its cliffs faint in the shadows. To his left, at the far edge of the yard by the rhododendron, a piece of gray clothing lay crumpled on the ground. Annalise's sweat shirt.

He almost vaulted through the window right then, put his hands on either side of the window frame and raised his foot to the sill. Then he let go of the frame and lowered his foot and hurried to the front hall, where he picked up his machete. In the kitchen he opened a cabinet and took out a flashlight and put it in his jeans pocket. Then he was out the back door, boots clomping across the porch and down the steps to the grass.

She had ten minutes on him, maybe more. She was sick and didn't know the area. But if she had found a path, she could have gained some ground. She could also have fallen into a ravine or tumbled into the lake or come across a bear. And while the days were getting longer, it would be dark soon enough in the valley.

When he reached the rhododendron at the edge of his yard, he stopped to pick up her sweat shirt, then looked uphill into the darkening woods. No sign of her, even though the rhododendron was broken here, a branch or two snapped back exactly as if someone had pushed through the bushes to get to the trees beyond. He paused, looked at the sweat shirt in his hand. Looked back at the cabin. Then he heard two distinct sounds from the direction of the cabin—a sharp cry of fear, followed almost immediately by a dry, insistent rattle.

He ran back across the yard, calling her name. She screamed in reply from the far side of the cabin, by the carport. He ran past the porch and rounded the corner to see Annalise on the ground, leaning back on her elbows, staring in terror at the rattlesnake coiled two yards from her feet. It was big, thick as his arm and at least four feet long, maybe five. "Don't move," he shouted. She was crying now but didn't take her eyes off the snake. Its head wavered a few inches off the ground, its tongue scenting the air. Its rattle sent up a sinister beat. Nick slowly approached from the side, holding the machete out in front of him. The snake's head pivoted in his direction. "Annalise," Nick said. "Very slowly, start crawling backward." Annalise continued to cry and did not move. The snake bobbed its head up and down, flicking its tongue at Nick. "Annalise," he said again. "Look at me. Look at me." She turned her face toward him, eyes wide with terror, tears streaking her cheeks. "It's going to be okay," he said, even as he was thinking he should have grabbed a walking stick, a fallen branch, something long enough to keep the rattlesnake at bay. "You need to crawl away from it. Slowly. Go slowly. I'll keep it distracted."

Tentatively, Annalise pulled one of her legs back, then the other. The snake dipped its head and slowly swung toward Annalise. She scooted backward about a foot, still crying. The snake paused, its head drawn back. Nick stamped his boot. The snake flinched and looked at Nick, its tongue flickering like a dark flame. The rattle sang. "*Go*," Nick hissed at Annalise. She crawled away, faster now. The snake moved, a hideous, smooth unspooling. Nick took two quick steps forward and raised the machete. Annalise screamed as the snake struck like a whiplash. It sank its fangs into Nick's right boot, just above the ankle. Nick raised his leg and kicked it to shake off the snake, but the snake had already withdrawn its fangs and was coiling itself again, the rattle high and shrill. Nick swung the machete up and then back down, striking the snake behind its head. The blade cut through the snake's body and struck the earth beneath, the impact jarring Nick's arm so the machete sprang out of his hand. The snake's head opened its mouth, the inside pearly white, displaying its two enormous curved fangs, and then bit at the air. Its headless body writhed and twisted, the rattle a staccato death beat.

Annalise was struggling to her feet. "Don't go near the head!" Nick shouted. "It can still bite." He backed away several steps and then sat heavily on the ground.

Annalise stumbled toward Nick, giving the snake's head a wide berth, and then fell on all fours next to him. "I'm sorry," she said. "I'm sorry."

"It's okay," Nick said. He was examining his boot where the snake had bitten him.

"We need to get you to a hospital," she said. She was pale and looked as if she were about to be violently sick, but she focused on Nick's boot. "Don't raise it too high—you don't want the venom to go to your heart."

Nick began unlacing the boot.

"What are you doing?" Annalise said, her voice rising. "You need to lie down. Where's your phone?"

"Don't have one," Nick said. He pulled the boot off.

She stared at him. "You don't have a phone?"

"Nope." He peeled off his sock and looked closely around his ankle.

She leaned closer to examine his ankle with a mixture of disgust and resolve on her face. "Do I need to suck the venom out or anything?"

Nick looked sharply at her. "Nobody does that," he said. "Except on TV. I'm okay. Look." He wiggled his toes. "Snake boots. They have multiple layers. Fangs didn't penetrate to my leg." He started putting his sock back on. "I need you to go around to the other side of the house and get the maul that's leaning against the woodpile. It's like a cross between an ax and a sledgehammer. Run and get it for me, please."

Thankfully Annalise didn't ask questions, just got up and left. Nick shoved his foot back into his boot and relaced it. By the time he was finished, Annalise had come back carrying the maul.

"Thanks," he said, standing up. He took the maul from her, then cautiously approached the snake.

"I think you killed it," Annalise said, although she remained several feet away.

He shook his head. The snake's body had ceased writhing and lay still. Its head was also still, the mouth gaping open. "Snakes are cold-blooded," he said. "Don't need a lot of oxygen. Right now the snake doesn't know its head has been cut off. It just feels pain."

He steadied himself, raised the maul, and then swung the blunt end down onto the snake's head. The maul crushed it, a small amount of blood spurting out of its mouth, staining the grass.

"It's dead now," Nick said. He turned to see Annalise staring in horror at the snake's crushed head, then at him, just before turning to one side and retching.

ANNALISE WAS BACK in the bed, trying to eat her reheated bowl of chicken-and-rice soup. Nick sat in the armchair by the windows, both of which were now closed. He felt exhausted, but his mind spun in circles around the snake, Annalise, his brother. He watched his niece sitting up in his bed, slurping soup from the bowl.

"You know how to use a spoon?" he asked.

She lowered the bowl from her mouth. "Easier this way, sitting in a bed. Don't spill as much."

Nick closed his eyes. He had to talk to her, understand what had happened to her parents, but he just needed a moment.

"Why did you come back?" Annalise said.

Nick forced his eyes open. She sat in the bed looking at him. "What?" he said.

"You were going to look for me in the woods. Why did you come back?" She looked drained, and he was sure by now that the adrenaline rush from the snake had faded, but she also looked like she would sit there waiting until he answered her.

"I heard you scream," he said.

She shook her head. "I was watching you from behind the house. You stopped at the edge of the woods and stood there for a minute, then turned back. I was going to run when I saw the snake and tripped. What made you stop?"

He tried to remember. "Your sweat shirt," he said. "It was lying on the ground. You would have put it on because it was getting colder and you're sick. It's a pullover, so it couldn't have just fallen off of you when you went into the woods. You dropped it there as a decoy, tried to get me to chase phantoms in the forest."

She looked impressed, begrudgingly, and despite himself, Nick felt a brief glow of satisfaction. "Were you like a cop or something?" Annalise asked.

"No," he said. "I taught history. What were you going to do if I went into the woods? Take my car and drive away?"

She nodded. "If I could find the keys. If not, I was going to walk up to the road and then hitch my way out of here."

"Because of what the deputy said?"

She fell silent, looked in her lap. Nodded.

"Where were you going to go?"

She shrugged, still looking in her lap. "Away," she said. "California, maybe."

"Why there?"

52

"Because it's about as far away from here as you can get without leaving the country."

"And once you got there, then what?" He heard the harsh tone in his voice, saw Annalise look up from her lap in surprise, but he kept going, as if he had released something bitter that needed to flood out. "You go live on a beach? Maybe go to Hollywood and become a movie star?"

"Fuck you," she said.

Stop it, Ellie said.

"Stop," Nick said aloud. He put his hands over his face. When he dropped them, he saw Annalise had slid farther down in the bed but was still glaring at him. "I'm sorry," he said. "I'm sorry, Annalise. You're scared and you've been through a horrible experience, and you don't know me and I'm just . . . I'm tired. I'm sorry."

She considered him as if weighing his apology. "Fuck you for being mean," she said. Her voice was weaker now, but it still rocked him back on his heels. "You did save my life and all," she continued, "but you don't get to yell at me."

"Okay," he said. "You're right. I'm sorry." He sighed. "And I didn't save your life. That rattlesnake wouldn't have killed you. Sent you to the hospital, yes."

"Okay," she said.

They sat there, looking past each other in the silence that followed. Then Annalise picked up the box of Theraflu from her tray and struggled briefly with the blister pack before popping two pills out. She swallowed them, chasing them with water. She sank back against the pillow. "I still need to tell you what happened . . ."

"Later," Nick said. "Get some rest."

"No," she said. "I need to tell you now. While I have the nerve to do it."

CHAPTER EIGHT

In the story Annalise told her uncle, she was dreaming that her phone was ringing and she was looking for it on the golf course, of all places. It was bright noon and she was the only one on the fairway, the only person she could see at all, in fact, as if she were the last person on earth. The phone continued to ring, insistent on being answered. She approached the green, walking across a sand trap, trying to follow the sound. Her phone seemed to be ringing from inside the hole, which had a limp red flag. She reached out toward the hole, and a sudden breeze made the red flag flap wildly—

She opened her eyes to find herself in Eric's bedroom. It was dark and her phone was ringing somewhere on the floor. Just as she started to get out of bed, it stopped ringing. She sat on the edge of the bed, still woozy from the vodka, and looked back at Eric. He was lying facedown on the bed, his head turned away from her. He was still naked, while she had pulled on her T-shirt and panties. She looked across the room at Eric's clock. It was 12:06 AM. They'd been asleep maybe an hour.

Her phone started ringing again, and now she registered the ring tone—"The Imperial March" from *The Empire Strikes Back*. Her father. Shit. She looked for her jeans on the floor and plucked her ringing phone out of the hip pocket, then hurried out of the bedroom into the hall and closed the door behind her so Eric wouldn't wake up, wouldn't hear her placating her father.

She took a breath and answered. "Hi, Daddy," she said, pacing the hallway.

"Thank God," her father said. "*Moosh*, I've been calling you."

Annalise groaned. Her father's insistence on calling her "mouse" in Dari—something his own mother, whom Annalise had never known, had called him when he was younger—was beyond embarrassing at this point, and she made a point of protesting whenever he used that term.

"Where are you?" he said. "Are you still at Eric's?"

"No," she said. She passed Eric's parents' bedroom—they were in Las Vegas. "I'm over at Kit's house. I told Mom I was going to sleep over?"

"*Moosh*, listen to me—"

Annalise groaned again.

"Annalise!" He snapped her name in a way that made her stop pacing. Her father rarely spoke with such urgency and . . . was that fear? "Your phone says you're at Eric's. Are you still there? It's okay, just tell me."

Anger flared in her briefly. *Your phone says you're at Eric's.* "Did you put spyware on my phone again?" she said.

"*Moosh*, please."

She paused, closed her eyes. "Yeah, I'm at Eric's."

"Okay," her father said. "Your mother and I are coming to get you. We—"

"Daddy, please," she said. "Don't do that, I'll . . . I'll come home—"

"*No*," her father said. "Listen to me, Annalise. We have to leave. All of us. Tonight."

"Leave? What do you . . . where are we *going*?"

"To your Uncle Nick's. Can you put me on speaker?"

"I . . . yeah, okay," Annalise said, and she held her phone away and tapped the icon so her father's voice was now on speaker. "What—"

His voice was tinny on the speaker, echoing in the dark hallway. "You need to disable location tracking on your phone," he said. "I'll walk you through it."

"What's going on, Dad?"

"There's no time, Annalise," he said. "I need you to do this."

She stood in the hallway, staring at her phone. "You're scaring me," she said.

"Good," he said. "I'm sorry, but I need you to pay attention. Go into your settings on your phone, okay? Then you—"

"I know how to disable location tracking, Dad."

"You need to do it for everything. No apps at all, nothing. Now."

"I just—Jesus! Okay, okay, I'm doing it." She started tapping. In fifteen seconds she was finished. "Done," she said. "Now tell me what's going on. We're going to Uncle Nick? Where does he even live?"

"North Carolina," he said. "In a town called Cashiers, in the mountains. Your mother and I will come pick you up soon, maybe half an hour. Be outside, okay? We might walk over there, so wait for us on Eric's patio."

"You might *walk* here?"

"Someone's watching the house. We can't drive—"

"Someone is *watching our house*?" she said. "What the fuck, Daddy?"

Eric's bedroom door cracked open, and Eric looked out. *What's going on?* he mouthed.

She waved him away, then turned the speaker on her phone back off and held it up to her ear. "Just call the police!" she said to her father.

"I can't do that, honey," her father said.

Eric walked into the hall, wearing a pair of boxers. "Are you in trouble or something?" he asked.

"Shut up," she hissed at him.

"Annalise?" her father said on the phone.

"Not you," she said to her father. She glared at Eric and waved him back toward the room. He shrugged and rolled his eyes and went back into the bedroom, closing the door behind him.

"What did you do, Dad?" she said. Her father's job as a contractor took him all around the world, and he dealt with lots of different people—some of them less than savory, as her best friend Kit would say. In the back of her mind ever since she was thirteen, she had this imagined scenario where the FBI or the IRS or some other alphabet agency would come to arrest her father for cheating on his taxes or bending some sort of business regulation to the breaking point. Her father was always looking for corners to cut, for the next easy deal, the next big pile of money. More often than not it eluded him, but he was successful just often enough to whet his appetite for more. And, as he was fond of pointing out, to keep her and her mother in the lifestyle to which they had become accustomed.

But this was different. Now her father was asking her to turn off her phone's location settings and meet him and her mom after midnight at her boyfriend's house, a boyfriend her father either ignored or vaguely disliked, depending on his mood, all so they could escape some unseen stalker and go see Uncle Nick, her father's older brother whom he never spoke about and whom she had never met. And he couldn't—or wouldn't—call the police.

"Annalise," her father said, ignoring her question about what he had done, "just in case, if you have to leave without us, you need to go to a public storage place on Benjamin Road by the airport and get something out of a locker. It's a backpack. There's cash in there and some clothes. There's also a piece of paper that's folded up with the cash. Take that paper to your uncle. You have to give it to him—no one else. The locker number is twelve and the code is your mother's birthday reversed. You can use the cash to help you get to your uncle. You fly to Atlanta and then take a bus up to north Georgia or South Carolina; you can find your way to Cashiers from there."

She shook her head. "I don't even understand what you're saying. And I'm not going anywhere without you. You're coming here, right?"

"We are," he said. "Just being careful. Here's your mother."

58

There was a fumbling sound, and then she heard her mother say, "Hi, baby." At the sound of her mother's voice, something in Annalise broke and she began crying, hard jags like her confusion and fear were trying to claw their way out of her.

"It's okay, baby," her mother said, which only made Annalise cry harder. "It's going to be all right. I'm with your father, and we'll both be with you very soon. Is Eric there with you?"

Annalise wiped her nose on her T-shirt. "Yeah," she said. "Yes, he is."

"Stay with him. We'll be there soon. Here's your father."

The same fumbling sound, and then her father said, "One more thing, about your uncle. If you get there before we do, he lives off of Whiteside Cove Road outside of Cashiers. Number 1066. And make sure it's really your Uncle Nick. Ask him how old I was when I fell off the roof."

"You fell off a roof?"

"No. That's the trick. *He* fell off the roof when he was ten. Only your uncle will know that story."

"This is the most bizarre phone call I have ever had," Annalise said.

Her father chuckled. "I love you, *moosh*."

"Love you too, Daddy."

"We'll see you soon. Wait outside with Eric." He hung up.

Annalise stood in the dark hallway, staring at her phone, until Eric poked his head back out of his room. "What was *that* all about?" he said. "Hey, are you crying?"

"Something's wrong," she said. "My dad and mom—something happened. They're coming over here to pick me up."

"Shit," Eric said. "Busted."

"You're not *listening*. It's not that. There's . . . someone's watching our house. My dad says we have to leave town."

"Wait," Eric said. "Someone's watching your house? You don't mean, like, a house sitter, right? Like surveillance or something?"

She nodded. "Dad sounded scared. He never sounds scared."

Eric frowned. "Why doesn't your dad just call the cops?"

"He said he can't."

Eric's frown deepened. "Why not?"

Annalise shook her head. He wasn't listening to her—didn't he get that something was really wrong? And yet his questions made perfect sense. Her father, as usual, had been long on drama, short on details.

"You're shivering," Eric said, and he hugged her. Annalise leaned her head against him and closed her eyes. Her eyes filled with tears. What was wrong with her? "It's okay," Eric said, rocking her gently. "Are your parents really coming?"

She nodded against his chest. "That's what they said. They wanted me to wait for them outside, on your patio. They're walking over from our house."

Eric didn't say anything for a moment, and Annalise wondered if he was trying to figure out some smartass thing to say. She loved him, but God, he could be such a *boy* sometimes.

"Then let's go out there and wait for them," he said. "And then we can figure out what to do." He leaned back to look at her face. "Okay?"

She nodded, relieved but also feeling guilty about thinking of him as a boy. Then she reached up on her tiptoes and kissed him. "Okay," she said.

They got dressed and went downstairs, through the kitchen—Annalise saw the empty shot glasses on the kitchen counter, and her stomach roiled—and then they were out the sliding glass door and on the stone patio. It was dark, but the tree frogs were singing up a storm. Past the trees at the edge of the backyard was the golf course, the vast empty stretch of the fairways lying under a quarter moon. She sat down on a chaise longue that had a good view of the seventh hole, and Eric sat next to her on the same chair. She scooted over to make room. They lay back in the seat together, Eric with his arm across the back of Annalise's shoulders, both looking out at the golf course, waiting for her parents to arrive.

ANNALISE WOKE UP suddenly. She was wet, covered in dew—in Florida at night the temp dropped but the humidity shot up, leaving a fine lace of water on everything. The chaise longue was damp, as was Eric, who lay next to her snoring softly. The house behind them was dark.

She pulled her phone out of her hip pocket and blinked her eyes clear of sleep. It was 1:27 in the morning. Panic stabbed her. Her father had called over an hour ago. Where was he?

She looked out at the golf course. Across the fairway, behind the mansions that fronted the golf course, was her house. She couldn't see it from here, but it was close. Then, as she watched, where it had been dark just a second ago there was now a flicker, like a candle moving among the trees. No, it was bigger than that, a ruddy orange glow. It wasn't a streetlight; it looked more like someone had started a—

She bolted up and out of the chaise longue, sprinting across the golf course. Behind her Eric called her name, but by that point she was already halfway across the fairway. It was the strangest run she had ever made in her life—the night air, the singing of the tree frogs, the wide-open fairways where, like in her earlier dream, she was the only person in sight. Her pulse beat in her throat, her lungs drawing in air and forcing it out. Then she reached the far side of the fairway and ran across the street without looking, right into the Andersons' yard. She went around the side of the Andersons' house and in their backyard skirted the blue glow of their swimming pool, heading for the gate in the privacy fence that separated their yard from her own. She could see a fiery glow reflected off the leaves of the trees above her.

When she opened the gate, the heat rolled over her first, and then the noise. It was as if her house were roaring. Her kitchen and den were already aflame, the windows like doorways to hell. Thick smoke boiled out the back door, which was open. She stood staring, arms slack at her sides, her brain refusing to process what she was seeing. Her home was on fire. She did not see her parents. "Dad!" she screamed. "Mom!"

That was when she saw the two men in her driveway. Her house had a side-entry garage, so she had a clear line of sight from the back gate all the way down the driveway to the street. The two men stood in the shadows, looking at her house on fire as if watching it on television. She couldn't see them clearly, but then part of the roof of the garage collapsed and flames shot up, throwing light on their faces. One of them had short blond hair and a sharp, stubbled jaw. Neither man made a move toward the house. Behind them, down on the street, she could see a car idling, a four-door sedan, someone in the driver's seat. "Hey!" she screamed. But the two men gave no sign of hearing her over the noise of the burning house. They walked down the driveway to the idling car, opened the back doors, and got in. As soon as they closed the doors, the car took off, vanishing from sight.

SITTING IN HER uncle's bed, Annalise drank half a glass of water, her throat sore and dry. She had told him everything except the part about the paper. It was still folded up and safely behind her driver's license in the sleeve on the back of her phone—she had checked earlier when her uncle had gone to make her tea. She lay back in the bed, feeling spent. Her uncle sat brooding in the chair by the window. When he spoke, she jumped, startled.

"Did you talk to the police?" he asked.

She shook her head. "I didn't wait," she said. "Maybe I should have. Maybe if I'd —"

Her uncle cut her off, although his tone was kind. "Your parents were dead," he told her. "Those men probably set the fire to cover up the crime, at least for long enough to give them a chance to get away. You couldn't have done anything, Annalise."

She didn't know how to respond to that, so she just sipped more water. A wave of fatigue swept over her. The Theraflu must have finally started working.

"What did you do next?" he asked.

"Eric drove me to the storage place," she said. "There was a backpack in the locker, like Dad said. It had a roll of cash in twenties and . . . some clothes. They were Dad's." For a moment she felt as if she would cry, and then she didn't. "Then Eric took me to the airport and I bought a plane ticket to Atlanta, worked my way up here."

"What about Eric?"

"He stayed home," she said. "He offered to come with me, but I said no. I didn't want him to get in trouble for skipping school and just taking off. His parents can be kind of psycho. I think he was relieved, to be honest."

Her uncle nodded, thinking. "Where's your backpack?" he asked.

"I lost it," she said. She was fading, but the shame cut through her exhaustion. "Somebody stole it from me. When I got off the plane in Atlanta, I was looking at my phone for a way to get to Cashiers, and someone snagged the backpack. I put it down for a second and then it was gone." She shook her head, angry. "I'd taken the cash out of it, thank God. All that was left in it was some of Dad's clothes."

"That must have hurt," her uncle said softly.

She nodded, then closed her eyes and rode another wave of fatigue.

"How'd you get here from Atlanta?" he asked.

"Took a bus to Gainesville," she said, her eyes still closed. "I went into a hardware store across from the bus station, bought a big knife. Felt like I needed some kind of protection."

"Next time buy a hammer," he said. The comment was so odd that she opened her eyes to stare at him. "Won't look as suspicious and it's easier to carry," he explained, then gave her a little smile. "What happened next?"

She closed her eyes again. She was so sleepy. "Called a taxi to take me to Clayton, then another one up here. Tried looking you up in the phone book at a gas station, but I couldn't find you listed. My phone was dead. Cell service sucked anyway. But Dad gave me your address, so I looked at a map on the gas station wall. I found it. Then I walked."

She couldn't open her eyes, but she heard her uncle say one last thing. "You were brave," he said. She was too worn out to process anything else, but as she slipped away, she held on to the understanding in her uncle's voice, the kindness. For the first time in three days, she felt safe.

A small voice deep in her mind said, *He's just a history teacher.* Then she struggled feebly to grasp another thought that lay just out of reach. Before she could, she slept.

CHAPTER NINE

Nick watched Annalise for a few minutes as she slept, then quietly got up, picked up the food tray with the soup bowl and plate, and took it to the kitchen. Then he went back to the bedroom, made sure Annalise was still sleeping, turned off the light, and closed the door.

The den was dark—he'd left the lights off, and the sun had already set. He turned on the lamp by his armchair and built a fire in the hearth, twisting old newspaper and putting it underneath the grate with two pieces of fatwood, then stacking three logs of hickory on top of that. When he struck a match and set it to the newspaper, the fire kindled and took hold swiftly. He poured himself a finger of whiskey and set the glass down on the side table next to his armchair.

Nick sat in his chair, thinking. Annalise was either telling the truth or she was a very skilled liar. Nick had met very skilled liars before. He needed to do some research, and for that he needed Internet access. The library in Cashiers had Wi-Fi and computers available for the public, but it was closed for renovations. He would have to drive to Highlands instead. But before that he would need to have a serious talk with Annalise. He picked up the glass of whiskey and looked at the amber liquid, then held it to his nose and breathed in. Sweet and spice, wood and grain.

Jay, he thought. *What the hell did you do?*

GROWING UP IN San Diego, Nick navigated the worlds of both middle and high school with relative ease. His father worked for USAID in San Diego, helping Afghan refugees relocate, and also taught an international relations class at San Diego City College. This was a far cry from his more exalted post as a USAID foreign service officer in Afghanistan, but he never complained, and Nick was proud of his father and of his job helping immigrants become American citizens.

Jay, by contrast, seemed to have chosen his mother's path of resistance, often asking what Afghanistan was like and why his father had made his mother leave. With his sneer and curled lip that he'd perfected ever since turning thirteen, Jay announced at breakfast one morning that he was going to take his mother's family name, Bashir.

Their father had paused, then put his coffee down on the breakfast table. "When you're eighteen, you can do as you like," he said, puzzled, as usual, by his youngest son. "Bashir is a fine name. It means 'bringer of good news' in Arabic."

Jay rolled his eyes. "I know what it means."

Nick glanced at their mother, who was busy at the stove, her back to them, pretending she wasn't listening. "What's wrong with Anthony?" he asked Jay. "That's our last name."

"I didn't choose it," Jay said.

Their father raised his hands in a calming gesture. "Afghans have always taken and borrowed names," he said. "Your great-grandfather was the first in his family to take a last name."

"This is stupid," Nick muttered.

"What's your problem?" Jay said.

"We were born in San Diego," Nick said. "You've never even *been* to Afghanistan."

"Only because Dad made Mâmân leave," Jay said.

"Jay," their father said.

There was a crash as their mother dropped a pan into the sink, and then she walked out of the kitchen, went upstairs, and slammed the door of the master bedroom.

Jay began frequenting the local mosque, a display of piety that made their mother happy. Little else did. If their father had returned home and Nick was an all-American teenager, their mother fought a rear-guard action against assimilation. She complained of the weather in California, the traffic, the noise, the women who walked around practically undressed, the strange food, the sun that was not their sun.

"It's the same sun that shines in Afghanistan, Mâmân," Nick said.

"It is not," their mother replied. "How can you even say such a thing?"

Her outrage extended to all of them, even Jay, whom she usually doted on, giving him extra sweets as a child, excusing his stubbornness as standing on principle and his dislike of school as evidence of a superior mind. Nick knew their mother was having a very bad day when she would turn on Jay, chastising him for letting his hair grow too long or for not perfectly reciting a verse from the Koran.

Their father got the worst of it, though. He was baffled by his wife's outbursts, even moved to tears of frustration. Some evenings she was kind and spoke lovingly to him, and others she would rail and curse at him for not making enough money. He had argued that he was lucky to have a job at all, let alone one that was similar to his previous career. The communist regime in Kabul had marked him as an intellectual and a possible dissident, and he was already under suspicion as an American. Once the Soviets had decided to invade, they'd had to flee. Didn't she see that?

But their mother would not be mollified. As Nick and his brother had grown older, she had become prone to rages so strong that her tongue would fail her and she would instead use her hands, slapping or pushing or punching. One evening when Jay was attending prayers at the mosque, she picked up a plate of kofta and hurled it at Nick, who ducked. The plate shattered against the wall, the spiced balls of ground lamb rolling across the floor. The shattering plate and his mother's cries brought his father running. "What's going on?" his father shouted. Her face red, mouth opened in a shriek, Nick's mother flew at her husband, slapping, hitting, shoving. His father fended her off with his arms but did not raise a hand to her. He let her expend her rage like a thunderstorm on him, and when she finally collapsed to the floor of the kitchen, sobbing, he picked her up like a child and carried her to their room, while Nick scraped up the mashed kofta from the kitchen floor.

That night, lying in bed and listening to Van Halen on his Walkman, Nick at first didn't hear the knock on his bedroom window. Then someone started pounding on the window so that it rattled in its frame. Nick sat up in bed and stared out the window at Jay, who stood outside in the dark, dress shirt untucked and dirty. *Let me in*, Jay mouthed. Nick took his headphones off, got up, and with a little difficulty opened the window. Jay climbed in clumsily, nearly falling on his face. "The hell is wrong with your window?" he said.

"What are you doing?" Nick demanded. His room and Jay's were on the lower floor of their split-level, their parents' bedroom just above. "You'll wake Mom and Dad up."

" 'Mom and Dad,' " Jay said, mocking Nick. "Relax, *beraadar*." *Beraadar* was Dari for brother. Jay used that term only to annoy Nick. He stood up, and as he did, the sharp medicinal smell of vodka hit Nick in the face.

"What the hell?" Nick said.

Jay chuckled. "It's good, I'm fine."

Nick grabbed Jay by the shoulders. Jay tried to brush his hands away but he kept chuckling, even when Nick shook him a little. "Oh no, *beraadar* is angry," Jay said, shaking with laughter.

"How did you get drunk?" Nick demanded.

Jay closed his eyes, contemplating the question. "Aaqil had the vodka. I didn't ask where he got it."

"I thought you were at the mosque. Have you not been going?"

Jay opened his eyes and managed to look offended. "I attend services. Tonight we left and Aaqil had vodka and orange juice and gave us some. It was very good."

Nick slung an arm across Jay's shoulders. "Come on, you're going to bed." Jay slumped against Nick but managed to move his feet enough to walk with his brother across the hallway to his own room. He fell across his bed, and Nick threw a blanket over him and closed the door. Nick returned to his room and slipped his headphones back on, but the music did little to calm his anger. What was his brother thinking? He was thirteen. Nick could scarcely imagine what their mother would do if she found Jay drunk.

The next morning, Saturday, their mother opened Nick's door and told him to get up if he wanted breakfast and that his father needed help moving some plants in the backyard. Nick muttered a greeting and got out of bed, yawning, and then with a shock remembered Jay. "Mâmân!" he called, scrambling out of bed. "I'll get Jay up!" Too late, he heard his mother open Jay's bedroom door. Shrieks and wails followed, and Nick ran across the hall. Their mother stood shouting over Jay, who was lying on his back in bed, bleary eyed, covered in his own reeking puke. "What?" Jay kept saying. "What?"

Their father appeared in the doorway, dressed in blue jeans and a long-sleeved T-shirt, a pair of gardening gloves in one hand. He wrinkled his nose at the smell. "He's drunk," he said.

Their mother's eyes seemed to swell with anger. "You are *drunk?*" she hissed at Jay, who cowered on his bed. She reached for him as if to strangle him, then withdrew her hands, disgusted by the puke on his shirt and bedsheets. "You drink alcohol and then vomit like a dog in my house? You miserable, useless child! You disgrace your family! I—"

"It's my fault, Mâmân," Nick said, the words coming out of his mouth the same instant they sprang to mind. "I . . . gave him the alcohol."

A stunned silence fell on the room.

His voice flat, their father said, "You gave him the alcohol."

Nick hung his head. "I'm sorry, Dad."

Their father folded his arms across his chest and frowned. Even his moustache registered disapproval. "Why would you do that?"

Nick glanced at Jay, who sat in his fouled T-shirt stained yellow from the orange juice, and at their mother, who stared dumbfounded. He remembered his mother throwing the plate of kofta at him the night before. "It was stupid," Nick said, looking at the floor. "I wanted to know how it felt to be drunk, and I offered some to Jay."

Their father stepped forward and slapped Nick across the face. The sound was like a green branch being snapped over a knee.

"You'll both work in the yard today, all day, as punishment," their father said. "No breakfast. Mâmân, would you please wash Jay's sheets and clothes?" He turned on his heel and walked out of the room without waiting for a reply. Their mother, nonplussed, muttered at Jay to take off his clothes and bring them with the bedsheets to the laundry room, then hurried after their father.

"Why did you do that?" Jay whispered.

Nick felt his cheek where his father had struck him. He didn't know which stung worse, the slap or the fact that his father had slapped him. "Because I didn't want Mom to lose it," he said.

"What are you talking about?" Jay looked down at himself and his bed, grimacing. "Shit."

"She threw a plate of food at me last night, Jay," Nick said. "A whole plate of kofta. She just chucked it across the room at me and started screaming."

"Why?"

"*Why*? Because she's *angry*. At everything. And she doesn't want to be here." Nick shook his head in disgust. "Get your clothes off. You stink." He turned to leave.

"Hey," Jay said, and Nick stopped in the doorway and turned back. Jay looked pale and bilious, but his expression was serious. "Dad only slapped you so Mom wouldn't," he said.

Nick nodded. "I know. But that doesn't make it any better."

SITTING IN HIS armchair, Nick held the glass of whiskey to his lips, not touching but so close. He remembered Clarence, a colleague at Oxford, talking to him over whiskey about Prince Hamlet, how students focused on his suicidal tendencies. "What they ignore," Clarence had said, refilling an honest-to-God pipe with tobacco while an interminable January rain fell outside the study windows, "is that the poor bugger doesn't want to kill himself as much as just cease to exist."

" 'O that this too too solid flesh would melt, / Thaw, and resolve itself into a dew,' " Nick had said, quoting from memory.

Clarence had smiled, a wrinkled, jowly expression of pleasure, and pointed his unlit pipe at Nick. "Just so." He had picked up his glass of whiskey and held it up in salute. "*Sláinte.*"

Now, sitting in his den with the fire crackling in the hearth, Nick contemplated the glass in his hand. A simple tilt of the wrist, and he could pour the whiskey into his mouth. The first sip of a long, slow slide into oblivion.

Then he stood and walked into the kitchen and poured the glass out in the sink.

In the tiny laundry room off the kitchen, he found and changed into a clean T-shirt and a pair of pajama pants, leaving his jeans and Henley on the floor, then padded out to the sofa and set up his pillow and blanket. After stoking the fire and adding one more log, he used the bathroom off the foyer and flushed, then went into his office, glancing as he always did at the picture of Ellie. He missed her smile. He missed her. He pulled open the top desk drawer and took out the pistol that lay there, then found the magazines in the drawer below it and loaded one into the pistol. He placed the pistol back into the top drawer, closed it, and went back to the sofa to stare at the fire as it crackled and hissed in the hearth.

CHAPTER TEN

THE PLANE CARRYING COLE AND HIS MEN TOUCHED DOWN AT CHARLIE Brown airport west of Atlanta. Everyone unbuckled, but Jonas, Hicks, and Waco remained in their seats. Randy the pilot told Cole he could be in the air and on the way to Hilton Head in under thirty minutes. Poncho and Dawes went to check on ground transportation, which they had arranged through a rental agency in Tampa.

Before leaving the plane, Cole huddled one last time with Jonas. "Just surveillance for now," Cole said. "Keep an eye on the grandparents. If you see the girl, call before doing anything else."

"Got it. Where will you be?"

"Gonna find a place to stay until we hear something different. And we need to resupply. Winslow's contact is in north Georgia. I'll keep you posted." Still Cole hesitated. He did not like breaking up the team, even though it made the most sense. With the girl in the wind, they needed to cover all possibilities in order to find her.

Jonas seemed to understand. "It's only an hour away," he said. "We'll be there before you know it. And we can get back fast, long as we have this ride."

"It's ours for as long as we need it," Cole said. "Whoever's hiring us has deep pockets."

"Best kind of client."

"Stay safe." Cole gently punched Jonas on the arm and then turned and stepped outside onto the stairs. The sky was dark—it was after midnight—although the county airport was brightly lit. Hopefully they could get a meal and a few hours' sleep before continuing the search. Speed was essential, but so was being prepared. Exhaustion led to careless mistakes. The thought reminded him of Winslow, and Cole grimaced like he had just smelled something rank. Winslow hadn't been exhausted, just stupid.

Cole walked down the stairs to the tarmac just as Poncho drove up in another Suburban. Cole helped Dawes and Zhang unload their gear from the plane and put it in the vehicle—they were the only people on the field this late at night, and Cole didn't want to draw any more attention to themselves than necessary. Cole looked back at the jet and saw Jonas watching from a window. Jonas nodded at him, and Cole tossed off a casual salute before stepping into the Suburban.

"Gentlemen," he said. "What are the sleeping arrangements this evening?"

It was an old setup to a long-running joke. Cole had asked this question when they had been humping across a desert, when they were trying not to drown in a jungle downpour, and once when they were in a Liberian prison before they could bribe their way out. Usually when Cole asked it, one of them would make a comment about which one of them was boning Waco, the youngest of them, or some other wiseass crack. This time, there was the barest pause after Cole asked the question, as if no one wanted to speak.

It was Dawes who answered him, as reliably no-drama as ever. "A Super Inn off I-20, just south of here," he said. "Got a Waffle House across the street."

Behind the wheel, Poncho groaned. "Fucking Waffle House, man."

"I *love* Waffle House," Cole said. "Eggs, steak, burgers, chicken salad, whatever you want, twenty-four/seven. Scattered, smothered, and covered."

Poncho nodded wearily but said nothing as he starting driving, the Suburban crossing the tarmac toward an exit gate.

Cole looked straight ahead through the windshield and said, "Why is everyone acting like someone just shit themselves?"

Silence except for the hum of the tires. Even Zhang's constant typing on his laptop had stopped.

In a quiet voice, Cole said, "Is there a problem?"

"No problem, boss," Poncho said, glancing over at Cole before returning his attention to the road. "Just tired, is all."

The fuck that's all, Cole thought. They were wary of him. Scared, even. Because of Winslow. He hadn't noticed on the plane because he had been talking with Jonas, and Jonas wasn't scared of anything this side of the grave. Some men who led squads of mercenaries or "security contractors" wanted to be feared. But fear wasn't the same as respect. Cole felt a small light in him grow dimmer. He stifled a sigh.

"Yeah, we're all tired," he said. "Zhang, where are we with the girl's phone?"

"Making progress," Zhang said, typing on his laptop. "Should get into their phone records in the next twenty-four hours."

Cole drummed his fingers on his knee. Hacking into a telecommunications company was tricky, especially if you wanted access to records without alerting the company or leaving a trace. But if Zhang said it would be done in a day, it would be done in a day.

"All right," Cole said. "We eat, check in, and get some rack time. Then we start looking."

THE NEXT MORNING, Zhang stayed in the motel room with his laptop, continuing to try to hack into the girl's cell phone carrier, while Cole, Dawes, and Poncho drove to the Atlanta airport. They left the

Suburban in short-term parking and made their way to Arrivals in the domestic terminal.

Hundreds of thousands of children and teenagers went missing each year in the US. The vast majority returned home alive within twelve months, but thousands slipped through the cracks. Police did their best but were often overwhelmed by sheer numbers, and teen runaways were a lower priority than young children who had disappeared. Cole was counting on that as he and his men spread out in the cavernous Arrivals lobby at Hartsfield-Jackson International Airport. Thousands of people passed through the space every hour; ten million passengers flowed through Hartsfield-Jackson a month. It was searching for a grain of rice in a snowbank. But they had to start somewhere.

True to his word, Kobayashi had called soon after dawn to tell them that the girl had not been on the manifest of any commercial flight in the United States since arriving in Atlanta yesterday. Assuming they could trust Kobayashi's information, and Cole thought that was a safe assumption, the girl had not left Atlanta by plane. She was too young to rent a car, and according to Zhang her phone was turned off, so she hadn't called for an Uber or Lyft, at least not on her own phone. Unless she had gotten another phone or somehow gotten in touch with a friend in Atlanta to come pick her up, that left taxi, bus, or MARTA, the regional public train system.

Dawes headed for the buses while Poncho took an escalator to the airport MARTA station. Cole bypassed the skycaps at baggage claim—the girl wouldn't have had any checked luggage—and went to the taxi stand outside. A man in a neon-green vest gazed at the line of taxis at the curb, but he snapped alert as soon as Cole walked up. "Where to, sir?"

"Actually, I need your help," Cole said. He held up a laminated ID card with a false name and his picture that read PRIVATE INVESTIGATOR. "I'm looking for a missing girl." With his other hand he held up his phone, which displayed a picture of Annalise that he'd taken from her father's phone. "She's sixteen years old, probably traveling alone, flew in around nine forty-five yesterday morning. See anyone like her?"

The man glanced at the picture but was already shaking his head. "Man, I don't know. So many people come through here . . ."

Cole put his ID back in his jacket pocket, and when he took his hand back out, he was holding two twenties. "Take another look," Cole said. "She's a runaway. Her father's really worried about her."

The man hesitated, then took the two twenties and peered at the picture of a smiling Annalise on the phone in Cole's hand. "Cute girl," he said. "But I didn't see her. And I was out here all yesterday morning too."

Cole spoke with two other green-vested men at the taxi stand and came up just as empty-handed. He looked at the long line of taxis that snaked back down the terminal drive. If he had to talk to every god-damned taxi driver in Atlanta, he would.

His phone buzzed. Dawes. Cole answered. "Tell me something good."

"I'm at the bus station," Dawes said. "Woman at the counter says she might have seen her."

Cole made his way back inside to the Greyhound bus station, where he found Dawes talking with the uniformed woman behind the counter. "Jerilyn here says she saw the girl," Dawes said. "But she's worried about telling anybody."

Cole nodded and smiled warmly at Jerilyn, who gave him a nervous smile in return. "I understand," Cole said. "A man walks up and wants to know if you've seen an underage girl, you wonder if he's on the up-and-up." He pulled out his ID and held it up to Jerilyn. "Mr. Smith here works for the same firm I do. We're just trying to get this girl back to her mom and dad."

Jerilyn glanced at Cole's ear and just as quickly looked away. Cole continued to smile at her. He was used to people staring at his chewed-up ear. He'd thought about wearing a watch cap to cover it, make him less memorable, but wearing a watch cap in June in Atlanta would be about as conspicuous as wearing a parka in the Sahara. Cole held out his phone with the picture of Annalise. "So you did see her?"

Jerilyn looked at the picture and gnawed briefly on her lower lip. "I don't know. I mean, yes, I saw her—"

"Was she okay?" Cole said, concern in his voice. "Did she seem upset?"

"She'd lost her backpack," Jerilyn said. "That's how come I remember her. She put it down for a minute, and somebody snatched it. You know how it is." Cole nodded in commiseration, and Jerilyn continued. "Anyway, she was freaking out, wanted us to make sure we didn't have her backpack behind the counter or anything."

"Did she find it?" Cole asked.

Jerilyn shook her head. "She started crying, said something about her dad. She was torn up about it."

Cole saw Dawes dart a glance at him at the mention of the girl's father. Cole kept his eyes on Jerilyn. "Did she get on a bus without it?" he asked.

Jerilyn opened her mouth, then shut it. "Maybe we should get the police, you know?" she said. "If this girl is missing like you say, we should tell them."

Cole nodded. "Understandable," he said, then lowered his voice just enough to render their conversation private, even though no one else was currently at the counter. "The thing is, this girl's father, he's the kind of person who wants to keep things about his family private. His daughter is running away to this man she met. He's a bad guy, Jerilyn. Exploits girls. She won't listen, of course. They're in love."

"That's terrible," Jerilyn said, her eyes wide.

"Her father doesn't want her name to get out there," Cole said. "Especially not with this scumbag of a boyfriend. That's why he hired us to find her. Keep it all discreet. If we call the cops, then the press finds out and the girl's life gets ruined forever." Cole leaned in just a hair, eyes on Jerilyn. "Please help us, Jerilyn. Help her."

Jerilyn worried her lower lip again, then said, "You can't tell anyone I told you. I could lose my job."

Cole smiled. "That's the last thing I would want to do," he said.

Jerilyn nodded solemnly, then took a deep breath. "She took a bus to Gainesville. Yesterday."

CHAPTER ELEVEN

Nick woke to the thrumming of his water pipes in the walls. He lay on his back, trying to orient himself, then realized he was on the couch in his living room where he had slept. Annalise must be taking a shower. He sat up and tossed the fleece blanket off. It was raining outside, Whiteside wreathed in tattered fog. There was a soft *ker-chunk* as the shower was turned off, followed by a rapid hammering in the walls. Air trapped in the pipes, he thought, or maybe a water pressure issue. Or both. He rubbed his face, then stood and went into the kitchen to make coffee, taking two mugs out of the cabinet.

When the coffee was ready, he carried both mugs to the bedroom door, which he again tapped with his foot before opening. The bed was empty, the covers kicked back, and he could hear the low hum of the exhaust fan in the bathroom. "Annalise," he called out. "It's me. I've got some coffee." He walked into the room and put the mugs down on the side table, then turned around and stopped cold. At the far end of the bathroom, in the doorway of the walk-in closet, Annalise had frozen, a white towel wrapped around her hair like a turban. She was wearing a red dress, sleeveless with the skirt flaring out and falling to just above her knees. Ellie's dress.

"ARE YOU REALLY ready to retire to the mountains?" Ellie had asked him.

They were at the Frog and Owl, a restaurant in a former gristmill outside Highlands. A celebratory dinner, trout and rack of lamb supported by a fantastic wine cellar, the night-darkened windows reflecting the candlelight.

"It's not retirement," Nick said. "Not really. I'll still be teaching."

Ellie's smile was warm and a little sad. "That's not what I meant," she said.

The waiter thankfully chose that moment to appear and refill their wineglasses. They sat back and regarded one another over the table as the waiter poured. Nick thought Ellie had never looked so lovely. She was wearing the red dress that he loved, the one she took out of its garment bag only for special occasions—her first promotion at the World Bank, his first teaching post in Cairo. And now they had closed on a house outside Cashiers. It needed some renovations, but it had a beautiful view of Whiteside and was exactly what Ellie wanted.

When the waiter left, Ellie took a sip of her wine. "Western Carolina isn't the same as Oxford," she said.

"Oxford," Nick said, as if enjoying the sound of the word. "Did I really teach there?"

"And you met me there. Best thing that ever happened to you."

"True," he said. "But we didn't really meet there. It's more like you stalked me."

She rolled her eyes. "I didn't stalk you."

"You went to the registrar and looked up my schedule so you could bump into me after class."

"That's strategic pursuing, not stalking." She eyed him wickedly over her glass. "How else was I going to get a hotshot young professor with his head up his own ass to notice me?"

He grinned back at her and sipped from his own glass. They sat in comfortable silence, enjoying the sight of each other. The waiter hovered in the background, and Nick gave him a subtle shake of the head, causing him to vanish. "I won't miss Oxford or the rest of it," Nick said. "Teaching here suits me just fine. And I'll get cable internet set up at the house so you can work from home."

"I'll still have to fly to DC sometimes."

"Absence makes the heart grow fonder."

Ellie laughed at that, a sound that drew attention not because it was loud but because it was pure, the kind of laughter that made everyone who heard it wish they were the one who had caused it. "You're such a cheeseball," she said, and he waggled his eyebrows, making her laugh again.

She sighed, content. "We're really going to move up here."

"We really are."

"Promise me something."

Nick set his glass down. "Anything."

"If you aren't happy, you'll tell me."

Now Nick laughed. "I'm very happy."

"I mean when we move here." Ellie leaned forward, still smiling, but behind the smile was that dogged focus Nick so often admired and at other times found exasperating. "It's so different from everywhere else we've lived. I just don't want you to regret it."

Nick reached across the table and took Ellie's hand. "You followed me for my career," he said. "And I'm done with that. With all of it."

Ellie looked straight at him. "All of it?"

And there it was, the shadow at the edge of the candlelight.

"All of it," he said, his eyes on hers, unwavering. And he meant it, at least at that moment. "Now I get to focus on us. On you. Just promise you won't get tired of me."

Ellie raised an eyebrow. "As long as you don't start wearing bathrobes past noon and shuffling around the house like an old man. I've got plans, mister. We're going to hike every trail in these mountains."

Nick groaned. "You and your death marches. You're going to kill me." He leaned forward to kiss her hand. "So be it."

Ellie squeezed his hand, then released it. "Need to use the ladies'," she said. Nick stood as she got up, then sat back down and watched her walk across the room. Ellie knew he was watching and moved her hips a bit more than usual, the red dress flaring at the bottom just below her knees to show off her calves. Nick felt an ache right then, a longing for her that was only partly about being together with her in bed later that night, or how they would hold each other afterward. It was as if he were already anticipating that he would lose her at some point in the future, although neither of them knew yet about the cancer brewing inside her. That night all Nick understood was that he would follow this woman anywhere.

Ellie glanced back over her shoulder with a hint of a smile, and then she turned the corner and was gone.

STANDING IN HIS bedroom, staring at Annalise wearing Ellie's red dress, Nick needed a moment to get his voice under control. "What are you doing?" he managed to say.

A guilty expression wavered in Annalise's face, and then something harder set in her features. "I needed something to wear," she said. "I just, I took a shower, and my clothes are disgusting, and I thought it'd be weird to grab one of your T-shirts—"

"So you thought you'd put on my wife's dress," he said. He was astonished at how angry he was, as if his anger were a thing separate from himself rather than some inherent defect.

Annalise looked down at herself as if seeing the dress for the first time, then back up at him. "Your wife?" she said. The open question was on her face.

Nick gestured to the mugs on the side table. "I brought you some coffee," he said. Then he turned and left the bedroom, closing the door behind him.

He marched across the great room into the kitchen, turned and marched back, going from kitchen table to fireplace to sofa to kitchen and then around again. If it weren't for the rain, he would walk outside around the lake, maybe take the long trail up to Whiteside and back to burn off his anger, like he had all those months ago after Ellie's death, trying to exhaust himself so he could fall asleep. But the rain was still coming down, so he paced inside like a caged animal.

It's all right, he could hear Ellie say.

No, it's not.

Yes.

No, damn it, no one else should be wearing it—it's yours.

I don't need it anymore.

I need it.

You don't need a dress, she said, a bit sadly. *You want it because you miss me.*

Damn her logic, replaying itself in his memory like a once-loved album that now annoyed you because you would never love it like you once had, never again be the person you were when you first heard it. "I don't . . . *want* this," he said aloud. His heart heaved once, an ugly, thudding piece of meat in his chest. He stood by the fireplace, now cold and dark, and put both hands up against the mantel and closed his eyes, as if he were bearing the weight of the stacked-stone chimney.

"Uncle Nick?" He turned and looked up to see Annalise, now wearing one of his T-shirts and her own jeans, standing outside the bedroom door, clasping her arms across her waist. Nick opened his mouth, words like daggers sharpened and ready to be flung, when he saw the hesitancy and fear in her eyes, in the way she seemed to be holding herself in a comfortless hug. His anger drained away.

"I'm sorry," he said.

Annalise shook her head. "No, I shouldn't have—"

"It's okay."

"No, it's not. I never should have messed with that dress."

"True," Nick conceded.

They looked at each other across the room.

"I hung the dress back up in the bag," Annalise said with all the honest naïveté of a child hoping her words would make everything better.

Nick said nothing, then sighed. Annalise looked at him warily.

"My wife," Nick began. Something swelled in his throat, and with an effort he swallowed. "She died, last year."

Something in Annalise's face shifted, but again that hardness was there like a wall. "That's awful," she said, her voice small.

"I gave away all of her clothes," he continued. "But I couldn't get rid of that dress. Sentimental, I guess. So when I saw you in it, I was . . . upset. You lose someone and it's . . . you get reminded and it's like you lose them again." Too late he brought himself up short, his face slack with shame. "God, Annalise, I'm sorry. Your parents—"

"It's fine," she said. Her voice was toneless. "I don't want to talk about that." She folded her arms across her chest and leaned against the wall, like she was waiting for a bus. Her eyes on the floor, she added, "Thank you for the coffee."

Nick looked at her, the studied blankness of her expression, her whole slumped posture trying to indicate boredom and indifference. She might as well have been wearing an actual suit of armor with spikes. He realized that the rain had stopped; through the window he saw the shadows of clouds race across the surface of the lake, followed by a swelling sunlight.

"Grab your sneakers," he said. "We're going on a walk."

CHAPTER TWELVE

They started out walking up the drive, Nick leading, the gravel crunching beneath their feet. Before the drive hooked left to follow the ridgeline of the hill on the eastern flank of the lake, Nick stepped through a break in the rhododendron onto a worn footpath that wound lazily up a gentler slope. He'd given Annalise a walking stick and a spare rain jacket that hung loosely from her shoulders. The rain had left the path muddy, but he clearly knew where he was going and where to step. "You okay?" he called, planting his own walking stick firmly on the ground as he moved forward.

Annalise glared at her uncle's back. "I'm great. I love walking around in the woods. Maybe we'll find another snake."

"That's why we have these," he said, holding up his own walking stick without turning around.

"What, so we can beat them to death?"

Nick thumped his stick on the ground. "No, so we can warn them we're coming."

Annalise muttered, "Fucking snakes."

What were they doing out here, hiking up a mountain? Okay, a big hill, but whatever. She had never liked hiking; walking to her was a means of getting somewhere. Her father had once planned a hike at Torrey Pines, a state reserve north of San Diego. We'll walk on the beach, we'll bond, it'll be fun, Dad had said. Ten-year-old Annalise asked if they could bring their old Labrador, Gus, with them. "Sure," Dad said, smiling. "The salt air will be good for his old bones." But when they'd driven all the way up the coast to the reserve, they saw the big sign that read NO DOGS ALLOWED. Dad cussed and made a big production about how they'd driven all that way, even though it had taken less than half an hour on a Saturday morning, and then he tried to get Annalise to sneak Gus into the reserve. She stood in the parking lot, holding Gus on his leash, with Gus looking miserable and sad eyed as her father insisted that they just go, it wasn't a big deal. And then a park ranger rolled up in a pickup truck and told her father that he was sorry, but dogs weren't allowed in the reserve. Annalise was convinced that her dad was going to pull out a twenty and try a bribe, but he just gave the ranger a jerky nod and then told Annalise to get back in the car. All the way home he said nothing, just glowered out the windshield, and Gus laid his head on his paws and gazed dolefully at Annalise.

That had been the only time her father tried to take her on a hike. One event in a long list of failed attempts and broken promises.

A defiant voice in her head said, *That's not all that he was.*

No, sometimes he was the guy who brought home suitcases full of cash, another voice said, bitter and resigned. *And sometimes he came home broke. Then there was the time we had to move because he could no longer afford the mortgage and he'd lost most of our savings.*

The defiant voice still spoke. *He took you dress shopping when Mom was sick with a stomach bug,* it said. *He helped you with algebra. He taught you how to drive a car. He called you* moosh.

At that last thought, Annalise stabbed her walking stick into the ground—if there had been a snake there, she would have speared it straight through. She was not going to dissolve into tears on this muddy path.

Soon they crested the hill. Annalise was breathing more heavily than she would have expected, her new T-shirt damp with sweat at the neck and under her arms. She leaned on her walking stick, a sturdy piece of polished hickory as tall as she was and at least an inch thick. Her uncle wasn't even winded. At the bottom of the slope before them, she could see a river twisting its way through the trees. Overhead, white clouds moved through a sky of blue, the sun painfully bright after the rain. Annalise shaded her eyes and turned back the way they had come to see her uncle's cabin at the foot of the lake, beyond which Whiteside spread across the near horizon like an enormous crooked horseshoe, its broken arms open and reaching toward them from the stone wall of its highest cliff face.

Nick sat on a stump and laid his walking stick across his lap, then rubbed his knees. When Annalise turned to look at him, he gave her a little smile. "My legs take a little while to warm up," he said.

She did not return his smile. Dismissively she said, "Nice view."

Nick looked around as if he hadn't noticed where they were until now and nodded. "It is. But that's not why I brought you up here."

Annalise folded her hands on top of her walking stick. "Is this where we have a heart-to-heart talk and then hug it out?"

"I have a confession to make," Nick said.

"What, are you Catholic now?"

"Muslim. Agnostic, really. Doesn't matter." He paused. "It's about your father."

Her heart fluttered at that, but she ignored it. "You going to tell me how he did bad things? Try to let me down gently? Trust me, I already know."

Nick shook his head. "No," he said. "I have to tell you about the last time I talked to him."

"Why?"

"Because I'm afraid it might be partly my fault that he died."

IT WAS EARLY the previous fall, rain coming down in a steady pour, the whole world wreathed in clouds, the forest green and not yet shading to gold and flame. Not that Nick had seen any of this—the trees could literally have been on fire and he wouldn't have noticed. In July he had buried Ellie. Two months later he sat in the darkened house, holding a glass of bourbon and gazing at it, considering whether or not to get drunk. Nothing mattered much anymore, aside from his grief, and he was already sick of that.

His phone rang. It was an older landline and sat on the kitchen counter. *Let it ring*, he thought, but he put the bourbon down and got up from his chair and answered. "Hello?"

"Nick?" a man said on the other end.

"Who is this?"

"It's Jay."

Nick gripped the handset and stared unseeing out the window at the oncoming night. A gust of wind scattered rain against the panes. "Jay," he managed.

"It's been a long time, brother."

"What do you want?"

A pause. "Almost twenty years and that's the first thing you ask?" Jay said.

Nick closed his eyes. *You had almost twenty years to call me*, he wanted to say. Instead he waited his brother out.

Jay sighed. "Fine. I need your help. Just a favor, really. I'm looking for someone who could connect me with the Syrian government."

Nick opened his eyes. "Why would you think I know anyone in the Syrian government?"

"Come on, give me some credit. You served in the Middle East, taught there for a while. You must know some people."

Standing in his dark house, Nick smiled—a cruel expression that did nothing to lighten his face. "The kind of people who like to broker information? Like about arms deals with the Kurds? Or maybe the Houthi in Yemen?"

Silence. Then his brother's voice, low and harsh. "How the hell do you—"

"Come on," Nick said, still smiling in the dark. "Give me some credit."

"This was a mistake," Jay said.

"Clearly," Nick said, and he hung up, then yanked the cord out of the wall. The next day, he had the phone disconnected.

WHEN NICK FINISHED, Annalise shook her head. "I don't understand," she said. "You argued with my dad last year, you hung up on him, and that's why somebody—" She grimaced.

"He was asking me for help," Nick said. "I didn't give him what he was looking for. So he went somewhere else, maybe asked the wrong person."

"Why didn't you just tell him what he wanted to know?"

"Because I don't know anyone in the Syrian government like that."

"So why did he think you did?"

"Because I lived in the Middle East for several years. I met a lot of people there. But the kind of people your father wanted to meet . . . they're dangerous."

"What do you mean, dangerous?" As soon as she asked the question, she knew the answer. The kind who would kill her parents and then torch her house. The kind who might be looking for her right now. Her heart was a stone in her throat; it was suddenly hard to breathe. She forced herself to take a deep breath, then another.

"Annalise, I'm sorry," Nick said. "Maybe I should have tried to help him." He shrugged and held up his hands as if in offering. "I'm sorry," he said again.

She let out a bark of a laugh that was more than half a sob. "You're *sorry*," she said, almost spitting the words, then hesitated. Her uncle sat on his stump, looked steadily at her. It would be so easy, she knew, to just unload on him, to release all her grief and rage onto him like a tsunami. And he was offering himself as a target.

She took in a ragged breath and let it out. "No," she said, shaking her head. "You didn't know what would happen. My father made a mistake.

He makes—*made* a lot of mistakes." Her eyes pricked with tears, but she gave Nick a shrug. "Life's a bitch and all that."

Calmly, as if reciting a fact out of a newspaper, Nick said, "Your parents are dead, Annalise."

The naked words stung her, but she refused to show any reaction. "No shit," she bit out.

"Someone killed them."

"Good to know you've been paying attention."

Nick said nothing but held his gaze on Annalise, who was determined not to look away first, to not even blink. She stared into her uncle's amber eyes, saw the pain and the pity in them. That angered her. He had no idea, no fucking clue how she felt. *Goddamn him*, she thought fiercely, her own fury startling her for a moment before it burned away her surprise and everything else.

"Why are you looking at me?" she said.

He didn't reply.

"Why the *fuck* are you looking at me?" she said, her voice rising to a shout.

He blinked slowly, irrationally causing her to briefly exult in winning the staring contest, but he didn't look away.

"Stop *looking* at me!" she shouted. "What are you, a pervert? Stop it!"

In the same calm tone he had spoken in before, Nick said, "I'm sorry they died."

"Shut up!"

"But they're gone," he said. "And you're not."

She threw her walking stick at him. It was a clumsy throw and the stick wobbled through the air like the world's shittiest spear and missed her uncle by a mile, clattering against the trunk of a nearby pine tree. Nick didn't even flinch. "I know what it feels like to lose someone you love," he said. "It's like the whole world stops, and—"

Annalise snatched a rock off the ground and hurled it at her uncle's head. This time her aim was true, and she knew as the rock left her hand that it would strike her uncle in the forehead, splitting the skin open. She knew it would draw blood, that it would hurt.

In a single, swift motion, Nick snatched the rock out of midair with his bare hand.

Annalise stood there, staring, not knowing what stunned her more, her uncle's reflexes or the fact that she had thrown the rock in the first place.

"It's like the whole world stops," her uncle continued. "But then the world moves on, and you can't believe it, because don't they know what happened? What you *lost*? That your heart just got ripped out of your chest and you're *bleeding* to death?"

Her eyes stung and she wanted her uncle to stop talking but she couldn't move, couldn't speak.

"And then you want to build a wall around you and shut off the pain," he said. "But it doesn't work. Trust me. You just drive people away and end up alone. And then it's even easier to be angry at the people who died on you."

She started crying—angry, frustrated sobs, like something ugly and barbed was being yanked out of her. "Fuck you!" she screamed, and she didn't know whether she was screaming at her uncle or at herself or both. She dropped to her knees, keening with pain as if she'd been gored by some horrible animal. *Mommy. Daddy.* She wanted to die in the face of that pain, to be obliterated, to feel nothing.

But slowly she came back to herself. First she realized her cries had grown softer, her throat aching with the force of her grief. She felt the dirt beneath her palms and understood that she had fallen onto all fours. She sat up, rubbing her palms across the slick front of her rain jacket and then wiping her tears from her face, even as she continued weeping. Her uncle still sat on his stump, watching her. He had made no movement toward her, offered her no hug or other sign of physical comfort. For that she felt a strange gratitude. He had allowed her a space to grieve. When their eyes met, he got to his feet and stepped closer and held out something. A wad of tissues. She laughed at that—a single hard *ha!*—and took the tissues from him and finished wiping her face, then blew her nose. When she was finished, she balled up the tissues and shoved them into her jacket pocket. "Crying is exhausting," she rasped.

Her uncle gave her a hint of a smile, nodded, and held out his hand. She took it, and he pulled her to her feet. "Let's get back down to the house," he said. "We have some plans to make."

CHAPTER THIRTEEN

Nɪᴄᴋ ᴍᴀᴅᴇ Aɴɴᴀʟɪꜱᴇ ᴇɢɢꜱ ᴀɴᴅ ᴛᴏᴀꜱᴛ ᴀɴᴅ ꜱɪᴘᴘᴇᴅ ᴀ ᴍᴜɢ ᴏꜰ ᴄᴏꜰꜰᴇᴇ while he watched her eat. When she devoured her breakfast, she took a sip from her glass of orange juice and then put the glass down and closed her eyes.

"You okay?" Nick said.

Annalise nodded, then opened her eyes. "I was thinking my legs hurt," she said. "From the hike. They hurt the same way they do after tennis practice, kind of like a burning pain? I was thinking that Coach Dunn would make us run suicides and my shins would burn the same way, and I just . . ." She paused, and Nick nodded at her encouragingly. "We had this dog, Gus? And he got old and really sick, and we had to put him to sleep. It was the right thing to do, but it sucked. And for weeks afterward I'd find all these old squeaky toys and chew bones of his, all over the house. Every time I found one it would hurt, like I was reminded all over again that Gus was gone." She took a breath, let it out. "And now I keep thinking about tennis practice, or my boyfriend Eric, or how my mom would have liked this view"—she waved a hand at the windows— "and it's the same thing, you know? It's like . . . it's . . ."

"It's like those memories jump you at the weirdest moments," Nick said.

Annalise nodded. "Yep," she said, and she gave him a halfhearted smile. Then she wiped her eyes and stood and carried her plate to the dishwasher.

She's strong, Ellie said.

I hope so, Nick thought. *I'm not exactly an expert on teenage girls.*

And whose fault is that? Ellie said. Her tone was teasing, but Nick set his mug down on the table hard enough to get Annalise's attention.

"Tell me about your dad," he said, and Annalise's eyes widened. "About his work," he clarified. "About how he was acting the past few weeks."

"Oh," she said. "Okay." She was standing by the kitchen sink and with her hand traced an invisible line on the counter. "Um, he was fine? Normal, I guess, whatever that is." She stared into space, thinking. "Actually, he seemed . . . happy."

"Was he not usually happy?"

Annalise shrugged. "He was usually stressed about something. Work, money. He traveled a lot, which was hard on Mom. Me too."

"Where did he travel?" Nick asked.

"The Middle East. Europe sometimes. Singapore. He went to the Gulf states a lot. Saudi Arabia, Bahrain, the UAE." She smiled briefly, like a flash of sunlight through trees, and then it was gone. "Sent me a picture of the Burj Khalifa once when I was a kid."

Nick rotated his mug on the table. "Did he tell you what kind of work he did?"

Annalise shrugged again. "He was a contractor. I don't know the details. He told me he made business deals. Mom asked him a couple of times if maybe he would go to work for an oil company—you know, steadier paycheck. But Dad liked being his own boss. Anyway, this last trip, maybe two weeks ago, he came home from Saudi Arabia with a diamond necklace for Mom and a new iPhone for me. Talking about how he'd made a big score. Wasn't the first time he'd said that—Dad talked a big game, you know?"

Nick gave her a sad smile. "Yeah," he said. "I do."

"What happened between you and Dad?" Annalise spoke as if the words came out of her mouth before she had given herself time to consider them. She seemed embarrassed by the bluntness of her own question—and, Nick guessed, by the look of surprise on his own face—but she plowed ahead. "Why didn't I ever know about you growing up?"

Nick met her eyes, but what he saw was a memory from the past, he and Jay in a hospital room, arguing. "We both made mistakes when we were younger," he said. "And we were both stubborn."

Annalise stood there, thinking. She looked older that she should, Nick thought, like an adult considering grave issues rather than a teenager who should be worrying about a history test or what to wear to prom. He needed to buy her some clothes.

Annalise reached into her back pocket and pulled something out and held it out over the kitchen counter to Nick. It was a piece of paper, folded down to the size of a credit card. "Dad wanted you to have this," she said.

Nick stared at her. "What is it?"

Annalise shrugged. "I don't know. But Dad said I had to give it to you. I'm sorry I didn't give it to you earlier, but I . . . I wanted to make sure."

Nick felt a strange quiver in his chest, not unlike the thrumming of the water pipes earlier. He reached out and took the paper. "Thank you," he said. Carefully he unfolded the piece of paper. It had been unfolded and refolded more than once, but it wasn't soft and furred yet—the creases were still sharp. It was a single sheet of paper and Nick flattened it on the table. He glanced at Annalise, who was still standing by the sink. "You can look at this too," he said, and he shifted over to make room for her. Annalise came out from behind the counter and stood next to Nick, peering down at the paper.

He guessed they were looking at a photograph that had been printed on a laser printer. It looked like a plat survey, dark-blue lines drawn on a grayish-white background. An arrow with an *N* pointed to the top of the page. There were a few blue lines packed closely together in concentric curves or arcs, like a topographic map showing elevations. Tiny numerical notations appeared at intervals next to the blue lines. Scattered across the page at differing intervals were what looked like tiny triangles with the bases extending beyond the other two arms, like capital As drawn by a young child. The word ANTICLINE was written against a straight blue line that stretched vertically across the page. The letters GH appeared at the extreme right-hand side of the page, as if they were the beginning of a word or phrase that had been cut off. Below that, in the bottom right-hand corner, was some sort of box or grid that had been cut off as well, but he could make out the letters CALIFO typed in the box. In the top right-hand corner was a handwritten word: ABQAIQ.

He had no idea what he was looking at. *Abqaiq* rang a very distant bell, though. He sat still and waited, but whatever faint associations he had with the word faded and then were gone. He held the paper close to his eyes to make sense of the numbers and to see if he could make out any other details, but the resolution of the photo wasn't high enough.

He turned the paper over and his pulse skipped a beat. Something was written in pencil. He held the paper up to the light and read the word *Halliwell*. Underneath it were the letters *FL*, followed by a ten-digit number.

"Is that a phone number?" Annalise said.

"Maybe. Does it look familiar?"

She shook her head. Nick read the writing again. *FL* might stand for Florida, but *Halliwell* meant nothing to him. Nick carefully scanned both sides of the paper, but there was nothing else written on it.

"Does this mean anything to you?" he asked Annalise.

She shook her head again. "No clue." She looked at him, her whole face a question. "Now what?"

He folded the paper back up. "Now I go get you some clothes," he said. "And make a phone call or two. I'm just going into town, won't be gone long. You stay here. Don't go outside, and stay away from the windows."

She nodded, and when she spoke, her voice was small but steady. "Do you think those men who killed my parents are looking for me?"

Nick stood and put the folded paper in his pocket. "That's one of the things I want to find out."

NICK DROVE OUT of the valley below Whiteside Mountain to Highway 107, the road cutting away from the Chattooga River which flowed through the valley. Farther south the Chattooga formed part of the border between South Carolina and Georgia and then dropped down from the hills into what eventually became Lake Hartwell, and then the Savannah River, and then the Atlantic. Everything connected in one long chain. Nick needed to find a different kind of chain, discover how events and facts lined up and connected to create a comprehensible story about his brother Jay and his death. But first he needed to buy Annalise some clothes.

The roads were already filling with cars and SUVs bearing license plates from Florida, Georgia, South Carolina, Tennessee, Virginia, even as far away as Vermont and Arizona. Fewer than two hundred people lived in Cashiers year-round, but over the past several years entire communities of vacation homes had sprung up on the mountains like mushrooms after rain. And now that summer had started, the tourists had begun arriving in full force.

When Nick got to the traffic light at the village green, he went straight through and then pulled into the white gravel parking lot of the Carolina Mountain Shop, a one-story white clapboard store with dark-green trim. The bell rang over the door as Nick entered the shop. The long front room held books, toys, candy, candles, crockery, postcards, walking sticks, kitchen gadgets, place mats, linen napkins, and an abundance of other bric-a-brac. A wide doorway led to another room, which contained sweaters, shirts, blouses, skirts, pants, and other clothing items.

In the back corner by the register stood Lettie Corden. She was being talked at by a customer, a tall, beefy, red-faced man wearing a white polo and chinos. The customer was saying something about maps, occasionally gesturing like he was directing a cavalry charge. Lettie, dressed in black pants and a red sweater set with pearls, her blue-gray hair perfectly coiffed, listened calmly while the man spoke and waved his hands.

"They told me to go to Panther Valley," the man said. "I just need a map."

Lettie had her hands on a bin next to the register whose several slots held various maps of western North Carolina. "It's Panthertown," she said.

The man shook his head. "There's no *town* there," he insisted.

"I didn't say there was," Lettie said. "But that's the name of the valley." She pulled out a map and handed it to the man.

He looked at it. "This is Sapphire Valley," he said, thrusting it back at her. "I need Panther Valley."

Lettie leaned over the bin and scanned the maps, lifting a hand to brush her strand of pearls. "I'm looking for it."

The red-face man smiled, halfway to a sneer. "You've lost it, you mean," he said. "Not very good with maps, are you?"

Lettie straightened and looked the man square in the eye. "I don't need a map to know where I am," she said. "Or where I'm going."

The man glared at Lettie, but under her steady gaze he began to sputter, then harrumphed and turned and hurried past Nick and out the door, the bell jangling in his wake.

"I think you lost a sale," Nick said.

"Jackass," Lettie murmured. She smoothed the front of her skirt. "The customer is always right, until he's a jackass. Might have to get that in needlepoint and hang it by the cash register." She shook her head, then smiled at Nick. "What can I do for you, Professor?"

"May I borrow your phone? I hate to ask, but—"

"But you don't have a phone anymore," Lettie said. "Sometimes I wish I didn't have a phone myself. Only keep it so I can call 911 and get harassed by telemarketers." She nodded toward the door behind the register. "Just don't order anything illegal. And don't go through my files."

"You hiding state secrets in your desk drawers?"

Lettie smiled. "Wouldn't you like to know."

Behind the door was an office, cramped but neat as a pin. Nick closed the door behind him and from his pocket took out the folded piece of paper Annalise had given him before he sat down at Lettie's desk. She had an old black push-button telephone, and he picked up the handset and dialed the number on the back of the paper.

The phone rang twice and then Nick heard a man's voice, an automatic message. *You've reached Lapidus Investigations. For appointments, press 1. For office hours and address, press 2.*

Nick pressed 2. Now a pleasant female voice stated that office hours were eight AM to four thirty PM, Monday through Friday, with on-call services available for current clients 24/7. The recording then rattled off an address in Charlotte, which Nick wrote down on a notepad on Lettie's desk. After a pause, the original message replayed, and Nick pressed 1 for appointments.

There was a beep, followed by the same female voice as before, except live this time. "Lapidus Investigations. How may I help you?"

"I need to speak with the investigator hired by Jay Bashir, please," Nick said.

"I apologize, sir, we cannot reveal the names of our clients."

Nick squeezed the handset, but his voice remained calm. "I appreciate your sense of privacy, but this is an emergency."

"Sir, we cannot reveal the names of our clients."

"Your client is dead," Nick said.

Silence on the other end of the line. When the woman spoke again, her voice was tight with tension. "What is your name, sir?"

"I'm Jay Bashir's brother," Nick said.

Another, shorter silence. "Hold, please," she said.

Nick sat hunched forward, staring at the floor, as jazz played over the line. In less than a minute, the music cut out and a new voice, a man's, said, "This is Frank Lapidus. Who am I speaking with?"

"My name is Nick Anthony," Nick said. "My brother is Jay Bashir. Was. He was killed three days ago. I'm in possession of some sort of map that he sent me. Your phone number is on the back, along with the word Halliwell."

Lapidus sounded like a two-pack-a-day smoker, as if his voice had been dredged through gravel. "You said killed. How?"

"He and his wife were tortured. Then someone lit their house on fire and left them inside."

"Jesus," Lapidus said.

"Why is your number written on this map?" Nick said. "And who is Halliwell?"

"I don't know anything about a map, Mr. Anthony," Lapidus said. "But I have something for you. How far away are you from Charlotte?"

"About three hours. What do you mean you have something for me?"

"I'd rather not say over the phone," Lapidus said. "Can you get here this afternoon? By, say, two o'clock?"

"I'll be there."

"Two o'clock, then," Lapidus said, and hung up.

Nick dropped the handset onto the cradle and sat in thought for a moment. Then he picked the phone back up and dialed another number, this one from memory. As the phone rang on the other end, he sat back in the chair and looked out the window at a wall of pine trees.

On the third ring a voice said, "Hello?"

"Jean-Jacques," Nick said. "It's Nick Anthony."

The barest fraction of a pause. "Nick," Jean-Jacques said. "This is a pleasant surprise. How are you? Are you in DC?"

"No, I'm in North Carolina. I'm sorry to bother you. How's Georgetown?"

Jean-Jacques's *hmph* was a particularly Gallic expression that landed somewhere between indifference and a grudging acceptance of reality. "The students keep getting younger. As you have probably noticed. And you are not bothering me. I'm grading papers."

"That bad?"

"Allow me to read you an opening line. 'The fundamentals of international finance law as applied to a region such as Lebanon leave something to be desired,' end quote."

"Lebanon is a region?"

"Apparently."

"Please tell me you spoke with that student."

"He has an appointment with me this afternoon to go over his paper. I'm sharpening my knives."

Jean-Jacques Christophe was the child of a French deputy minister of finance and a Lebanese photographer. He had followed in his father's footsteps and spent two decades enticing Western countries to invest in Lebanon. He and Nick had met at a conference in Beirut, where they soon became thick as thieves.

"Jean-Jacques, I have a favor to ask," Nick said. "I'm trying to track down a contractor, an American who was doing business in the Middle East."

"That should narrow it down to several thousand people."

"This one was trying to make contact with the Syrian government last fall. His name was Jay Bashir."

"Bashir, Bashir," Jean-Jacques mused. "What was the nature of his business with the Syrians?"

"I'm not sure, but I'm guessing either information or arms."

Another pause. "I don't do that, Nick."

"I know you don't, Jean-Jacques. But he wouldn't have known that. And you know everyone worth knowing in the Middle East."

"Hardly. But I vaguely recall a Jay Bashir looking for an entrée to the Assad regime. The kind of man who wants to impress and thinks he has, even when he hasn't."

The description of Jay made Nick smile while at the same time he had to throttle back a sob. He cleared his throat. "That sounds like him. Do you remember anything else?"

"I told him he was foolish to consider doing any sort of back-deal business with Syria. He seemed to understand. I got the sense he had several irons in the fire, as it were. Said he had an appointment with a Saudi minister. That was his parting shot."

Syria and the Saudis. Nick stared out the window at the pine trees. What had Jay been up to?

Jean-Jacques coughed politely. "May I ask why you want to know?"

"He's my brother," Nick said, continuing to stare at the pine trees. "Just trying to keep track of him."

"I understand," Jean-Jacques said. "Family is important." He sighed. "Nick, how are you doing, really? I know this past year . . . it must have been terrible. You should come up for a visit. Yvette would love to see you, as would I. You're welcome anytime."

Nick closed his eyes. "I appreciate that, Jean-Jacques. Thank you. Give Yvette my best." Nick hung up before the other man could say anything more. Jean-Jacques and Yvette had been good friends when he and Ellie lived in Beirut. But Nick could bear only so much sympathy—responding to it was like smiling with a mouthful of razors.

The kind of man who wants to impress and thinks he has, even when he hasn't, Jean-Jacques had said about Jay. Always looking for the deal, always selling something, even if what he was selling was just smoke.

When Nick had been offered a scholarship at San Diego State, he'd seized it, choosing to double-major in medieval European history and Arabic studies. "You're literally a child of two worlds," his father had said when Nick announced his intended course of study. Nick liked that idea, standing astride two different but intertwined cultures that had often clashed in the very part of the world where the earliest human civilizations had flourished. Nick enjoyed college, where he studied and drank and had sex and avoided going home as much as possible, but it felt more like a way station, a crossroads where none of the paths before him were clear. He thought he wanted to be a professor, which made his father proud, and he applied to the master's program in history at UC Davis with the potential to work toward a PhD. He had a sharp mind and was quick to absorb whatever he learned, and he earned the respect of his professors. But somewhere at the back of his head, behind a door he mostly kept closed, lurked the feeling that, for him, spending several more years in school was an indulgence, a way to escape the real world, to distance himself from his own family.

Meanwhile, Jay had stopped attending the mosque and started dressing like a businessman in suits and silk ties. After high school, he had not followed Nick to college but borrowed money, often from Afghan refugees his parents knew, to finance real estate deals. Many failed, but one investment paid off well enough that Jay was able to invest in other ventures. Soon he was driving a Porsche and wearing a watch that was close enough to a Rolex to impress at a distance.

If Jay made Nick roll his eyes, their mother broke his heart. Her world had dwindled to their house, the market, and the mosque. She refused to watch television, convinced the government was spying on them through the screen. She also thought the electric company was running a scam, so she left all the lights off, sitting in perpetual dusk in the house. Flashlights were okay, however, so when she was home she was either cooking by candlelight or peering at her Koran, a yellow plastic Eveready in one hand throwing a circle of light on the page.

"She needs to see a psychiatrist," Nick said to his father one Friday evening when his mother was at the mosque. They were in the kitchen with the overhead light on—Nick knew his father was watching the clock and would turn the light off before his mother was due to return home. "This isn't normal, Dad. She isn't well."

His father shook his head. "Don't you think I've tried?" he said. When Nick started to argue, his father raised a hand to cut him off. His hair thinning, a paunch visible above his belt, his father looked weary. "She refuses to go to any doctor. I've even tried to speak with the imam." As his father was a committed agnostic who despised organized religion, Nick knew he must be supremely concerned to have talked to the imam.

Later, Nick realized that he never should have gone to Jay for help, that instead he should have taken his mother to a doctor himself, even if that meant carrying her over his shoulder to a psychiatrist's office. But at the time, Jay seemed the best of a narrowing set of unpleasant choices. Nick got his brother to meet him at a coffeehouse near campus. Jay walked in wearing a gray suit and pink shirt with no tie, his fake Rolex glinting on his wrist. "This the best place you can find to get coffee?" he said as he slid into the booth across from Nick.

"Good to see you too," Nick said.

Jay looked around the room. "Any service around here?"

"You order at the counter," Nick said. "I need your help, Jay. It's about Mom."

Jay grunted. "Yeah, well, Mom needs help."

"She won't listen to Dad," Nick said. "And she sure won't listen to me."

Jay's eyebrows rose, the beginnings of a sneer on his face. "And you think she'll listen to me?"

"You're her favorite," Nick said. "If anyone can get her to go see a doctor, it's you."

Jay snorted. "Poor Nick," he said. "Firstborn disappointment."

"That's a nice suit," Nick said. "Wear that when you talk to Mom. She would like it."

Jay laughed. "God, you're so transparent. You think you can flatter me, say I'm the golden child and get me to take our mother to a doctor?"

It's working, Nick thought, watching as his younger brother absently ran a hand down a lapel on his suit jacket. Nick sat there, coffee cold in his cup, willing himself to say nothing.

Jay tapped a finger on the table, thinking. "I need a favor," he said finally.

Nick waited.

Jay sighed. "It's not a big deal. Basically you'd just stand in the background. You wouldn't even have to say anything. Easy."

Nick let the moment of silence stretch until he saw Jay was about to say something, then cut him off. "Remember Brandon Deeker?"

Jay frowned. "Kid in junior high?"

"He was bullying you. You told me if I went with you to stand up to him, he'd get scared and back down."

Jay waved his hand as if dispelling smoke. "That was a long—"

"He went to the principal and had us suspended for threatening to beat him up."

Jay opened his hands to encompass the room. "You see a principal here? Somebody going to suspend us?" He leaned forward. "I need a favor," he said. "You help me, I'll deal with Mom."

The favor involved Nick showing up the next evening at his brother's office, a rented box of rooms in a strip mall in El Cajon. It was a cool night, the sun still flaring red beyond the horizon and the sky above a deep blue, but it wasn't cool enough for the front door of Jay's office to be left swinging open. Nick glanced around the mostly empty parking lot, then eased through the open door. He stepped into an anodyne waiting room, an unmanned mahogany-veneer desk presiding over beige carpet and floral-print furniture. The overhead fluorescents were off, but yellow light and men's voices spilled from another open door at the back of the waiting room. Nick picked up a glass paperweight from the front desk and put it in his pocket, then strode to the open door.

Beyond was an office the same size as the waiting room, but with wood paneling and a thicker carpet and a nicer desk. Jay, wearing a navy silk suit with an open-collared white shirt, was backed against the desk, three men standing in front of him. Two wore off-the-rack suits, one gray, one brown, like TV cops. Nick was certain neither of them was a cop. The third man had a mullet and tight jeans and a purple Members Only jacket and was thrusting a finger into Jay's chest. "It's bullshit is what it is," he was saying, his voice nasal and grating. "You fucked me, Bashir, so now it's your turn."

When Jay saw Nick over the man's shoulder, relief shone from his face. In that moment, Nick hated his brother.

The three men turned to look at Nick. "What?" the man with the Members Only jacket snapped.

Nick saw a slight bulge underneath Brown Suit's jacket, another at Gray Suit's waist. Both men flanked Members Only and stood one deferential step back from him. He was clearly the leader. Nick ignored all of them and fixed his eyes on his brother. In Dari, he shouted, "Keep your mouth shut and don't say anything unless I tell you to."

"The fuck is this?" Members Only said. The two goons scowled.

Nick kept his eyes on Jay. In English, he said, "What is it this time, Bashir? TV sets? Cars? What?" Jay opened his mouth, seemed to remember Nick's earlier warning, and closed it again. Exasperated, Nick turned to Members Only. "What did he take from you?"

Members Only managed to look astonished and outraged at the same time. "What the fuck do you—"

"What," Nick said, "did he take from you?"

Members Only blinked. "Cigarettes," he said.

Nick glared at Jay, incredulous. "*Cigarettes*? You wrong these men for cigarettes? Do you *know* what Mustafa will do to you? I'll tell you what he'll do. He'll make you wear your tongue as a necktie."

"Who the fuck is Mustafa?" Members Only demanded.

Nick whirled so fast that one of the two goons nearly pulled his gun out from beneath his jacket, but Nick just stared at Members Only. Then slowly he smiled. "What's your name?" he asked kindly.

"Carl," Members Only said.

Nick nodded, as if he had expected nothing less. "Carl," he said, "we work for Mustafa Khan." He paused, waiting for a response.

"Who?" Carl said.

Nick stared. "Mustafa *Khan*," he said. "He moves half the heroin in California. And he does *not* stand for people who do stupid shit like this." Carl frowned slightly, and Nick shook his head. "No, no, no, no," he said. "Not you, Carl. This one"—nodding at Jay—"for trying to steal from you without permission from Mustafa. What did this *olagh* take from you? Fifty cartons? A hundred?"

"Two hundred," Carl said.

Nick looked at Jay and hissed, "You stole *two hundred* cartons from this man?" Then in Dari he said, "Tell me you have money here to pay him. Nod or shake your head."

Jay nodded.

Nick rolled his eyes. To Carl, he said, "This *koskesh* will pay you for the cigarettes, now. Just don't kill him." He leaned up against a wall and glanced at his watch, clearly bored by the whole ordeal. Jay, meanwhile, looked increasingly uncomfortable, even panicked.

Carl stared at Nick, then Jay, then at his own thugs, who looked like they were watching a movie. When Carl glanced at Nick again, Nick gave him a little shrug as if to say, *What? Go ahead.* Carl cleared his throat self-consciously and turned back to Jay, a snarl pasted over his features. "You don't fuck with me, Bashir," he said, and he slapped Jay across the face, first with his right hand, then with his left. The second slap caused Jay to stumble slightly, a fiery crimson blush on his cheeks. Carl spat on the floor at Jay's feet, then looked at Nick as if seeking approval. Nick gave none, just said to Jay, in a tired voice, "Pay the man."

Jay paid Carl with cash from a floor safe behind the desk, and Nick shook hands with Carl, then escorted him and his men out through the waiting room. As soon as they had closed the front door behind them, Nick slumped against a chair. He felt relieved and exhausted and strangely alert, his chest and head humming as if conducting current.

"Holy shit," Jay said. He stood in the center of the waiting room, staring at his brother in astonishment. "What was that story? That was amazing." He laughed. "Shit. And Mustafa Khan? Who the fuck is that?"

"He was the janitor on my dorm freshman year," Nick said. He took the glass paperweight out of his pocket. Jay glanced at it.

"Were you planning to hit him over the head with that if he didn't go along with your bullshit?" Jay asked. He shook his head, a man pulled back from the brink of a nasty fall, and gave another nervous laugh. "This calls for a drink," he said. He stepped forward, arm raised as if preparing to give Nick a high five. "Seriously, man, you saved—"

The paperweight in his hand, Nick drove his fist forward, right into Jay's stomach. Jay folded in half and fell to the floor, gasping for air. Nick looked down at his brother, then tossed the paperweight with a thud onto the mahogany-veneer desk. "I did you a favor," he said, walking to the door. "Now you take care of Mom."

WHEN NICK WALKED out of Lettie's office, he found her in the front room refolding a stack of linen napkins on a display table. "All done?" she asked.

Nick glanced around to make sure there weren't any other customers in the store. "I need some clothes," he said. "Women's clothes."

Lettie arched an eyebrow. "I didn't take you for that kind of man, but to each his own."

"They aren't for me."

"Say no more," Lettie said. "No judgment here. You'd be, what, a size eighteen?"

"They're for my niece. She's a teenager."

"A gift, then. You want them wrapped?"

"She's visiting. It's . . . complicated. A running-away kind of thing." He hesitated. "Lettie, can you keep this just between us? She's in trouble and I'm trying to help."

"Well," she said, "if you're helping her, she's in good hands. Mum's the word." She nodded once, as if they had shaken on a deal. "Now, what does she need?"

With Lettie's help, Nick bought some T-shirts, socks, cotton panties, a pair of jeans, and a pair of capri pants. He refused to even consider looking at brassieres and said he had no idea what her cup size would be, so Lettie added three different sizes of bras and told him to see which one fit best. Nick didn't like involving Lettie, or deceiving her, but Annalise needed clothes, and the less Lettie knew, the better. Even as he told himself this, he knew he could simply have driven down to Brevard and gone to the Walmart there, where he would be anonymous and could buy anything he needed without anyone giving him a second glance.

As if reading his thoughts, Lettie said, while ringing him up, "It's good to see you in here, Nick. It's been too long. You should come over for dinner sometime."

"Been busy," Nick said. "Always something to fix on a house."

Lettie nailed him with the same look she'd given the red-faced customer earlier. "When a lady invites a man to dinner, the man should say yes and offer to bring wine."

"Are you asking me on a date?"

Lettie rolled her eyes. "Men," she said. "Always convinced women are just falling all over themselves to attract one. No, you ignoramus, I'm asking you to dinner. A home-cooked meal from a neighbor. You understand *neighbor*? Or *friend*?"

Nick stood with his bag of clothing in his hands, feeling like a boy called on the carpet and trying to decide how to respond. Exasperated, Lettie saved him the trouble by shoving him out the door. "Just goes to show that you can go to school and even write books and still be an imbecile," she said.

Nick took one step toward his car, then turned around, looking up the short flight of steps to the door. "You know I wrote books?" he said.

Lettie closed the door in his face.

CHAPTER FOURTEEN

AFTER HER UNCLE LEFT TO GET HER CLOTHES, ANNALISE SAT IN THE great room and paged through a dusty coffee table book of Ansel Adams photographs that had been abandoned on the bottom shelf of a side table. Through the back windows of the great room, she saw the sun trying to break through the puffy white clouds overhead. Across the lake she could see the cliff face of Whiteside, stark and striking against the fringe of trees around it, like the moon had landed on Earth and was trying to disguise itself as a mountain. After a while she closed the Ansel Adams book and wandered through the great room, looking around and occasionally picking up items, then putting them back down—a wooden clock on a side table, a red ballpoint pen with the text CASHIERS FIRE DEPT on the barrel, a little statue of a knight on a horse that sat on the fireplace mantel. The statue of the knight was lightweight, made out of tin or maybe aluminum, and aside from the books stacked everywhere it was the only item she saw in the great room that seemed unique, belonging to a specific person.

The books eventually drew her full attention, not only because she had always liked reading but also because you could tell a lot about a person by the kinds of books they read. And she was definitely curious about her uncle. After a few minutes of looking through the stacks of books, it was clear that Uncle Nick was maybe a little obsessed with the Middle Ages—almost all the books were about medieval history or works of medieval lit. Made sense for a history professor, she guessed. But he'd said he was retired. She tried to imagine being a widow, holing up in a mountain cabin with her grief and the remnants of her career as a professor. It seemed sad and almost perverse, like her uncle was playing at being a hermit, inviting people to ask him if he was okay just so he could tell them to get lost.

She realized she was still hungry and went to raid the kitchen for food. She made herself some more toast even though her uncle didn't have any jam or jelly—seriously, why have bread for toast without any kind of jelly?—and scarfed it down, along with a full glass of water, and then sat at the kitchen table for a minute, tracing the wood grain of the table with her finger. She got up and rinsed her dish off in the sink and put it and her glass in the dishwasher, because her mother hated it when she left a mess in the kitchen, and that brought a wave of quiet sobs that seemed like they would never recede. She stood in the kitchen, hands braced on the counter—unknowingly in the same position her uncle had been in two days earlier—and rode out the sobs like she was a tiny raft bobbing on an ocean of grief. *I'm going to get really sick of crying*, she thought.

She wiped her face and blew her nose on some paper towels, and after she threw the towels away, she looked up from the trash can and saw, through the office entryway, a framed photograph on a desk. It was of a woman. Annalise walked into the office, a small wood-paneled room with more bookshelves and a window, under which sat the desk with the photograph. Annalise picked the photograph up. The woman in the picture was standing in a field. She had long blond hair and was looking back over her shoulder at the photographer and laughing. Her skin was fair, and she looked like an elf or a sprite caught dancing in the wilderness.

That was my aunt, Annalise thought, and she felt an empty ache in her chest. How strange to miss someone she had never met. The woman in the picture was beautiful. And now she was dead. Suddenly Annalise felt cold, and she put the photograph back down on the desk.

The shelves held more books, most of them with academic-sounding titles. One of them snagged her attention, a slim volume with a rich red spine and the title in gold print: *The Lion and the Prince.* The author's name was Nicholas Anthony. She pulled the book off the shelf. The front cover showed a medieval illustration of two knights on horseback, jousting. The back cover described the book as offering new insight into the relationship between English king Richard I, the "Lionheart," and the great Muslim sultan and general Saladin. Annalise looked at the inside flap and saw a picture of a younger Uncle Nick, a slight smile on his lips. The book had been published a decade earlier. The dedication page read simply, "To Ellie, as always." Annalise looked back at the photograph on the desk. Aunt Ellie.

She put the book back on the shelf and trailed her hand over other volumes—*A World Lit Only by Fire, How the Irish Saved Civilization, Eleanor of Aquitaine: A Life.* She had heard of Eleanor of Aquitaine. Kind of a badass queen, if she remembered correctly. She pulled the book off the shelf, and as she did, an envelope fell to the floor. When she picked up the envelope, she lifted the flap and saw a few photographs that were beginning to yellow with age.

The book forgotten for the moment, Annalise sat at the desk with the photographs. The first was of a split-level house, the walls a light green and the front walk made of stepping stones. The second picture stopped her heart. It was a photo of a man and two boys standing at the front door of the same split-level house. The man, tall with a dark moustache, was stiff with formality in his white button-down shirt and dark slacks. Next to him was one of the boys, maybe ten or twelve, hair thick and black as oil and his mouth open in a happy shriek. Then there was the second boy, a few years older and taller, arm slung over the younger boy's shoulders.

He smiled easily at the camera, his hair dark and over his ears, eyes the color of honey in a brown face. It was her uncle. Which meant that the boy he had under his arm was most likely his brother—her father. Even as she thought it, she saw her father's features in the boy's face, the nose and lips and even the cast of the eyes, the mischievous glint. Through her tears she smiled at the picture. "Hi, Daddy," she said.

Reluctantly she put the picture down on the desk and looked at the others. There was a woman in a red hijab or head scarf that framed a tired but smiling face, Annalise's father hanging from her arm, while the moustached man in the white shirt and dark pants stood unfocused in the background, a watchful phantom. Another picture of the boys showed them both standing in the driveway of the split-level and striking muscle poses. And then there was one of the man and the woman, clearly the boys' parents, Annalise's grandparents, sitting on a yellowish-green sofa, the woman raising one hand to her hijab as if tucking it more securely around her face, the man looking at her with a smile. That was the last of the photographs. Annalise looked inside the empty envelope, then turned over each picture to see if anything was written on the backs, but found nothing.

Annalise knew her father's family had left Afghanistan before the Russians invaded, emigrating to the United States. She guessed the photos showed when they had first moved to the US—the split-level house, the clothing, the age of the pictures all suggested as much. She looked at her grandparents, her grandfather's grin, her grandmother's weary smile. Her grandfather had been American, some sort of government employee, and had met her grandmother in Afghanistan. Annalise thought it must have been a truly romantic love story. And then they had moved halfway around the world to a country that must have seemed almost alien to her grandmother. She wondered if her grandmother had been welcomed, if her grandfather had helped her adapt. She knew very little about her father's family. He had usually changed the subject whenever it was brought up. Maybe her uncle could tell her about them, lift the veil on that part of her family's history.

Maybe there were some more photographs in the desk. She pulled open the top drawer. She stared. In the drawer was a gun.

She looked at the gun as if it would coil and strike at the first hint of motion. It was the color of graphite, an ugly chunk of metal lying in a drawer. Lots of people owned guns, she knew. Up here in the mountains, she guessed several people shot deer and rabbits and who knew what else for food. But she was pretty certain her uncle wasn't hunting deer with a pistol. Maybe he had it for home protection. He lived pretty much in the middle of nowhere, far from any immediate help from the police or sheriff.

She closed the drawer. She could hear the gun shift in the drawer when she closed it. She told herself it was fine, it was just a gun in a desk. But if that were true, then why did her skin feel prickly, like she was standing outside just before a summer thunderstorm struck?

She opened the lower desk drawer and found a box of magazines she assumed were for the pistol. Behind the box, at the back of the drawer, was a Ziploc bag with some sort of booklets in them. She picked up the Ziploc bad and opened it, then dumped the booklets out onto the desk. Even as she did it, she realized they weren't booklets. They were passports, half a dozen of them. She picked up one and opened it to see her uncle's photo staring back at her, a pleasantly neutral look on his face. But the passport cover read REPUBLIC OF LEBANON, and it identified her uncle as Amir Haddad. She stared at the passport, then picked up another one with a bright-green cover. On the outside was KINGDOM OF SAUDI ARABIA printed in gold. Inside was another picture of her uncle, this time staring seriously at the camera. According to that passport, her uncle's name was Mohammed Al-Salhi.

The rain started again, a sudden downpour that beat against the roof, lashing at the windows like waves battering a ship. She ignored it and looked through the other passports. A French one in the name of Jean Dubois. Another identifying her uncle as an Afghan named Farman Ghosh, and yet another saying he was Sanjay Reddy from India. The sixth and last one, a Mexican passport in the name of Pablo Jesús Rodríguez Zapatero, made her snort with laughter, as if the name were too much, the final entry in an absurd parade of identities. All too soon, she choked off her laughter, tears pricking her eyes. What the hell was this? Why did her uncle have six different passports, all from different countries and in different names? And why did he have a gun—a gun, she noted as if tabulating evidence in her mind, that was in a desk drawer rather than locked in a safe or a gun box?

He didn't tell the cop you were here, she thought.

Of course he wouldn't tell the cop. He had a gun and a bunch of fake passports. Who knew what other shady shit he might have going on?

He saved you from the rattlesnake, she thought. *And he took care of you when you had a fever. And he said he would help you.*

Help her. How could he help her? He was a retired history professor. Or maybe not, she thought, looking at the passports on the desk. Maybe he was some sort of undercover cop, or a criminal. And he had a gun.

So do the other guys, she thought.

With the sense of finding herself at the bottom of a deep, dark well, Annalise was struck by how alone she truly was. Her parents were dead, and she was in a cabin in the North Carolina mountains waiting for her uncle, a man she didn't truly know, a man with a gun and multiple passports whom her father had ignored all of Annalise's life until a few days ago. A man who might not be safe.

In the kitchen, the door to the carport opened, the rain outside suddenly louder. The sound struck Annalise like a bolt of lightning, and she froze. "Hey," someone called—a man, maybe her uncle, maybe not. The door closed. He was inside the house. Annalise's heart was in her throat. Then, her hand shaking, she yanked open the top drawer.

CHAPTER FIFTEEN

Nick turned off Whiteside Cove onto the dirt road that led to his house. He needed to order another load of gravel to spread on the road before it got completely washed out. As it was, he jounced and swayed along the hillside and past the lake. Even now he saw a line of dark clouds through a break in the green wall of trees. People were always struck by how leafy and green Cashiers was. While it had its share of beautiful sunny days, Cashiers also got over seven inches of rain a month, making it one of the rainiest places in the eastern US. No wonder the woods were almost primordial.

And then another flash of memory: a canteen lying in the dirt, water spilling out. A bloody hand next to it.

Nick hit the brakes, jerking to a stop, and squeezed his eyes shut. When he opened them, the memory had faded. He continued down the road, the sky growing darker.

The clouds broke just as he pulled up to the cabin. He parked in the carport, grabbed his bag from Lettie's shop, and opened the car door to the thunderous roar of the rain. He unlocked the door to the kitchen and went inside. "Hey," he called to Annalise, and he kicked the door shut behind him, which diminished the roar of the rain a little. It pinged off the chimney cap, echoing down the flue, and made a steady drumbeat on the roof. Just above the din, he could hear water pouring in a stream from the gutter outside his office. He'd just had the gutters replaced—maybe it wasn't fit tightly enough to the fascia. Something else to have to repair.

He put the shopping bags down on the kitchen counter and turned to face Annalise standing in the office doorway, pointing a pistol at him with both hands. "Don't move," she said.

He held his hands up, palms facing her. "Annalise, what—"

"Shut up," she said. Her eyes were wide with terror, but that hardness was back. "Who are you? Who the fuck are you?"

Nick glanced past her into the office and saw the passports scattered across his desk. Shit.

"Who are you?" she said, more loudly now. The pistol trembled in her hands.

"I'm your uncle, Annalise," he said, keeping his voice calm.

"Why do you have a gun?" she said.

"I keep the gun for protection," he said. He didn't move, didn't consider moving.

"Why do you have a bunch of fake fucking passports?"

"Annalise, please, just put the gun down."

"Do you think I'm stupid?" The pistol began to waver more erratically.

"I think you're scared," Nick said. "And you have every right to be. But I don't think you're stupid. You found me, all by yourself. Let me help you. Please. I won't hurt you."

The pistol began to waver less, as if focusing all its attention on Nick's chest. Annalise still looked scared, her eyes shining with tears, but her face was set, determined, backed by a mulish stubbornness. "Why do you have all these passports?" she demanded. "You a smuggler? A criminal?"

Nick smiled. He couldn't help it.

"What," Annalise said, "is so funny?"

"Sorry," he said. "I just . . . you reminded me of Ellie."

Annalise raised the pistol so it aimed at his face. "Don't play me," she said.

Nick shook his head. "I'm not. Honest. She did the same thing once. Ellie. Your aunt. She busted me. She didn't point a gun at me, but it was a—pretty tense situation."

"What do you mean, she busted you? Were you cheating on her or something?"

"No," Nick said. "I never cheated on her. She wanted to know the same thing you do. Who I am. Who I was."

The pistol remained steady, aimed directly at his nose. "What did you tell her?" Annalise said.

"That I was a spy," Nick said.

THEY HAD BEEN in Cairo then. Early morning, before sunrise. Nick remembered hearing the muezzin calling the faithful of Cairo to the pre-dawn Fajr prayer, the sidewalks almost completely empty as he hurried down Kamel Al Shenawy Street and turned into the court of his apartment building, his footsteps echoing off the stone. He fumbled his keys out of his pocket, his bandaged hand giving him trouble, and opened the door into the building as quietly as he could. Despite the call of the muezzin, no other tenants were stirring at this hour. Nick took the stairs rather than waiting for the elevator, which was old and loud. When he reached his floor, he padded down the hallway to his apartment, inserted another key, and was inside, the door shut behind him. He allowed himself a moment to breathe.

A snap of a light switch and Nick froze, the apartment springing into view, lamps and couches and tables and doorways. And Ellie, in a red robe, sitting in her usual chair by the window.

"Shit," Nick said. "You scared me."

Ellie narrowed her eyes in a frown. "Likewise. It's five in the morning, Nick. Where have you been?"

Nick put his hands in his pockets and leaned back against the door. "I thought you had a conference in Berlin."

The coolness of her tone made Nick wince. "I came home early to surprise you," she said. She sat forward. "What's wrong with your face? Nick?"

Slowly Nick stepped out of the shadowed foyer into the lamp-lit living room. Ellie's eyes widened. "Oh my God, Nick, what happened?"

"It looks worse than it is," Nick said, but Ellie was already out of her chair and hurrying across the room. She stopped outside of hugging distance.

"Who did this to you?"

"I fell into the street. Clumsy—"

"The street didn't give you a black eye, Nick."

"Streets are hard."

"Stop bullshitting me." Ellie glanced down at his pockets. "Show me your hands."

"Ellie—"

"Now."

Nick took his hands out of his pockets, revealing his bandaged hand. "Did the street do that too?" Ellie asked.

He was so tired. He hadn't slept all night, of course, and he was long past the adrenaline rush of earlier. But he was also weary to the bone of keeping this part of his life, of himself, from Ellie. "No," he said. "The street didn't do that." He gestured with his uninjured hand to the couch. "Let's sit."

Ellie didn't move, arms crossed. "I'd prefer to stand."

"Well, I'm sitting. I don't want to fall over and lose whatever dignity I have left." Nick walked past Ellie and sat on the couch, his head back on the cushion. After a few moments, Ellie came and sat on the far end of the couch.

Nick looked up at the ceiling as he spoke. "I had a meeting last night."

"A meeting."

"It wasn't an academic meeting." He closed his eyes, which felt like they'd been scoured with sand. "It was with a very frightened man from Sudan. Let's call him Ahmed."

"Ahmed from Sudan."

"Exactly."

"Why were you meeting with Ahmed from Sudan?"

"Because he had some information he wanted to share."

"With a professor of medieval studies?"

Nick opened his eyes and turned his head to look directly at Ellie. "I'm not just a professor of medieval studies," he said.

She looked back at him, her face inscrutable. "Go on," she said.

He was so tired. He could fall asleep right here, looking at his wife. And yet he also knew he was standing at the edge of a cliff, and so was Ellie, and he wanted to be able to step back from that cliff with her. One wrong step and he would fall. Or Ellie might push him.

"I was asked to meet with Ahmed and talk with him, find out if the information he wanted to share was valuable. He would only meet with an American, in a public place."

"Where?"

"The Barrel Bar at the Windsor. I had to wear this straw hat, a fedora—you would have laughed your ass off. Anyway, I can see him from a mile away, he's so nervous he's practically vibrating. Took him two drinks to calm down. He's convinced the waiter is listening to our conversation, so I call the waiter over and give him a nice tip and tell him to leave us alone for a while, which he does. And Ahmed starts talking." Nick paused. "Would you please get me a glass of water? My throat's dry."

Ellie got up and went into the kitchen and Nick laid his head back again. Outside, a car horn beeped and another responded. Ellie returned with a glass of water. Nick drank half the glass down and put it on the coffee table. "Thank you," he said.

"What did Ahmed want to talk about?" she asked.

"How some people in the Sudanese government were supporting terrorists," Nick said. "Ahmed used to be an intelligence officer. He claimed to have lots of secrets."

The dark sky outside the window was shading to gray, the sounds of street traffic rising as the city awoke. Ellie looked pale and exhausted and beautiful. "This is the part where you tell me how you got hurt," she said.

Nick nodded. "Ahmed wanted a hotel room. He thought the Windsor would do nicely, but I told him I knew of another place, more discreet, where he would be safe. A private hotel out in Heliopolis. He agreed, so I paid the tab and we left. Outside, I started walking toward the metro, but Ahmed refused—too crowded, too easy for a stranger in the crowd to stick a knife between his ribs and then vanish. He wanted to take a taxi, all the way to Heliopolis. We were standing on the sidewalk, arguing." Nick took another sip of water. "And that's when they hit us."

"They?"

"Three of them. They walked up behind us on the street and muscled us into an alley like we'd all practiced it together." Nick closed his eyes again.

In a low voice, Ellie said, "And you went into hero mode."

His eyes still closed, Nick said, "They were going to kill him. I couldn't let that happen."

"Yes, you could."

Nick's eyes opened. He stared at Ellie.

Ellie's voice barely kept her fury in check. "Don't give me that look. You are a fucking *history professor*."

"I was a Marine too."

"You're not a Marine now. I don't know what you are."

"I'm your husband who couldn't let a man be killed in front of him."

Ellie raised a hand as if to slap him, held it in midair, then let it drop. "Did you kill those men?" she said.

He nodded, still looking at her.

"You couldn't let a man be killed, so instead you killed three."

"I didn't—" Nick shook his head. "They were going to murder him, Ellie. And then they would have killed me. He came to me—"

"He didn't come to you," Ellie said.

"I was the one who was there," Nick said. "I was the one who met him. So he was my responsibility right then."

She sighed and closed her eyes. After a long pause, she said, "Who were they? The three men."

"Local thugs. They were hired by someone in Sudan to take care of Ahmed, probably."

She opened her eyes. "What happened to them? The—bodies?"

"The Egyptians took care of it."

She gestured toward his bandaged hand. "Did they take care of that too?"

Nick looked at his hand, wrapped in gauze. "One of the thugs pulled a knife. It's not serious. A Marine corpsman wrapped it up, actually."

"A Marine corpsman," Ellie said. "What, he just happened to be walking by?"

"He was at the US embassy, actually. Where I had to explain what happened to the deputy chief of mission. Ahmed practically begged for asylum. The DCM was pissed."

For the first time, Ellie smiled. "Fitzgerald? I bet he was. He's hated your guts ever since you made him look like a jerk in front of Ambassador Yarsawich."

"In my defense, Fitzgerald was hitting on my wife at that embassy party."

Her smile faded as she considered Nick. "So you're one of the alphabet boys," she said. "Military intelligence? CIA?"

"The second one."

"Since when?"

He held her gaze. "Since I got out of the Marines."

She stood and walked the length of the room, arms folded across her midriff, then walked back. "Jesus, Nick."

"I know," he said. "I'm sorry. I should have told you sooner."

Ellie continued pacing the floor. "Why didn't you? And don't give me any 'sworn to secrecy' bullshit."

He reached out and took her hand, stopping her. "I didn't want to make you worry," he said. "It was stupid. I'm sorry."

She didn't look at him. She also didn't remove her hand from his. He sat there on the couch, in the lightening dawn, holding his wife's hand in his unbandaged one while she stood half turned away.

She let go of his hand. As soon as she did, he missed her touch. Then, to his relief, she sat down on the couch next to him. "So now what?"

"Now," he said, "I have to prep for a lecture on the First Crusade this afternoon, and I don't know where my notes are."

"That's not what I mean."

"I know." God, his eyes, they were so dry. And he was so tired. "I can quit. It'll take a few months, but I'll do it." *And we could have kids*, he almost said, but he stopped himself. He wasn't going to pretend his career—either of his careers—was what made him not want to have children. He wouldn't lie about that, not to Ellie. And he wouldn't offer the possibility of having children as some sort of peace offering. He'd been dishonest enough.

"You'd have to quit your teaching job," she said, a question posed as a statement.

"This one, yes, probably," he said. "But there are other schools."

She took his bandaged hand in hers and looked at it as if searching for something in the folds of gauze. "You don't want to quit," she said, and for a moment he had no response to that simple, undeniable fact.

"I was actually worried that maybe you were having an affair," she said.

He let out a bark of laughter. "That's ridiculous," he said. "I would never—"

"More ridiculous than you being a CIA agent?"

"Officer," he said, and when she raised an eyebrow, he said, "We prefer *intelligence officer* to *agent*."

She looked at him for so long that he grew scared, imagined her walking out the door and never returning. That would break him, he knew.

Then she raised his bandaged hand to her lips and kissed it. "Oh for fuck's sake," she said.

"WHAT DO YOU mean, you're a spy?" Annalise said. She was still aiming the pistol at Nick's face.

"Was," Nick said. "I was a spy. I retired from that too." He nodded toward the passports on the desk. "I kept those as insurance, I guess. If I needed to go somewhere without anyone knowing who I am."

He could see Annalise was struggling to digest this. "So you weren't a professor?"

"No, I was. I was a professor."

"So that was, what, your cover?"

"Sort of," he said. "I was an actual professor. Taught classes. Wrote books."

Annalise lowered the gun so now it pointed in the general vicinity of his stomach. "I saw the one on your shelf about Richard the Lionheart and Saladin."

"You did?"

She nodded.

"Annalise?" Nick said. "Can I put my hands down now? My arms are getting tired."

She looked warily at him. "You won't hurt me?"

"I won't hurt you," he said. "I swear on Ellie's grave."

They stood there for a moment, eyeing each other. Then Annalise laid the pistol down on the table.

He was able to refrain from sighing with relief, but it was a close thing. Instead he lowered his hands and gestured at the shopping bags. "I got you some clothes. I hope they fit."

"Okay," she said. "Thank you." She shifted from one foot to the other but didn't make a move toward the bags. Nick felt like they were two awkward dancers who didn't understand the music.

"I need to leave in a few minutes," he said. "I have to make a short trip. Do some research."

She stood very still. "Is this about whatever my dad wanted me to give you? That map?"

125

"Yes. And about whoever wants it."

"What kind of research? I mean, can't you just look on the internet?"

"Need Wi-Fi for that."

"No Wi-Fi, no phone." Annalise sounded like she was stranded on an island, taking stock of the situation. "Wait, when you go back out, can you get a charger for my phone? I can pay for it. I'll pay you back for all the clothes and everything—"

He waved her off. "Don't worry about the clothes. And a cell phone will work fine in town, but off the main roads the reception is pretty bad. Won't work out here."

She nodded, thinking. "You said you had to make a trip. Where are you going?"

"Charlotte."

Her eyes widened. "How far away is that?"

"I'll be back by tonight."

"I'm coming with you."

Nick shook his head. "Nuh-uh. You stay here. You've got clothes, there's food in—"

"No way," she said. "I'm not staying here alone all day. I'm going with you. What's in Charlotte, anyway?"

"Annalise—"

"You're not leaving me here alone," she said.

They stared at one another for a long moment. Nick thought about how she would be a distraction, how he would have to make her stay in the car while he did whatever he needed to do.

You'll be worried about her even more if you leave her here, Ellie said.

"Please," Annalise said, and Nick could see the fear in her eyes.

Don't leave her alone, Ellie said.

Nick sighed. "Go use the bathroom and get changed. We're leaving in fifteen minutes."

Annalise smiled and went to grab the shopping bags, walking past the pistol on the table without giving it a second look. As soon as she left the room with the bags, Nick went to the laundry room off his kitchen and grabbed a small day pack, then retrieved the pistol from the table. By the time Annalise reappeared, in a red T-shirt and new jeans, Nick had the day pack over his shoulder, the pistol buried in the bottom of the pack under a red plastic poncho.

"Clothes fit okay?" he asked, getting two bottles of water from the fridge.

"Yeah, thanks," she said. "I mean, these are mom jeans, but they're comfortable. No offense," she added. "I'm just glad to have new jeans. And underwear. And, well, everything. Thank you."

Nick refrained from smiling. "Grab that blanket off the couch," he said.

Annalise picked up the blanket. "Why do you need this?"

Nick headed for the door to the carport. "Actually, that's for you."

CHAPTER SIXTEEN

Nɪᴄᴋ ᴍᴀᴅᴇ Aɴɴᴀʟɪꜱᴇ ʟɪᴇ ᴏɴ ᴛʜᴇ ꜰʟᴏᴏʀ ᴏꜰ ᴛʜᴇ ʙᴀᴄᴋ ꜱᴇᴀᴛ ᴡɪᴛʜ ᴛʜᴇ blanket over her until he had driven through Cashiers all the way to Lake Toxaway, nearly half an hour. "*Now* can I sit up?" Annalise asked for the fifth time.

"Yes," Nick said, eyes on the road.

Annalise threw the blanket off and crawled up onto the back seat. "God, I'm going to barf," she said.

Nick pressed a button to roll down the back window. "Take deep breaths," he said. "We'll be out of the big turns in a few minutes."

Annalise leaned against the door, eyes shut, hair whipping around from the open window.

"You okay?" Nick asked, glancing in the rearview mirror.

She kept her eyes shut. "Trying not to puke here."

Nick took the hint and shut up. Ten minutes later, when they had come down the worst of the hairpin turns, Annalise was sitting up straighter and Nick had put the windows back up. "God, that sucked," Annalise said.

"Mountain roads can do a number on your stomach."

"Especially if you're lying on the floor of a car under a blanket."

"Didn't want to risk somebody in town seeing you." Without taking his eyes off the road, Nick picked up a cap from the front seat and held it back to Annalise. "Speaking of, put your hair back and put this on."

Annalise took the cap. "Bass Pro Shop," she read off the cap. "Awesome. Why am I wearing this?"

"You want to get back under the blanket?"

Annalise made a face, but she took an elastic band off her wrist and pulled her hair into a ponytail, then slapped the cap on her head. "Sweet hat," she said. "This is a serious look. Do you have any water?"

"There's a bottle in the door cupholder back there."

Annalise opened a bottle and sipped. "So," she said, tightening the cap back on the bottle, "why are we going to Charlotte?"

"There was a phone number on the back of the piece of paper you gave me. It's for a private investigator in Charlotte. I called it from the store where I got you the clothes. Guy says he has something for me."

"Who, Halliwell? You think my dad hired this Halliwell guy?"

"Place is called Lapidus Investigations. Don't know what Halliwell is. Lapidus wouldn't say over the phone."

"Oh," Annalise said. "That's the *FL* in front of the number. Think that's Lapidus' name or whatever?"

"That's one of the things I'll find out."

"We," Annalise said. "That we are going to find out."

Nick didn't respond, just tightened his grip on the steering wheel slightly.

THE RAIN HAD moved off for good and the sun shone in a clear sky. They drove through small towns in a long valley arrowing to the northeast. Mountains rose on either side like the rounded shoulders of giants.

"I'm hungry," Annalise said.

"You wanted to throw up half an hour ago."

"Well, now I'm hungry. I'm a teenager—it's a metabolism thing."

"Let's get to the highway first."

"There's a Burger King right over there."

Nick shot her another look in the rearview mirror. "We're stopping once for gas and for food, and we'll do it at the highway."

"Sheesh, okay," Annalise said, holding up her hands in surrender.

When they hit I-26 in Fletcher, Nick filled up at a gas station. When he went inside to pay, he also grabbed a pair of sunglasses. He walked back to the car and found that Annalise had moved up to the front passenger seat, still wearing the Bass Pro Shop cap.

"Perfect," Annalise said when he handed her the sunglasses. "Now I'll look like I'm fleeing the paparazzi. No gas station candy?"

"Candy?"

"Everybody knows gas station candy is the best. They have stuff you can't buy in Target or whatever. Like Now and Laters, and Hot Tamales. Giant Twix." She looked at him expectantly.

Nick got back in the driver's seat and started the car. "I'm not going back in to buy candy," he said.

Annalise rolled her eyes. "Fine. Can I turn on the radio?"

"No."

Annalise put the sunglasses on and turned to look out her window.

They drove to a nearby Wendy's and got in line for the drive-through. "What do you want?" Nick asked.

She shrugged, still looking out the side window.

"Annalise," he said.

"I don't care," she said, still looking out her window.

Nick failed to bite back a sigh.

She turned to look at him. "I'm sorry," she said, "am I annoying you?"

"A little."

"Whatever," she said, turning back to the window. Then: "A double-bacon cheeseburger. Large fries, large Coke. And a smoothie."

"You sure that's enough?"

"This is the worst road trip ever."

"I did want you to stay at my house."

"Shit," Annalise said, then again, louder, "*Shit.*"

"What?"

"I left my phone at your house. I wanted to get a charger. *Shit.*"

TWENTY MINUTES LATER they were on the interstate. Annalise had devoured all her food and sat slumped in the passenger seat, the cap pulled down low. She hadn't said a word since they'd left the Wendy's. Nick left her alone and drove. They were making good time, and he thought they would reach Charlotte before two. But Annalise's silence filled the car.

"I don't know how to do this," Nick said.

Annalise turned her head toward him, her face largely hidden behind the sunglasses.

He kept his eyes on the road. "I'm sorry for saying you were annoying earlier."

Silence.

"It's just a lot to process," he said.

"I can relate," Annalise said.

Don't be a smartass, Ellie said. *She's hurt and scared and still angry. Be kind.*

"I just met you," Nick continued. "And you don't really know me at all." He glanced at her, then back at the road. "And I know you're scared and pissed off. I get it. I am too."

Annalise continued looking at him, and just as he was about to open his mouth and ask something inane, like *are you okay*, she said, "Good." She shifted in her seat. "So were you really a spy?"

"Yeah."

"How did that happen?" she asked. "Becoming a spy?"

He hesitated, the old habits of secrecy, of compartmentalizing his life, raising their walls. Slowly he said, "They recruited me when I got out of the Marines. They knew I wanted to get my PhD and be a professor. They helped make that happen, helped pay for school."

"And in return you, what, spied on other professors or something?"

He shook his head. "Nothing like that. I taught overseas and gathered information that might be helpful, passed it on."

She didn't say anything in response, and when he glanced over at her, even her sunglasses couldn't hide her look of disappointment. It was almost funny. "I'm not James Bond," he said. "Sorry."

"I was thinking more like Jason Bourne," she said, then gave him a little smile to show she was joking. Mostly. "So, what's the plan?"

"Plan?"

"When we get to Charlotte."

Nick thought of the pistol in his day pack, which was stowed beneath his seat.

"We'll go to this Lapidus Investigations office," Nick said. "I've got an address."

Annalise glanced at the dash. "And you've got GPS. Nice. Welcome to the twenty-first century."

"I aim to please."

"So we go to this Lapidus Investigations. Then what?"

"We see if we can find out why your dad hired them."

Annalise shifted in her seat again, as if trying to get comfortable and not succeeding. "And that might help us figure out who—who's chasing me?"

Nick noted that she had left out *who killed my parents.*

"Yep," he said.

ANNALISE DOZED, HER mouth slightly open. At one point she began snorting softly, cleared her throat, and fell back asleep. At Columbus, Nick turned onto US 74 and continued driving east. After an hour, on the other side of Kings Mountain, he merged onto I-85. Traffic grew heavier and the highway broadened from three lanes to four, like a river widening as it approached its mouth. The hills were behind them and they drove across flat plains, green trees bordering either side of the highway.

Billboards proliferated on the roadside. They crossed the Catawba River and Nick got on 478, which circled Charlotte. According to his GPS, Lapidus Investigations was in an office park south of the airport.

With a snort Annalise bolted upright in her seat, the sunglasses sliding down her nose. "Where are we?" she asked, her voice furred with sleep. She wiped the back of her hand across her mouth, then pushed the sunglasses back up.

"Outside of Charlotte," Nick said.

An eighteen-wheeler passed on the left, their car rocking slightly like a rowboat in the wake of a whale.

"I need to pee," Annalise said.

Nick nodded and at the next exit took the off-ramp and steered into a gas station. They parked at the pump, and Nick topped off the tank while Annalise went inside to use the restroom. She was still there when Nick went inside to pay. At the counter he hesitated, then went to look at the candy aisle.

He was back in the car when Annalise came out of the station, her sunglasses pushed back on top of her head. When she got in the car, Nick handed her a plastic bag. "Thought you could refuel before we get there," he said.

She opened the bag and stared. Inside Nick had thrown an assortment of giant Twix bars, Now and Laters, Starbursts, M&M's, and a box of Fudge Rounds.

"Gas station candy," Nick said. "They didn't have any Hot Tamales."

Annalise's eyes welled up and she covered her face with her hands. She released a strangled sob, her shoulders shaking with the effort.

"Hey," Nick said. He put his hand on her shoulder, hoping she'd find it comforting. Then a car pulled in behind him, waiting for the pump, and Nick pulled forward and drove across the station parking lot. He parked at the far end, away from the pumps and other customers, and turned off the engine. Annalise continued to cry behind her hands and Nick just sat behind the wheel, waiting it out.

Annalise lifted her face from her hands, then wiped her arm across her eyes. "Here," Nick said, handing her some clean napkins left over from lunch. Annalise wiped her eyes and blew her nose, then sat blinking away tears.

"Mom always bought gas station candy," she said, staring at the glove compartment. "Whenever we went on a road trip. Dad hated it, but Mom always insisted. It was like our dumb girls-only thing."

Nick nodded. "Sounds like a nice ritual."

Annalise looked at him. "Yeah," she said. She reached into the bag in her lap and pulled out a pack of Starbursts. She held it out to Nick, who opened it.

"Who liked the Starbursts, you or your mom?" he asked.

"Both of us," she said. "Mom would eat all of them if she could. Except the yellow ones—she said they tasted like furniture polish."

Nick took the first Starburst in the pack—it was yellow—and he unwrapped it and popped it in his mouth. "Your mom was right," he said, chewing. "Tastes like a square piece of Pledge."

Annalise held out her hand and Nick handed her the Starbursts, then started the car so the air conditioning would run. They sat there, eating Starbursts, watching traffic pass on the interstate a hundred yards away. Nick was aware of time ticking on, but he needed to give Annalise a moment.

"Can I ask you something about my dad?" Annalise asked.

"Shoot," Nick said.

"Were you all ever close?"

Nick looked out across the highway and turned the question over in his mind. "When we were kids," he said. "He followed me everywhere. I taught him how to swim." He stopped, surprised. He had forgotten that.

"You taught him how to swim?"

"Yeah," Nick said. "This girl in our neighborhood, Dorothy Sullivan, had a pool, and the neighborhood kids would go over sometimes. And in the summer when we weren't in school, our mother would either hover

over Jay and baby him to death or kick both of us out of the house. So we spent a lot of time in Dorothy Sullivan's pool, and I taught Jay how to swim. I mean, he could dog-paddle, but I taught him how to hold his breath and actually swim and all that." He paused, remembering a six-year-old Jay popping up out of the water after swimming the length of the pool and back, the smile on his face brighter than the sunlight glancing off the water. *I did it, Nick!* he had crowed. *Did you see me? I did it!*

"Dad taught me to swim," Annalise said. "Actually, he took me to lessons at the Y, but he would get in the water, too, to help me practice. I'd hold on to the side of the pool and then he'd say 'Green light!' and I'd have to kick like crazy, then 'Red light!' and I'd stop."

Nick smiled. "I taught him that."

"Really?"

"Uh-huh. He loved it."

Annalise grinned, then balled up a couple of Starburst wrappers and dropped them into a cupholder. "So," she said, "where is this private investigator's office?"

Nick nodded and put the car in gear. "Another exit down the highway," he said.

CHAPTER SEVENTEEN

In his dream, Cole was standing in the backyard of his childhood home, a brick ranch in Columbia, Missouri. He was holding a G.I. Joe action figure, a favorite toy. The sky was dark, clouds roiling overhead. Wind pulled at his hair, made the stand of pine trees at the back of the yard sway and creak like ship masts. Light faded, then shifted to a greenish hue. His ears popped. Somewhere beyond the house there was a moaning roar.

From behind the screen door to the kitchen, his father shouted, "Get in the house, boy!"

Cole didn't move, partly from fear, partly out of spite for his father.

"Goddammit, boy, get in this house!"

Cole balled his fists, the G.I. Joe figure pressing into his palm, and stood his ground. The wind thundered around him now, scraps of paper and leaves and roof tiles whirling past. The gas grill scraped across the concrete patio as if pushed by invisible hands. A loud *crack* and the top half of a dead pine tree toppled into the yard.

The screen door burst open, but instead of his father it was Winslow, a charred bullet hole in his forehead, flesh rotted and slimy with seaweed, wrapped in his father's barn coat. Winslow stalked down the stairs toward Cole. "I told you to get in the house," he said with a leer. A baby eel slid out of his mouth and dropped wriggling to the ground.

Cole backed away, Winslow advancing with the same leer. Cole threw the G.I. Joe figure at Winslow, who batted it away. The wind screamed, the ground shuddered. Behind Winslow, the house blew apart in a black whirlwind. And Winslow's hands, leprous, sea-changed, reached for Cole's throat.

When a hand touched Cole's shoulder, he shot up out of bed, grabbing and twisting the arm of the person who had touched him.

"Jesus, Cole!" Zhang cried out.

Breathing heavily, Cole realized he had Zhang on the floor of their hotel room in an armlock that threatened to break the man's arm at the elbow. He released Zhang, who stumbled to his feet. "The fuck?" Zhang said, holding his arm.

"Dream," Cole said thickly. "Sorry." He sat on the floor, leaning back against the bed. Slowly it came back to him—they were in a hotel outside Gainesville, Georgia. Looking for the girl. They'd spent yesterday afternoon canvassing hotels and found nothing. "I'm sorry," Cole said, rubbing his eyes with the heels of his hands. "You just startled me, is all. You okay?"

Zhang gently bent his arm at the elbow. "Yeah," he said. "It's good." He hesitated, then held out his hand to help Cole stand up. Cole took it and pulled himself to his feet, then clapped Zhang on the shoulder. "What have you got?" he asked, his tone brisk.

"I got it," Zhang said.

Cole glanced at Zhang's laptop, open on the desk across the room. "Where is she?"

"Her phone last pinged a tower in Dillard, north of here."

"When?"

"Yesterday at eighteen thirty-four. That's not all. I looked at Jay Bashir's cell records, and last week he tried to call an 828 number twice. That's in western North Carolina. Dillard is less than a mile from the

North Carolina border. The number's disconnected; I haven't found it yet."

"Call Jonas," Cole said. "Get them back here ASAP. Have them meet us in Dillard." He took a pair of pants out of his duffel on the floor, started pulling them on. "We'll drive there ourselves, pick up the girl's scent."

"I looked up our resupply contact," Zhang said. "We could stop on the way to Dillard."

Cole had a flash of Winslow from his dream, wrapped in his daddy's barn coat, reaching out with his rotting hands. He shoved the memory aside and kept his voice steady. "Then that's what we'll do. Keep looking for that North Carolina number."

Zhang nodded and pulled out his cell phone. Cole went into the bathroom and closed the door, then braced his hands on the sink. Jesus, the dream had been so real. He looked up at his reflection in the spotty mirror, saw the dark smudges under his eyes, the gray in his blond hair and in the stubble on his jaw. At least he didn't look like his old man. That asshole had been dead for twenty years, thankfully. Cole took a deep breath, let it out. Goddamn Winslow. Cole didn't believe in ghosts any more than he believed in the Loch Ness monster, but he had a feeling Winslow might haunt his dreams for a while to come. And he'd nearly broken Zhang's arm. He turned on the faucet and splashed water on his face. Fuck it, he thought. Focus on the girl. Get the girl, finish the job. Nothing else mattered.

DAWES DROVE THE Suburban north on 23 out of Gainesville. The land sloped up in gentle blue folds at the horizon. Before Tallulah Falls they took a two-lane road and headed west toward pine-covered foothills reaching down from the Blue Ridge Mountains like long stony fingers.

A few miles later Zhang, from the back seat, directed Dawes down a dirt road, the ruts wide with only an occasional spray of weeds in between. "Stop here," Zhang said, consulting a map on his phone. The Suburban rolled to a stop on the side of the road, engine idling. Kudzu swarmed over the hillside here, choking the tree trunks and twisting halfway up a power pole. From the back seat, Poncho got out of the Suburban, a rifle slung over one shoulder, and tossed off a casual salute before disappearing into the kudzu.

"Where's Jonas?" Cole said.

"Got delayed in Hilton Head," Zhang said. He stifled a yawn. "Tropical storm going up the coast grounded air travel. He'll let us know when they can fly out."

"How long do we wait here?" Dawes asked.

Cole leaned back in the front passenger seat. "Twenty minutes," he said. "Keep the engine on. Hot as balls out there."

Buying weapons always required care. In America, if you needed a rifle or a shotgun or a semiautomatic pistol, you could practically pick one up off the sidewalk. Anything beyond that and you entered thickets of legalese and local, state, and federal laws. Licensed gun dealers kept records, which meant a paper trail. Of course, some were willing to deal under the table, but that could be hit or miss in terms of the reliability of the dealer, the quality of the product, and the amount available. Cole preferred that when they took a job, the client provided all their weapons up front. And if they needed to buy their own, Cole knew dealers throughout Africa, Asia, the Middle East, even Europe. But Cole didn't operate in the States often, so whenever they had a job here he had relied on Winslow, who had been their quartermaster, to purchase their weapons. And Winslow's primary dealer in the Southeast sold out of a barn down this dirt road in Georgia. The fact that the dealer was conveniently located on their way to the last known signal from the girl's phone wasn't lost on Cole. Karma, perhaps—another sign of order in the universe.

Cole reached into a pocket of his tactical pants and pulled out a slim paperback of *The Art of War*. Time for a little reading. He hadn't finished the book yet.

Aside from the air conditioning and the idling engine, the only thing Cole could hear was Zhang softly snoring behind him. Cole was sure

Zhang was wearing those big-ass noise-canceling headphones that even Waco gave him shit about—he'd put them on anytime he could take a nap. Well, the man had been up all night hacking into Annalise Bashir's cell phone carrier. And after he had damn near broken Zhang's arm that morning, Cole wasn't going to deny him some shut-eye. He went back to Sun Tzu: *To secure ourselves against defeat lies in our own hands, but the opportunity of defeating the enemy is provided by the enemy himself.*

Dawes shifted in the driver's seat, then unbuckled his seat belt. Cole, concentrating on his book, waited for Dawes to step out of the Suburban, figuring he needed to take a leak. Several moments passed, the silence stretching. Cole looked up from the page to see Dawes sitting behind the wheel, staring off into the distance.

"What?" Cole said.

Dawes jerked his head, startled. "Shit," he said. He reached out to grasp the steering wheel, then withdrew his hands. "Sorry, Cole."

Cole glanced out the windshield. "You see something?"

"Nope," Dawes said. He shook his head. "Nothing."

Cole narrowed his eyes. Aside from Jonas, Dawes was usually the most rock solid of his men, and now he was acting like a teenager caught sneaking home after curfew. "What's on your mind?" he asked.

Dawes opened his mouth, closed it, looked in the rearview mirror at Zhang passed out in the back seat. Cole waited patiently. Then Dawes sighed like a man facing a fuckup. "You ever been married?" he asked.

Cole laughed. "Jesus," he said. "No. I haven't."

"Right," Dawes said. "Sorry. Didn't mean to pry."

Cole grunted. "Idea never interested me," he said. He laid his open book down on his lap. "And this line of work isn't exactly conducive to the bonds of matrimony."

"No," Dawes said. "I mean, that's true." He made to reach for the wheel again, and again he withdrew his hands as if he didn't know what to do with them.

"Dawes, what the fuck," Cole said.

"Huh?"

"You're acting like a kid on his first date. What is it?"

Dawes turned a miserable face to Cole, who was utterly baffled. And then it clicked into place and Cole stared at Dawes, gobsmacked. "Jesus," he said. "Are *you* thinking about getting married?"

Dawes shrugged. "Maybe," he said, his voice low. "Yeah."

Cole had nothing to say, or rather, he had plenty to say about the subject—how being married could make you vulnerable, how it could distract you from the job at hand, which, in their business, could mean getting a bullet in the head. How being a mercenary for hire often meant dropping everything to fly halfway around the world with less than forty-eight hours' notice. It wasn't a lack of things to say that made Cole hesitate; it was that he wasn't sure which objection to voice first.

In that moment while Cole paused, Dawes started talking, words pouring out of him like water from a burst dam. "I met her when I was in the Army—she was a waitress at a bar. How cliché is that? My whole table flirted with her, but she only flirted back with me, and we've been together since. I told Mandy—that's her name, Mandy—I told her I'm a security consultant, she's cool with me being gone when I'm on a job, but I'm worried she's gonna think I'm not serious. I've got a plan and everything. When we're done with this job, I'm gonna fly back to LA and surprise her. I've got a ring all picked out; this jeweler in Century City is holding on to it for me. So I'll fly in to LA and pick up the ring and take Mandy to this beach near Malibu, and that's when I'm gonna ask her." Dawes abruptly stopped talking and looked at Cole with a kind of sick hopefulness. "Am I being stupid?" he asked.

Cole looked down at the open book in his lap. Not that Sun Tzu had anything to say about marriage, at least not in the parts of the book Cole had managed to read. He picked up his book and closed it, then tossed it onto the dashboard. "My old man used to smack my mother around," Cole said. "Not every day, or every week, but he did it. Kicked my ass if I tried to stop him. I was ten years old, and I tackled him once when he was shoving her into a wall. It was like running into a tree. He just turned and backhanded me across the room, swatted me away like a puppy, then started laying into my mother again. Day I turned seventeen, I kicked his ass for once. Broke his nose and laid him out on the kitchen floor." Cole turned to Dawes with an ugly smile. "And my mother called the cops on me. I took off and never turned back."

Dawes blinked, as if trying to process what Cole had said, maybe trying to process the fact that Cole had shared any of this. "Jesus," he said.

Cole shrugged. "I'm just saying I'm probably not the best person to ask for advice about marriage. It's not like I had any great role model in the first place."

They sat in silence after that, looking out the windshield as if the answer to Dawes's question lay out in the kudzu. Cole let his thoughts drift to the idea of a home, a place to return to after a mission, a woman waiting for him. He couldn't picture it. He lived out of a duffel bag. He knew Jonas had a place in Chicago and a woman he'd had an on-again, off-again relationship with for years. And Winslow would crash with his sister. *Used to* crash. He shook his head at the thought of Winslow, at all of it, the whole domestic-bliss bullshit. He liked his freedom to move where and when he wanted, and as for women, he had no problems on that score and preferred to keep his relationships casual. Any home he had was with his men, but that wasn't the kind of thing you could share aloud. He'd shared enough. He looked at his phone. It had been nineteen minutes. "Let's roll," he said, loud enough that Zhang woke with a start in the back seat. Dawes put the Suburban in gear and continued down the road without another word.

Another half mile down the road and they saw a mailbox peppered by more than one blast of buckshot. Dawes turned left down a gravel drive past the mailbox and up a short rise. They crested the rise and drove down into a wide, shallow bowl like a moon crater. At the bottom of the bowl was a white ranch house with a covered porch across the entire front. To the right of the house sat a graying hulk of a barn. Cole made out two men on the porch of the ranch house, one sitting on a chair, the other standing at the top of the porch steps.

"Ten and three o'clock," Dawes said. Cole squinted—damn, he needed glasses. He'd seen movement by the barn to his right, and sure enough, there was a big old boy with a beard the size of a shovel blade standing in the open doorway of the barn, an AR15 in his hands. But he'd missed the smaller man who had stepped around the far left corner of the house, cradling a shotgun.

"Welcoming committee," Cole said.

Dawes stopped the Suburban about ten meters away from the front steps of the ranch and turned off the engine, leaving the keys in the ignition. "They look itchy," he said.

"Let's play nice," Cole said. He opened his door and stepped out of the Suburban, as did Zhang and Dawes. Cole had a blue duffel bag in one hand, his faded Hawaiian shirt untucked to cover the Glock in his waistband. He took a few steps toward the porch, Zhang on his right flank. "Mr. Toomey!" he called out, raising his free hand.

The man at the top of the porch steps didn't move, but the seated man stood up from his rocker. His face was leathered and lined and said his age was anywhere from forty to sixty. "You Cole?" he said.

"Yessir," Cole said, smiling. He made sure to hold his hands slightly out from his body, nonthreatening and friendly. In his periphery he saw Dawes doing the same, moving to stand by the left front tire of the Suburban.

Toomey walked across the porch, a board popping beneath his feet, and came down the steps, trailed by the other man, who put on a straw cowboy hat as he stepped into the sunlight. At the bottom of the steps Toomey stopped and put his hands on his hips. "Usually deal with Winslow," he said.

Cole nodded. "He couldn't make it today. You got my message, though."

Toomey said nothing, just continued to look at Cole, who looked back. A crow called out somewhere behind the house.

" 'Kay," Toomey said finally. "You got the cash?"

Cole held up the duffel bag. "You want to check it, of course."

Toomey grunted and moved toward Cole, the man in the cowboy hat following. The bearded man with the AR took a step or two closer, as did the fourth man at the corner of the house. When Toomey stopped just out of arm's reach, Cole raised the duffel bag and slowly unzipped it, then held the bag open so Toomey could see the stacks of bills.

Toomey leaned forward a little and peered at the contents of the bag, then frowned. "That ain't right," he said, sounding puzzled.

Cole glanced down at the bag even as he automatically took a half step back. The half step ruined Toomey's punch so it glanced off Cole's forehead instead of breaking his nose. Still, the blow was powerful enough to nearly send Cole to one knee. In less than a second he had regained his balance and dropped the bag to free both his hands, but now Toomey pointed a revolver in Cole's face. The man in the cowboy hat had a pistol trained on Zhang. On the other side of the Suburban, Dawes was holding his hands up, covered by the man with the shotgun.

"You treat all your customers this way?" Cole said.

Toomey's face was a closed door. "Where's Winslow?" he asked.

"Like I said, he couldn't make it."

Toomey took a step closer, the barrel of his revolver inches from Cole's forehead. "On your knees," he said.

Behind him, Zhang shifted his feet. "Don't move, motherfucker," the man in the cowboy hat said.

"It's okay," Cole said to Zhang, his eyes on Toomey. Slowly, he knelt in the yard, the grass here worn to dirt. "Mr. Toomey," he said, keeping his voice calm and measured, "I'm just here to make a deal."

"Did you kill him?" Toomey said.

Cole looked around the barrel directly into Toomey's eyes. "No. He's on another job."

"Bullshit."

"Why do you think that's bullshit?" Cole said.

Toomey didn't waver. Neither did the revolver. "Because he's my cousin, you asshole. And he *never* sends anyone to me without coming himself. So unless you want me to start lighting parts of you on fire, you tell me where he is."

Cole saw the grief and rage in Toomey's face, knew the man meant what he said. He sighed. "Zamboni," he said.

Toomey frowned, a question on his lips, when the other man's cowboy hat flew off his head, followed by the crack of a rifle shot. The man toppled to the ground, dust pluming around his body. Toomey jerked his head up, looking for the source of the shot. Cole drew his knife from his boot and stood, sweeping one arm to brush Toomey's gun hand to the side. With the other hand he stabbed upward into Toomey's gut, the blade just below the sternum, seeking for the heart. Toomey grunted, his mouth dropping open, and he sagged against Cole, who let go of the knife and shoved Toomey away. Zhang was shouting, and then a shotgun blast from the far side of the Suburban was punctuated by three pistol shots—Dawes. The bearded man by the barn let loose with his AR, stitching the dirt up to and past Cole, missing him by a foot. Cole pulled his Glock from beneath his Hawaiian shirt, crouched, and let off two rounds in the man's direction. Behind him Zhang was also shooting. More jackhammering from the AR, then the bearded man spun and collided with the side of the barn as another rifle shot cracked across the sky. The bearded man tried to lift the AR, but Cole put three rounds into his chest and dropped him.

"Dawes?" he called out. "Zhang?"

"All clear," Dawes called back.

"Clear," Zhang said.

Cole rose, still holding the Glock in both hands. He kicked the revolver away from Toomey's outstretched hand. Toomey was still breathing in shallow gasps, bright-red blood threading from his mouth. Cole bent to look Toomey in the face. The man's eyes were wide and rolling, but they came to focus on Cole.

"Fuck," Toomey breathed. "You."

"Yeah," Cole said. He stood and aimed the Glock and shot Toomey in the head.

He, Dawes, and Zhang started searching all four bodies. Dawes knelt next to the man with the straw cowboy hat and checked his pockets while Cole crouched by Toomey. Zhang was at the far corner of the house, checking out the guy with the shotgun. Absently, Cole scratched at his ear. "Hey," he said quietly, and Dawes looked up.

"That girl," Cole said. "Mandy. She make you happy? Beyond just getting laid?"

Dawes stared at him for a moment. "Yeah," he said. "Yeah, she does."

Cole nodded. "Then you oughta marry her," he said, and went back to searching Toomey's corpse.

Cole had just retrieved a ring of keys from Toomey's belt when Poncho jogged double-time out from behind a nearby stand of trees. He had slung his sniper rifle across his back so the barrel rose over his shoulder like an empty flagpole. A few moments later he reached them, slightly winded after his run from the far rim of the bowl. "The fuck happened?" he asked.

Dawes glanced at Cole, who was looking through the ring of keys. "Guy in charge wanted to know where Winslow was."

"I heard that part," Poncho said. "At least I heard Cole over his mic. Dude think you all were cops or something?"

Dawes glanced again at Cole, who continued examining the keys, and said nothing. Then Zhang, who had finished with his body and was now examining the Suburban for any bullet damage, spoke up. "He said he was Winslow's cousin."

Poncho's eyes widened. "Shit."

Cole, still looking at the keys, said, "Good thing the throat mics work. How far was that, Poncho? Half mile?"

Poncho nodded. "More or less. Heard you clear as a bell. Is Zamboni even a real word?"

"It's one of those ice rink machines," Dawes said. "Goes around and smooths out the ice." He picked up the straw cowboy hat from where it lay in the dirt. "About my size."

Poncho grinned. "Got a hole in it."

Dawes looked into the crown of the hat. "Kinda messy now too."

Cole found the kind of key he had been looking for. "Barn," he said, and the four of them headed for the barn, Dawes dropping the hat next to its former owner, the top of the man's head a shattered wreck. They stepped over the body of the bearded man where it lay across the barn entrance. Inside the barn, the air slightly cool and smelling of ancient horseshit, they found a stack of hard cases in a stall, covered by a tarp. They were padlocked, and Cole used the key from Toomey's ring to unlock the cases. Each held either an MP5 submachine gun or loaded magazines—what they had arranged to buy.

"My guess is there's a lot more guns around here somewhere," Zhang said.

"Just take what we need," Cole said. "Somebody heard that shooting."

"I saw another road out through the back fields," Poncho said. "Loops back around to that two-lane."

They put the cases into the back of the Suburban, threw the tarp over them, and drove around the side of the ranch and through the back fields on the route Poncho had found, leaving the bodies to the flies already swirling above them.

CHAPTER EIGHTEEN

Lapidus Investigations was located at one end of an office park. The two-story buildings were nondescript brick boxes with doors leading to various offices. The building that housed Lapidus Investigations also held a dental practice, an accounting firm, and a real estate office. The PI firm was at the far-right end of the building, next to the real estate office.

Nick parked the car in a far corner of the mostly empty parking lot. From their spot, Annalise could see the front door and the side of the building. The windows were all closed, the blinds drawn.

"What do we do now?" Annalise asked.

"You stay here," Nick said. He reached underneath his seat. "Keep an eye out for anyone."

"Meaning what?"

Nick retrieved his day pack from beneath the driver's seat. "Honk the horn if you need me."

"And call attention to the teenage girl all alone in a car? No thanks." Annalise unclipped her seat belt and opened the car door. "I'm coming with you."

"Wait a minute," Nick said, but she was already out of the car and had closed the door behind her. No way was her uncle leaving her alone in the car. He got out on his side, cursing under his breath. Annalise stood a few feet away, looking at him expectantly.

"You follow me and let me do the talking." Nick threw the day pack over his shoulder and started walking across the parking lot, Annalise following.

They opened the door and entered a small waiting room furnished with overstuffed beige chairs and a scarred coffee table holding a spread of last month's magazines. A frosted glass partition divided the waiting room from a receptionist's desk. The partition was open, revealing a woman in a purple sweater set seated behind a desktop monitor. "Can I help you?" the woman asked.

"I have a two o'clock appointment with Mr. Lapidus," Nick said.

A door to the right of the frosted glass partition opened, and a man in a gray suit and tie looked out. His hair was shorn close to his skull, and he had a long face that gave him a hangdog look. "Mr. Anthony? I'm Frank Lapidus. Come on back." He stepped aside to let Nick walk through. Then he saw Annalise and narrowed his eyes slightly as if trying to get a bead on her. She ducked her head and followed her uncle through the doorway.

Lapidus led them down a hallway to his office, which held two straight-backed chairs in front of a solid but battered mahogany desk. Plate glass windows behind the desk were covered by blinds which were shut. There were a few bookcases and a pair of Army green filing cabinets. A framed poster of Aruba hung incongruously on one wall, the only splash of bright color in the room.

Lapidus gestured at the two straight-backed chairs and remained standing behind his desk until they sat, then lowered himself into his own seat. He glanced at Annalise, then returned his gaze to Nick. "May I see some identification, please?"

Annalise stared at her uncle—*what the hell?*—but Nick reached into his back pocket, retrieved his wallet, slid his driver's license out, and leaned forward to hand it to Lapidus. Lapidus took it and examined it closely, then handed it back across his desk. "You too, young lady," he said.

"I don't have any," she said. When Nick turned to look at her, she shrugged. "It's in a sleeve on the back of my phone. I left it at your house."

Lapidus gazed at her, then shook his head. "If I were you," he said to Nick, "I'd be careful driving. If a state trooper pulls you over and finds a teen girl with no ID in your car, you'll have a lot of explaining to do."

"She's my niece," Nick said. "Annalise Bashir."

She saw her last name register with Lapidus. "I'm sorry for your loss," he said to her.

"You said you had something for me," Nick said.

Lapidus nodded. "I apologize for asking for ID," he said. "I was given specific instructions about passing this along." He opened a desk drawer and took out a sealed envelope, then passed it across the desk to Nick. "I was to give it only to Jay Bashir, his wife, his daughter, or his brother."

Nick held the envelope but didn't open it. "Who gave you instructions?"

"Your brother," Lapidus said, dipping his head slightly as if out of respect.

Nick considered the envelope, then looked at Annalise. She nodded and he opened the flap, the tearing sound loud in the silent office. Nick reached into the open envelope and held up a flash drive, the kind you would plug into your laptop and save files on.

"What's on it?" Nick asked.

"I don't know," Lapidus said. "I didn't look at it. He asked me to keep it safe, and I did."

Nick hesitated, then put the flash drive back into the envelope and dropped the envelope into his day pack, which was on the floor between his feet. "Why did he hire you, Mr. Lapidus?" he asked.

Lapidus clasped his hands together on his desk. "I promise my clients complete privacy and confidentiality, Mr. Anthony."

"I'm sure Jay appreciates that," Nick said coldly.

Annalise stifled a gasp. Nick's comment brought Lapidus up short, too, but only for a moment. "In this state, legally and ethically, it's unclear whether the confidentiality between a private investigator and a client extends beyond death."

"Come on, Lapidus."

"As I said—"

"What did my brother hire you to do?"

Annalise wanted to scream at both of them to stop measuring their dicks, but she was distracted by a wastebasket in her line of sight. It sat on the floor at one end of Lapidus's desk, and it was empty save for a single leaflet. Her eyes were drawn to the one word she could see at the top of the leaflet: *HALLIWELL*. She glanced at the two men, who were facing each other and clearly growing irritated. Neither paid her any attention. She leaned forward and fished out the leaflet, which was folded in thirds. Now she saw the full title: *HALLIWELL—Securing the Future of Energy*.

"It's not a person," Annalise said aloud, still looking at the leaflet. Both men stopped arguing and looked at her. "Halliwell's not a person," she said, looking at her uncle. She held up the leaflet. He took it from her hand and scanned the front, then unfolded it, holding it so Annalise could see it as well. Inside were color photographs of a sunset sky behind the black outline of an oil derrick, a group of smiling men and women around a conference table, a field of wind turbines under a dazzling blue sky.

"It's an energy company," Nick said, reading the text. "Here in Charlotte."

Lapidus tried to hide his annoyance and failed. He sighed and shook his head, then spread his hands across the top of his desk, like a dealer acknowledging the end of a card game.

And a memory dropped into Annalise's mind, bright and shiny as a new coin. "Did you talk to my dad on the phone last Friday, Mr. Lapidus?" she asked.

Her uncle glanced up from the leaflet, but she ignored him, her eyes fixed on Lapidus. Her dad had been grilling chicken in the backyard, she remembered. She had gone outside to ask him when dinner would be ready, and Dad had been on his phone, pacing across the patio. "Yes, Hollywood," she thought her dad had said into the phone. "That's the one. Is the package safe?" Then Dad had spotted Annalise and smiled, pointed at the phone, and rolled his eyes. *Just a minute*, he had mouthed, and Annalise had nodded and gone back inside to watch TikTok videos and forgotten all about it. But now she realized her father had not said *Yes, Hollywood*. What he had actually said was *Yes, Halliwell*.

Lapidus looked like he was sucking on a sour tooth. Then he smiled thinly at Annalise. She wasn't sure whether or not the smile was an improvement. "I did, yes," he said. "I had flown into Tampa and picked up something from him earlier that afternoon at the airport. By the time I got back to Charlotte, he'd left a voice mail asking me to do some digging into a particular company. I called him back to double-check the name of the company he wanted me to investigate."

"Why did he want you to look into Halliwell?" Nick said.

"I don't know," Lapidus said. "He didn't tell me, and I didn't ask. All I knew was he wanted me to look into Halliwell's business dealings with Saudi Arabia."

"Did you find anything?" Nick asked.

"Halliwell has contracts with Saudi Arabia to upgrade their oil and natural gas production systems," Lapidus said. "They're not alone. Lots of energy companies from the States and around the world do this kind of business with the Saudis."

"How much are Halliwell's contracts worth?"

"About a billion dollars." Lapidus shrugged and gave a little smile, as if he found the amount ludicrous. "This isn't top-secret information. Just some good old-fashioned research."

Nick nodded. "But it's not readily apparent information either," he said. "Probably mentioned in trade magazines or buried in a business prospectus."

Lapidus shrugged again but gave Nick a nod, conceding the point. "That's the nature of my business," he said. "I do mostly corporate investigation. No divorce cases for me." He glanced at his wristwatch, then stood up. "I'm sorry, but that's all I have to share with you. I never even had a chance to tell Mr. Bashir any of this. I was going to send him a preliminary report on Monday." Lapidus pursed his lips and shook his head. "Again, I'm very sorry for your loss."

"What package?" Annalise said, and when Lapidus blinked slowly at her, she said, "What my father asked you about. The package. What was that?"

"It's what your father handed to me in the Tampa airport," Lapidus said. "He told me to keep it locked away for him." He nodded toward Nick. "It's what I just gave your uncle."

THEY WERE BACK in the car but had not yet left the parking lot. Nick sat behind the steering wheel, brooding, while Annalise waited for him to say something.

"I don't like him," Annalise said finally.

Nick blinked, his thoughts interrupted. "What?"

"Do you think he's in on it or something?"

"Who? Lapidus?" Nick shook his head. "He just wanted to show us he was the boss. You ever have a teacher who liked making sure everyone knew they were in charge?"

"Mr. Montgomery," Annalise said promptly. "Always tried to bust kids for dress code violations. He was practically a Nazi."

Nick gave a little smile. "Lapidus is no Nazi, but he's an officious bastard."

Annalise smiled back. "Totally." Then the smile slid off her face. "What did my dad do?" she asked, her voice sounding small in her own ears. "Why did he want this Lapidus guy to investigate some energy company?"

"Your dad was a contractor," Nick said. "Maybe he was thinking of working for Halliwell and wanted to check them out. Or maybe he'd worked for them before and learned something, something he wanted to know more about."

"Or maybe a lot of things," Annalise said. "We don't know *anything*."

"That's not entirely true," Nick said. "We know what Halliwell is. We know your father hired Lapidus to investigate Halliwell's ties to Saudi Arabia. And we know your father sent the flash drive to Lapidus for safekeeping and wanted one of us to have it."

"Yeah, but *why*?" Annalise said. "And what do you think is on that thing?"

"I don't know," Nick said. "But I plan to find out." He turned the key in the ignition, starting the car. "First, we try to beat five o'clock traffic and get back home."

CHAPTER NINETEEN

GETTING OUT OF CHARLOTTE PROVED HARDER THAT DRIVING IN, AND Nick spent the better part of an hour grinding through ten miles of interstate before the logjam of traffic finally broke. After a short time of asking questions and wanting to know what Nick thought, especially about the flash drive, Annalise fell asleep, her Bass Pro Shop cap pulled down over her face.

Nick drove west into the setting sun, squinting behind his sunglasses. Occasionally he would glance at Annalise, this teenager who had dropped into his life. She was growing to trust him, but she didn't accept everything he said at face value. Grudgingly, he admired her for it. She would need that kind of wariness. His brother had never had that sense of caution. Nick signaled a lane switch and passed a pair of trucks, then smoothly returned to the right-hand lane.

It grew darker, the sun behind the hills and the road rising to meet them, and Nick drove past the signs of gas stations and fast-food restaurants glowing in the dusk. He had ditched his sunglasses and paid attention to the road, but in his mind he was traveling a well-worn path through his memory, a path that paradoxically led to him right now in the present, driving his sleeping niece into the dark foothills as he brooded on the past.

HE HAD MADE his brother take care of getting their mother to a doctor, made Jay be the responsible one for once. In a just world, they would have done it together. But in a just world, their mother wouldn't need to be taken care of, wouldn't be crazy.

And to be fair, Jay had tried. He'd found a psychiatrist willing to see their mother, called their father to tell him about the appointment, arranged to show up unannounced at their parents' home on the day of the appointment to convince their mother to go. He called Nick the night before to ask if he would come with him. No, Nick told him; if they both showed up, their mother would feel they were ganging up on her. This needed a soft touch. You can do this, Nick assured him—"You could sell cookies to Girl Scouts." Jay laughed at that and said he would call Nick from the psychiatrist's office.

The next day Nick was in a senior seminar on the Crusades when a knock on the open classroom door interrupted the professor, and Nick along with his classmates turned to see the dean of studies in the doorway, along with a uniformed campus security officer. "Nick Anthony?" the dean said, wearing the expression of a man who did not want to find the person he was looking for.

Nick ran every red light and stop sign on his drive to the hospital, which almost finished off his decrepit VW Bug—it shuddered to a stop in the UC San Diego hospital parking lot, wreathed in an oily, burning fume of exhaust. He found Jay standing in the cardiac intensive care unit, staring at their father in a hospital bed, tubed and wired to various machines. Their father looked gray and shrunken, like he wasn't even a person but a fake prop in a movie. As Nick watched, a nurse turned off one machine, then another, the screens going blank.

A doctor in blue scrubs told them their father had suffered a heart attack. He had been in the parking lot outside the psychiatrist's office, trying with Jay to get their mother to go inside, when his heart had shut tight as a stone fist, dropping him to the ground. The doctor said they had done their best, but there was significant plaque buildup in their father's arteries, and his heart had been too weak to continue.

"They were shouting," Jay said. He was still gazing at their father in the hospital bed. "Mom refused to go inside. She got in the car to go, but on the ride there she changed her mind. She was screaming at Dad in the parking lot and he shouted back at her, and then he just—dropped."

Nick was too stunned to cry, although he could feel his grief biding its time, waiting to overwhelm him. "Where's Mom?" he asked.

Jay raised his eyes to Nick's, and his look of pain and fury made Nick take half a step back. Jay spoke as if every word were being ripped out of his throat. "She ran out into the street. I tried to stop her, but she was too fast. There was a bus—" Jay gritted his teeth and closed his eyes.

Horrified, Nick looked at the doctor, who held up a hand and shook his head. "Your mother wasn't hit," he said. "She ran in front of a bus, but it swerved and missed her. She fell down in the street and hit her head. We admitted her, and she's under observation upstairs."

Nick looked from the doctor to his father in the bed, then to his brother, who stood with his eyes closed and jaw clenched as if trying very hard to keep some powerful emotion from erupting. Their mother was alive and their father was dead. How had this happened? Hesitantly, Nick raised a hand to put on Jay's shoulder. "Jay, I'm—"

Jay flung Nick's hand away, his eyes open and burning. "Don't you *fucking* say you're sorry," he said. "You *left* me there with them. You told me it was better if I did it alone. I needed your help, and you *weren't there*."

The words were a knife sawing at his heart. "I'm sorry," Nick said. He had never realized how feeble those words could be. "We . . . we decided it would be better if you—"

"*You* decided," Jay spit at him. "You told me to do it alone because you didn't want to be *bothered*."

The doctor spread his hands. "I am so sorry for your loss," he said, "but please, there are other patients, other families here. I can find you a room to talk."

"That's not necessary," Jay said. "There's nothing left to talk about."

"Jay," Nick said.

"Don't say another word. I'm done."

Anger kindled in Nick's chest, burning through the shock. "This isn't just about you. What about Mom? Don't be dramatic and walk—"

"*Dramatic*? Our father is *dead*, and you think I'm being *dramatic*?"

"Hey," the doctor said, raising his voice and his hands, and Jay turned away in disgust and stalked out, pushing past Nick to the door.

Nick stood in the aftermath of Jay's departure, head bowed, fists clenched. Slowly he realized the doctor was still talking to him, trying to usher him out of the unit. He turned back to what remained of his father, bent over the hospital bed, and kissed his cold brow. "Where is my mother?" he asked.

The doctor hesitated, and Nick turned from his father to look at the man. "You said she was upstairs for observation," Nick said. "Where?"

The doctor rode with Nick in the elevator up one floor and walked with him down a long white corridor. A pair of closed doors barred their way. A sign on one door read PSYCHIATRIC WARD. Nick stared at the doctor.

"We placed her on a seventy-two-hour hold," the doctor said. "The admitting physician said she presented a clear threat to herself."

On the ward, Nick was led to a room where he found his mother in a hospital bed just like the one his father lay on one floor below, but his mother was restrained to her bed by her wrists and ankles. "Nick," she said, so softly Nick almost didn't hear her. "Nick, where is Bâbâ? Where is Jay?"

Nick sat on a stool next to the bed and stroked his mother's hair. "Shh, Mâmân," he said, watching tears well up in his mother's eyes. His own eyes were dry, his heart cold. He made himself smile gently. "I'm here. I'm not going anywhere."

IT WAS FULLY dark by the time they got to Cashiers, the lights of the town center briefly illuminating the interior of the car and then swallowed by the black trees as they passed. By the time he turned onto the gravel drive and trundled down the hill to his house, Whiteside rose like a pale ghost of a mountain above them.

Annalise was muttering in her sleep when Nick pulled into his carport. In the overhead light when he opened the car door, she looked flushed, and her forehead was warm beneath Nick's wrist. She was disoriented for a moment when he woke her up, her features bleary with sleep, and he half carried her inside and to the bedroom. He helped her take her sneakers off as she lay on the bed, then got her to swallow two Advil before she turned onto her side and fell asleep. He stood in the doorway of the bedroom, watching her breath evenly, then turned off the light and closed the door.

He brought the day pack into the house and started a fire, then quickly scrambled some eggs in a saucepan and ate them quickly with a piece of toast. His hunger satisfied, he took the pistol out of his day pack and put it back into his desk drawer, then sat down in his chair by the fire with the flash drive and his laptop. He glanced at his closed bedroom door, knowing Annalise would want to know what was on the flash drive, but he was afraid he had pushed her too much today with the hike and then the long car ride, plus the meeting with Lapidus. He would look at it tonight and talk to her in the morning.

As soon as he tried to plug the flash drive into his laptop, he cursed. It was an older flash drive that used a standard USB-A connector. His laptop was a newer model with a squarer USB-C port. He would need a different computer to take a look at the flash drive. That would mean a trip to the Highlands library tomorrow.

He sat in the chair for a long time, staring into the fire and thinking about Jay and his parents and Annalise. The bottle of whiskey sat on his bar, forgotten.

CHAPTER TWENTY

Nick awoke in his chair, stiff and needing to pee. The fire was a bed of ash, and the morning outside the window was brightening. He used the hall bathroom and flushed, then splashed some water on his face and went into the kitchen. By the time he had scrambled some eggs and made coffee, Annalise had come out of the bedroom, bedraggled but smiling. "Coffee?" she said.

Nick nodded at the coffeemaker. "Help yourself."

Annalise stirred a spoonful of sugar into her mug and drank it standing at the counter as Nick plated the food. They sat at the table to eat, Annalise wolfing her food down. "Starving," she said, her mouth full of egg and toast.

"Apparently," Nick said, and when Annalise shot him a look, he gave her a slow smile, which she returned.

"Did you look at the flash drive?" she said.

"Doesn't fit in my laptop. Have to go to the public library in Highlands."

Annalise nodded, then swallowed the last of her coffee. "Let me take a shower and we'll go."

Nick shook his head. "You stay here. You had a fever again last night. Plus you don't need to be showing your face in public. That sheriff's deputy is looking for you. And he's not the only one."

"You let me go with you to Charlotte yesterday," she said.

"Only because you hid under a blanket in the back seat until we got down off the mountain. You can stay here. Highlands is less than half an hour away." He finished his own coffee, set the mug down on the table. "If you give me your phone, I'll take it with me and charge it while I'm at the library."

Annalise nodded and stood up to take her plate into the kitchen. Then she winced and put a hand on her belly.

"Are you okay?" Nick asked.

She nodded. "Just a cramp," she said. "I'll be—" She stopped, her eyes widening. "What's the date?" she asked.

He told her, then saw her do some mental calculations. Whatever result she got, she apparently didn't like—she closed her eyes and groaned, putting one hand out to lean against the kitchen counter, the other hand still on her belly.

"What is it?" He stood and went to her. "Talk to me, Annalise. What's wrong?"

"I'm *fine*," she said, not looking at him.

A thought shot through him like a bolt. "You aren't . . . you aren't pregnant, are you?"

Still leaning against the counter, she turned her head toward him and glared. "I'm having my *period*," she said. "But thanks for making this even more awkward." She straightened and stalked out of the kitchen to the bedroom.

Nick followed, horrified. "Annalise, I'm—"

"Whatever," she said, cutting him off. "Just—can you get me some tampons when you go out?" She closed the bedroom door in his face. "Please," she added from the other side of the door.

Oh, for fuck's sake, he heard Ellie say.

NICK STOOD IN the pharmacy aisle at Ingles, scanning the shelves. The last time he'd gone shopping for tampons was in London, when Ellie had been laid up in bed with a sprained ankle. Now it seemed things had advanced in the field of feminine hygiene. Nick was bemused by the variety of brands and products. He picked up one box, realized it contained pads instead of tampons, and set it down. A young mother waiting at the pharmacy counter, a toddler clinging to one leg while another child sat in her shopping cart, gave Nick a knowing smile of sympathy.

Nick finally selected a box of tampons—slim, unscented—and turned to find himself facing Deputy Sams, who was standing a few feet away by the shaving lotions, holding a plastic shopping basket in one hand and a can of Gillette shaving cream in the other. He was wearing jeans and a blue chambray shirt instead of his deputy's uniform.

"Professor," Sams said.

"Deputy," Nick replied.

With a nod, Sams indicated the box of tampons in Nick's hand. "Doing some shopping?"

Nick paused only a heartbeat. "Donation," he said. "For the women's shelter in Highlands." He took two more boxes of tampons off the shelf for good measure.

"Here." Sams held out his plastic shopping basket. "Looks like you need this more than I do."

Awkwardly Nick held the three boxes in his arm and took the basket from Sams with his free hand, then dropped the boxes into the basket. "Thanks," he said. He fought the instinct to walk away and instead asked, "Any more news?"

Sams shook his head. "Not that I've heard, I'm sorry to say. I'm off duty today, though, but if I hear anything, I'll let you know." He looked pointedly at the tampons in Nick's basket, then back at Nick. "No sign of your niece?"

"No," Nick said. "But if I see her, you'll be the first one I call." He nodded good-bye and walked down the aisle toward the front registers. He glanced back at the end of the aisle and saw Sams still watching him.

Nick stood in line to pay for the tampons, snagging a phone charger from an endcap. He paid for the tampons and the phone charger and walked outside with his bags, not looking back until he was in his car. He didn't see Sams anywhere. He drove out of the parking lot, turning right on 64 toward the BP station. When he stopped at the traffic light, he was hardly surprised when he glanced in his rearview and saw Sams's blue pickup, a Chevy Colorado, three cars behind him.

If he were in a city, he could lose the deputy easily, but there were few options on these mountain roads, and trying to shake him would be obvious. Plus, if he did that, the deputy would probably just go to his house to wait for him, and he would find Annalise there. So when the light turned green, instead of turning left toward home Nick continued straight through the intersection, heading to Highlands. The road here was a long straightaway, and he saw Sams was still following at a comfortable distance, now two cars back. He hoped Annalise would be okay without the tampons for another hour or so.

Outside Cashiers, the road curved and continued to rise, hugging the side of the mountains as the valley fell to his left. The rain had stopped, and blue sky was peeking through the heavy white clouds. The curving road kept Nick from seeing very far in his rearview mirror, but every once in a while he glimpsed Sams's blue pickup still behind him. Occasionally Nick passed new residential communities—Mountaintop Golf Club, Highlands Cove, GlenCove by Old Edwards. Ellie had hated the idea of moving into a subdivision, had wanted to live alone with Nick on the edge of a lake. Now Ellie was gone, and golf courses and million-dollar homes with mountain views were encroaching.

He started into another curve, like any other curve in the road, but something about this one struck him—the angle of the slope to his right, the scree of fallen rocks at the road's edge. He had been on a road like this before.

The canteen, spilling its water into the dirt. A bloody hand. Firelight on stones. Muzzle flashes like pinpoints of fire in the night. And screaming.

Nick realized his foot had let off the accelerator and he was slowing down. He stomped on the pedal and his car jerked forward, the engine whining. He wobbled coming out of the turn but stayed in his lane. He blinked and glanced back up at the slope to his right. Ranks of green trees, dappled in the sunlight, spread across the slope. It wasn't the same place at all. This was home now.

With a suddenness that was expected yet still always surprised him somehow, the trees fell away on the left-hand side of the road, revealing the north face of Whiteside Mountain. It was a panoramic view: Whiteside rose to the right, lower ridges hid Cashiers just beyond, and the single curved cliffside of Rock Mountain glimmered in the far distance. Then he was past the view and the road turned sharply right and away.

He passed more country clubs and private communities and the Highlands-Cashiers hospital, and a few minutes later Highlands sprang out of the trees, a mountain town that even with just under a thousand year-round residents dwarfed Cashiers. "Going to town" in Cashiers usually meant you were driving to Highlands, a cluster of a dozen or so town blocks centered on an actual Main Street with inns, bistros, banks, boutiques, antiques stores, an art gallery or two, a hardware store, and a gourmet market. If you wanted to go to the movies or the theater, you went to Highlands. It was also in neighboring Macon County, and Nick hoped that crossing the county line would deter Sams from trying to interfere with him in any sort of official capacity. After he'd finished at the library, Nick would figure out how to shake Sams and get home to Annalise.

Nick turned left onto Main Street and then pulled into the Hudson Library parking lot. The library was built like a mountain lodge, with an impressive peaked porte cochere over the main entrance. Nick parked his SUV, then took one box of tampons out of the Ingles bag and pushed the box under the front passenger seat. He got out of his car with the Ingles bag containing the other two boxes and the phone charger, locked the car, and walked down the parking lot to the street.

The Church of the Incarnation, located next door to the library, had an active outreach ministry and regularly solicited donations. Nick spent a few minutes in the church with a kind older woman who thanked him for his gift, fending off her polite request that he fill out a visitor form. Then he walked back over to the library, the new phone charger in his pocket. Across the street, Sams's blue pickup was parked at the curb, but

Nick ignored it as he headed for the library entrance. He hoped he could find a free computer.

Inside, Nick walked past the circulation desk, where a masked librarian was helping an elderly man in a red-and-black checked flannel shirt find a book on Audubon. A sign indicated the computers available for public use, desktops on heavy wooden tables. A young girl with a red bow in her hair was seated at one computer, avidly staring at her screen. Sitting in an armchair a few feet away, an adult woman was reading an *Outlander* novel. She glanced over her book at the girl with the bow. "Julia, you okay?" the woman asked.

"Yes, Mommy," the girl answered, eyes on the screen.

There was a computer directly opposite the young girl, and Nick sat in front of it. He put the flash drive Lapidus had given him on the table next to the computer keyboard and then put the folded sheet of paper next to it. He entered his library card information into the computer and pulled up the default browser. Then he remembered— Annalise's phone. He stood to take both her phone and the charger out of his pockets, then plugged one end of the charger into a power strip on the computer table.

"I'm researching whales," someone said, and Nick glanced up to see the girl with the red hair bow looking at him from her seat across the table.

Nick raised his eyebrows. "Is that a fact?" he said.

The girl nodded. "People think they're fish, but they're not. They're *mammals*—like us. I like sperm whales because they have teeth and really big heads and sometimes they eat giant squid."

Her mother stirred, distracted from her novel. "Oh, Julia, don't bother the nice man." She looked at Nick with a pained smile. "I'm sorry. She's *very* curious and she loves to share. Maybe too much."

"Not at all," Nick said. He smiled at Julia. Then he plugged the other end of the charger into Annalise's phone. In a few seconds, the Apple logo appeared on the screen as the iPhone began rebooting.

CHAPTER TWENTY-ONE

COLE AND ZHANG SAT IN THE SUBURBAN IN THE PARKING LOT OF A barbecue joint in Dillard, eating a quick lunch. They had been canvassing hotels, playing the private investigator angle—the runaway girl, the concerned father, the bad boyfriend—for two days. So far every hotel manager and employee they had spoken to had been accommodating, eager to help them find a young woman in trouble, but no luck yet. Cole put a lid on his growing unease. They just had to keep working their search grid. Dillard wasn't a sprawling city like Atlanta—they would find something. And Jonas and the others were finally en route from Hilton Head in the private jet. They'd been delayed by a tropical storm, and then by an engine problem requiring a mechanical fix, but now they were on their way. Once they arrived, Cole's team could cover more ground. Right now Dawes and Poncho were still out searching. As soon as Cole finished his sandwich, he would rejoin them. The sandwich was good but greasy. Sauce coated his chin and he wiped it off with a napkin.

"Boss," Zhang said from the back seat.

"You find that 828 number?" Cole asked. He balled up his napkin and dropped it in his cupholder.

"The girl's phone just pinged another tower."

Cole turned around to face Zhang. "Where?"

"Outside of Highlands, North Carolina," Zhang said. "Sixteen miles away."

Cole called Dawes on his cell. "You and Poncho get back here, now. The girl's phone is back on."

THE SUBURBAN RACED up Highway 23 through Dillard, passing other cars when the road widened to four lanes, riding impatiently behind a family in a Land Rover when the road narrowed. Once they were through Dillard, they turned right onto a two-lane road that wound up into the mountains.

Cole was driving, Poncho now in the passenger's seat and relegated to navigator.

"How far?" Cole said.

Poncho consulted the map on his phone. "Twenty-three minutes," he said.

"Zhang?" Cole said, eyes on the road. It was well paved but turned and corkscrewed like a bitch.

"Still pinging," Zhang said. "But this only tells me the tower, not the actual location of the phone. She could be anywhere in a twenty-mile radius of the tower."

"Not in these mountains," Cole said, passing a slow-moving Escalade. "Signal won't travel as far. Can we triangulate?"

"Working on it," Zhang said, hunched over his laptop.

Cole powered around another turn. It was like driving into a living tunnel of green—on either side of the road was a wall of trees, and in most places tree branches grew over the road, creating a canopy.

"Tell me something good, Zhang," he said.

"Trying to find a second cell tower," Zhang said.

"Dawes, where's Jonas?" Cole said.

"Still in the air but should be on the ground soon," Dawes said. "Closest airfield is about twenty minutes outside of Dillard."

"When he lands, tell him to set up in Dillard and wait for my call."

CHAPTER TWENTY-TWO

On the library computer, Nick ran a Google search for house fires in Tampa. The top story was about his brother—*Local Businessman, Wife Found Dead in Tampa House Fire.* He clicked the link to the local Tampa news outlet. The story said Jay and Carol Bashir had died in a house fire in the early morning hours of Wednesday. Evidence suggested an accident, a bad electrical outlet and polyurethane-soaked rags—the same story Deputy Sams had told him. But the article also said the police had not completely ruled out foul play and mentioned that the Bashirs' daughter, Annalise, was missing and wanted for questioning. The article included a smiling photo of Annalise, probably her school picture.

There was also a link to a story about another missing teen, Eric Morgan, who had disappeared sometime Wednesday evening. He, too, was wanted by the police for questioning with regard to the Bashir house fire. The article noted that he was a classmate of Annalise Bashir's and that the two had been reportedly dating.

Nick found other links on the story and read them too, but they added nothing substantial. Most simply reported the facts, although they hinted that Annalise and Eric were possible suspects. Other links led to Tampa-area bloggers posting about a fatal Romeo-and-Juliet couple who had set fire to her parents' house before running off into the night.

Nick knew Eric Morgan was probably not just missing but dead. Men willing to torture a married couple and then burn their house down were not likely to treat the missing daughter's boyfriend gently.

And they were doing all of this in order to retrieve whatever was on the flash drive that Jay had sent Lapidus. They thought Annalise had it.

He picked up the piece of paper and unfolded it and stared at it, the blue lines on the white background. Jay had sent this to him on purpose. It was presumably a map, but of what Nick wasn't sure. Perhaps the numerical notations were elevations, like he'd wondered earlier. He didn't know what to make of the tiny triangles, the shortened capital As. Then he saw the word ANTICLINE again on the sheet—plat, map, whatever—and typed it into the Google search box.

"Whatcha doing?" Julia asked, startling Nick. The little girl was standing next to him. How had she gotten out of her chair and crept up on him? He really was getting old.

"Research," he said. "Like you. But I'm not looking at whales." He picked up the sheet of paper with the blue lines. "I'm trying to figure out what this is."

Julia tilted her head and frowned. "It looks like a really bad map," she said. "Like somebody drew all the roads squiggly."

Nick nodded. "That's what I thought too."

Julia's eyes got big. In a husky whisper, she said, "Is it a treasure map?"

"Maybe." The desktop screen had gone to sleep, and he clicked the mouse to wake it up and get back to his Google search. "So now I'm looking up this word that was written on the map."

"Julia," her mother said faintly from her chair. Nick looked over his shoulder. She hadn't even looked up from her book. "Don't bother the man."

"I'm helping him, Mommy," Julia announced.

"Mm-hmm," her mother said.

Nick pulled up the first entry, a definition from Oxford Languages. *Anticline*, Nick read. *NOUN (GEOLOGY) A ridge-shaped fold of stratified rock in which the strata slope downward from the crest.*

"What does that mean?" Julia asked.

The next link was to Wikipedia. Nick clicked on it and scanned the article. "Well," he said, pointing to a picture on the screen, "it's a fold in the rock. Like a fold in a blanket, only a big one, like on the side of a hill."

"Like a valley!" Julia said.

"This kind only goes up," Nick said. "The point where it bends is at the top."

"Ohhh," Julia said. She looked at the screen for a moment, then turned to Nick. "Did you know blue whales are the biggest creatures on earth?"

Nick glanced at Julia's mother, who was still engrossed in her novel. He wondered if this was what parents did during the summer months, use strangers in libraries to babysit their children.

"I did know that about blue whales," Nick said to Julia. "Did you know most whales don't have teeth?"

"Sperm whales do," Julia said proudly.

"That's right. And killer whales."

"They're called *orcas*," Julia said.

"Like in *Free Willy*."

Julia frowned. "What's that?"

"It's a movie." Maybe *Free Willy* was too old for this girl to have seen. It hadn't come out that long ago, had it? Not that he'd seen it—he just remembered the trailer. "Tell you what," he said, "go look it up online. It's about a killer wh—I mean, an orca who gets trapped in a theme park and wants to go back to the ocean."

"Okay," said Julia. She went back to her computer and started typing. In her armchair, her mother continued to read her novel, oblivious to anything else.

Nick returned his attention to the sheet of paper. So he was looking at a map or plat that contained geological information. The vertical line running just a few degrees east of true north was marked as an anticline. Why would that be information people were willing to kill for?

He went back to the Wikipedia entry and read it more carefully, then stopped at the following line: "Anticlines, structural domes, fault zones and stratigraphic traps are very favorable locations for oil and natural gas drilling."

Oil and natural gas.

Nick double-checked the sheet, even though he knew the word he was looking for, and he found it again, written by hand in the upper-right-hand corner: ABQAIQ. Now he remembered what it meant, but he Googled the word to confirm. Abqaiq was the biggest oil-processing facility in Saudi Arabia. It was owned by Saudi Aramco, a national petroleum and natural gas company, one of the most profitable companies in the world.

Nick knew that Abqaiq was located just northeast of the Ghawar oil field, the largest oil field on the planet. That must be what the GH on the right-hand edge of the page meant—GHAWAR had been cropped out. And CALIFO in the bottom right-hand corner was most likely CALIFORNIA. Before the Saudis named their petroleum company Aramco, it had been California Arabian Standard Oil. They had changed the name in the 1940s.

The sheet wasn't a surface-level map with elevations. It was a field survey, an old one, of the northern part of the Ghawar oil field.

Nick sat back in his chair for a moment, thinking. His brother had sent Annalise to him with a picture of an old field survey. And the notes on the back had led them to Lapidus and the flash drive. He leaned forward and did some more searching online, and within a few minutes, on the website of an association of petroleum geologists, he found a nearly identical image of the same field survey. This was public knowledge, in other words. Rather technical knowledge, true, with no context provided, no other information. Just a field survey.

He Googled *Halliwell Energy* and quickly read through several news stories about Halliwell's rise in the crowded field of energy companies, its early forays into shale oil production in North America, and its efforts to modernize and improve production at various oil fields around the world. He then Googled *Halliwell Energy* and *Ghawar* and found a single mention of Halliwell Energy in a list of energy companies working with Saudi Arabia to ramp up the kingdom's oil and natural gas production in Ghawar.

Which left the flash drive.

He inserted it into the older USB port on the desktop computer, then opened the Finder window to display the contents of the drive. After a moment, the flash drive appeared as UNTITLED. There was a single file listed, a string of alphanumerics without an extension at the end to indicate what kind of file it was. Nick stared at it for a moment. He would bet anything the file was encrypted and that it had something to do with the Ghawar oil field. What he needed was a team of technicians who could open an encrypted file. What he had was a ten-year-old desktop computer at the public library.

Suspecting he would regret it, Nick clicked on the file.

A *Loading* message appeared on the screen, and then a message box popped up. The computer was unable to locate the correct program to open the file.

CHAPTER TWENTY-THREE

"Boss," Zhang said, his tone urgent.

"You find that second tower?" Cole said, close behind a Mini Cooper as they hugged a turn. If only they could hit a straight piece of road so he could pass.

"Someone just tried to access the file on that flash drive," Zhang said.

Kobayashi had set them up to receive alerts from the file on the flash drive. Anytime someone tried to open the file on a computer connected to the internet, the file would generate an alert without notifying whoever was opening the file. The alert would be sent via email to designated users.

"Can you tell where she is?" Cole said.

"Getting the IP address now," Zhang said.

They hit a straightaway, and Cole blasted past the Mini Cooper. "Time," he called out.

"Ten minutes," Poncho said.

"Got it," Zhang said from the back seat. "IP belongs to a computer owned by the Fontana Regional Library system."

Poncho looked up from navigating on his phone. "There's no town named Fontana around here. I see a Fontana Lake, but"—he tapped on the phone—"it's like an hour and a half away."

"It's just the name of the library system," Zhang said. "Covers three counties, including this one. But I can't trace the IP on a map to a specific computer."

"The girl's phone is here," Cole barked, gripping the steering wheel so hard it looked like he was about to bend it. "So look for a local library." He flew over a short hill and took a curve fast enough to make the tires squeal.

"Already got one," Zhang said. "Hudson Library."

"Poncho?" Cole asked.

"It's in Highlands," Poncho said, reading off his phone. "Eight minutes."

CHAPTER TWENTY-FOUR

Nᴜᴄᴋ ꜱᴘᴇɴᴛ ᴀɴᴏᴛʜᴇʀ ᴍɪɴᴜᴛᴇ ᴏʀ ᴛᴡᴏ ᴛʀʏɪɴɢ ᴛᴏ ꜰɪɢᴜʀᴇ ᴏᴜᴛ ʜᴏᴡ to open the file, then gave it up. Someone else with experience in decryption would need to take a look at this. But he knew he had exhausted his own meager resources. He needed to make a phone call.

Nick closed all the windows he had opened and ejected the flash drive, then stood and put it in his pocket.

"Are you leaving?" Julia said from her computer.

"For now," Nick said. He folded the land survey and put it in his pocket with the flash drive, then unplugged Annalise's cell phone and grabbed the phone charger as well. "Did you find the movie?"

"It's *sad*!" Julia said. "They take the whale from his family, and there's a boy who doesn't have a family either!"

Julia's mother stirred and looked over her novel at them. "What movie?" she said.

"*Free Willy*," Julia said.

"I mentioned it because of whales," Nick said. "I'm sorry if I upset her."

The mother looked anxiously at Julia, then relaxed. "She's not upset," she said.

"Can I watch it, Mommy? Please?" Julia said.

Nick tipped a wave at them both and headed to the front door. What he needed was in his car.

NICK HAD NO reliable cellular service at the cabin and had gotten rid of his landline after Ellie's death. But he had not cut himself off from the outside world completely. He walked out the library's front door and headed straight to his car. From his glove compartment he retrieved what looked like a cell phone clipped into a thick case with a fat, stubby antenna the width of a child's pencil. He made sure the phone was charged, then enabled an app to allow him to use the SatSleeve, which turned his cell phone into a functioning satellite phone. There was good cell service in Highlands, but the SatSleeve made his phone a bit more secure. He had never used it, had kept it only for emergencies. He figured this qualified. He dug in his memory for the phone number he wanted, then dialed it. Overhead a hawk circled lazily on the thermals.

The phone was picked up on the second ring. "DDA's office, Danvers speaking," a woman said.

"I need to speak with DDA Bhandari, please," Nick said.

"The DDA is unavailable right now—"

"Bottlecap," Nick said.

He felt as much as heard the woman's pause. "Did you say *Bottlecap*?"

"Yes," Nick said. "Give her that word. I'll wait."

Another, much briefer pause, and then the woman said, "Hold, please." The hold music was Beethoven, he was pretty sure, although he didn't know the name of the piece.

Less than three minutes later, the Beethoven was cut off. Then Nick heard a woman's angry, rasping voice. "You stupid, ball-scratching goat fucker."

"Thanks for taking my call," Nick said.

"I'm not taking anything, you son of a bitch. And how dare you use that word to get access to me."

"It was the only way I knew for certain you would get on the phone."

"Tell me you're in a Turkish prison. No, a *Russian* prison."

"I need your help, Rita."

She laughed, a raucous sound that made him think of macaws. "Definitely a Russian prison, then."

"My brother was murdered," Nick said. He hadn't planned on starting out with that fact, but it was the central issue, wasn't it?

Silence on the other end of the line. "I'm sorry, Nick," Bhandari said.

Nick was momentarily taken aback. Chitrita Bhandari acting human? He shook it off. "I need to know how he found me," he said. "How he knew where I live."

"He's your brother."

"We hadn't spoken in twenty years."

"Jesus, Nick, what the fuck?"

"Was he working for you?" Nick said. "Or the military? I know he was a contractor."

"How should I know?"

"I'm off the grid," Nick said. "Unlisted address. But he found me. Which means whoever killed him can find me too."

"Why do you think someone would want to find you?"

"Jay sent me something," Nick said. "A field survey of the Ghawar oil field in Saudi Arabia. There's a flash drive too. It's encrypted—I can't open it."

"Sent it how?"

"With his daughter. My niece. She brought it to me." He realized he was tightening his grip on the phone, forced himself to relax his hand. "She says a small group of men killed her parents and set their house on fire. In Tampa, four days ago. I need help."

"Where are you?"

"In Highlands, North Carolina. I'm at the Hudson Library on Main Street."

"Stay there. Don't fucking move." The line went dead.

Nick hung up, closed the SatSleeve app, powered down the phone, and put it back into his car's glove compartment. He put Annalise's phone and the charger in there as well. As he was bent down into his car, he heard a large vehicle, a truck or maybe an SUV, pull into the library parking lot. When he straightened up, he saw the vehicle, a black Suburban, pull up to the front door of the library.

Two men got out of the Suburban—both average height, medium build, short-cropped hair, one white, the other Latino. They wore light jackets that weren't completely unnecessary at this altitude, although by now the day had warmed into the low seventies. It was more the way both men carried themselves, a certain squared-away military bearing, that caught Nick's eye. He noted Georgia plates on the Suburban as it drove down the other side of the parking lot, then looked back toward the two men. They were approaching the library doors. The Latino man opened one door, keeping his right hand free. The other man walked in, head sweeping left and right, and the Latino man gave him half a beat and then followed him through the door.

The easiest thing to do would be to stay out here. It's what Bhandari had told him to do—ordered, actually. It was that order as much as anything else that led him to instead follow the two men inside.

CHAPTER TWENTY-FIVE

As soon as he walked back into the library, Nick saw the two men by the computer station, one of them crouched next to Julia. His first instinct was to tell the men to get away from the girl. His second was to turn and walk back outside. But before he could do anything, Julia looked over and recognized him. "There he is," she said, pointing at Nick. The man crouched next to Julia turned to look at him. So did the Latino man standing near Julia's mother.

Nick turned to his left and passed the front desk, heading for a short hallway that led to the periodicals room. As he went by the front desk, he saw a red stainless-steel water bottle standing on the counter, and without pausing he reached out and grabbed it before walking down the hallway. At the end of the hall he stepped into the periodicals room, where magazines and newspapers sat on shelves, covers facing out, and two couches and a few chairs were scattered about the room for readers. There were metal folding chairs leaning up against a couple of walls. No one else was in the room. Good. There was a closed door to the right that Nick knew led to a storage room and, through that, to a long community room at the back of the library. Nick walked to the closed door and opened it a few inches. Then he retreated behind a nearby shelf of *National Geographics* and crouched low, gripping the water bottle upside down by its neck. He breathed through his open mouth to make as little noise as possible and tried to will his heart to slow down.

He heard the soft scuffing of shoes on carpet. Someone was coming down the hall, more than one person. A bitter taste flooded his mouth as if he had a penny on his tongue—that was the adrenaline. One of his knees ached from crouching. He ignored it and gripped the water bottle tighter.

The two men Nick had followed into the library stepped out of the hall, eyes sweeping the periodicals room. Nick's nerves were taut, yet a familiar calm settled over him, everything reduced to this room and the two other men in it. The taller man saw the door that Nick had left ajar and snapped his fingers at his Latino partner, then pointed at the door. His partner nodded and both men advanced toward the door, passing Nick's hiding place behind the shelves. The taller man opened the door with his left hand, his right hand reaching underneath his jacket as he stepped through the doorway.

As soon as the taller man had entered the storage room, Nick rushed the second man. The man's reflexes were good—he either heard Nick or saw him move out of the corner of his eye and began to turn toward him, just as Nick swung the stainless-steel water bottle, clubbing the man on the skull with a hollow *thok*. The man staggered back into another shelf, then fell to the floor, stunned.

Nick dropped the bottle he had just used as a billy club and grabbed a nearby folding chair. He placed the chair up and under the doorknob of the door leading to the storage room, effectively jamming the door shut. The man on the other side shouted something, then hit the door. The chair held it shut. The man hit it again, but the door held.

The sound of magazines sliding and falling to the floor gave Nick enough warning to turn and see the Latino man sit up against the shelf and reach into his jacket. Nick took two quick steps and kicked out just as the man pulled a pistol. Nick's foot connected with the man's hand and sent the pistol flying, but Nick was off-balance enough for the other man to lash out with his own foot. He kicked Nick in the hip and sent him reeling back against another rack of shelves.

The man pulled himself to his feet. He had a large purple welt on his forehead from where Nick had hit him with the bottle. In his hand he held a knife. The long blade had a black oxide coating—so it wouldn't reflect light, Nick knew. Nick had a similar knife, locked in a trunk in his attic.

The man slashed at Nick's face, forcing him back. Nick's hip was a bright-red flare of pain—he couldn't trust that leg. He grabbed a magazine off a shelf and rapidly rolled it into a tube. The man advanced, jabbing the knife at Nick, who used the rolled-up magazine to smack it away. Then Nick bumped up against a wall—no more room to retreat. The man smiled just before Nick whacked him across the face with his magazine, then stepped in to jab a hand at his throat. The man ducked, and Nick dropped the magazine and grabbed the man's knife arm.

They struggled for the knife, caroming off more library shelves, magazines falling to the floor like leaves in a storm. "Hey!" someone shouted. It was the librarian from the front desk, standing in the hallway, hands on her hips. Her look of disapproval vanished and she gaped at the two men fighting over the knife. The man used the distraction to head-butt Nick, the impact sending Nick staggering to the center of the room. The librarian squawked and vanished.

The man stepped out from the shelves, knife blade up and out, just as Nick hurled another metal folding chair at him. The chair bounced off the man's arm, causing him to shout in pain. Nick threw another chair, but this time the man just sidestepped it, cursing in Spanish. When Nick pulled an entire shelf down between them, the man tried to leap over it. He tripped and fell, but he didn't drop the knife. He got to one knee and looked up just in time to receive a blast of chemical powder directly in his face. He rocked back on his knees and dropped his knife, screaming and wiping at his burning eyes. Then Nick stepped forward, holding the fire extinguisher he'd ripped off the wall, and brought the metal cylinder down on the man's head. The impact drove the man flat to the floor, where he lay, unmoving.

Gasping, Nick leaned back against a wall. Yellow dust from the fire extinguisher covered the floor and the unconscious man, and there was an acrid, ammonia-like smell cutting the air. Nick was drenched in sweat and his hip was on fire. He would have a spectacular bruise there by tomorrow. *Too old for this*, he thought.

A faint alarm rang in the back of his mind, but by the time he remembered the other man, he felt cold metal pressed against the side of his head.

"Don't move," the man said. "Hands out and away from your body, now."

Nick complied, the gun barrel still pressed to his head. Then he heard the man behind him murmur, "I've got him. Poncho's down; I'm gonna need—"

"Freeze!" a voice shouted from the hall.

As soon as the man spun around, taking the gun away from Nick's head, Nick dropped to the floor in a fetal position and covered his head with his arms. A gunshot roared, the short hallway amplifying the sound and nearly deafening him. A second gunshot, and then the man fell on the floor, right in front of Nick. His chest was bloody and he gaped like a fish who had been yanked out of a river and tossed onto the bank. As Nick watched, the man's mouth moved in an effort to speak.

"I wanted . . ." the man said. "I wanted to take her . . . to Malibu." And then he just stopped, his eyes fixed on a spot above Nick's head.

Through his ringing ears, Nick could dimly hear cries and shouts from farther back in the library. He slowly started to sit up.

"Don't move," he heard, and Deputy Sams stepped out of the hallway, holding a revolver in a two-handed grip. The revolver was pointed directly at Nick.

"Thought you were off duty," Nick said. His own voice sounded muffled to him, and he felt hot and nauseous. His shirt clung to his back with sweat.

Sams took one of his large hands off the revolver, which he kept pointed at Nick, and crouched down next to the man he had shot. With his free hand he touched the man's neck, checking for a pulse. After a few moments he withdrew his hand and returned to a two-hand grip on his revolver.

"Thought you were just a professor," Sams said.

CHAPTER TWENTY-SIX

As jails went, the Highlands Police Department jail was spartan but very clean. The cell consisted of three cinder-block walls, a concrete floor, two metal bunks built into the back wall, and a stainless-steel sink-and-toilet combination that gleamed as if it had just been polished by a crack team of Cub Scouts. Currently Nick was the only inmate, and so he had his pick of the two bunks and the toilet all to himself.

The fourth wall of the cell was entirely made of white metal bars, a portion of which was a hinged door, now locked. Outside the cell stood five men, two of them engaged in conversation, all of them ignoring Nick, who was sitting on the lower bunk.

"I want my phone call," Nick said.

"In a minute," Chief Ted Davies said. Chief Davies was pushing sixty, with the eyeglasses and haircut of a successful accountant. He wore a white uniform shirt with a black tie, his chief's badge, and a salad bar of multicolored service ribbons. With him were Deputy Sams, two Highlands police officers in dark-blue duty uniforms, and a man with wind-tousled blond hair in a linen suit and pink tie who was the town manager, Bill Kettle.

"The mayor is apoplectic," Kettle was saying. "A shootout in the library? In *Highlands*? Do you know what kind of panic this will cause? How much media attention this will draw?"

"I'm well aware, Bill," Chief Davies said.

"Then you know what kind of fallout we might have. Summer just started, and we're barely up from last year in terms of visitors. Restaurant reservations are still down, hotels, guides—"

"I'm aware of that too," Chief Davies said. He glanced at Nick, who was still sitting on the lower cell bunk, then returned his attention to the town manager. "I've already talked to the mayor. We'll issue a statement within the half hour, saying this was an isolated incident and that we have the participants in custody."

"What about him?" Kettle said, pointing at Sams, who was flanked by the two Highlands police officers. "A sheriff's deputy from a neighboring county walks into the library like it's the Wild West and starts shooting up the place?"

Sams spoke, his voice flat. "I told the suspect to freeze."

"And then you shot him," Kettle said. "And now he's in the county morgue, and there's another man in the hospital."

In the cell, Nick raised his hand. "That one was my fault."

"You can just shut it," Kettle said. "Chief, why isn't Deputy Sams sitting in there with Mr. Anthony?"

Chief Davies's patient expression was wearing thin. "I spoke with Sheriff Faye over in Jackson County. There will be an incident review board hearing for Deputy Sams, and he will be on administrative leave in the meantime." Kettle opened his mouth, but Chief Davies cut him off. "And he'll be cleared, Bill. It was a justified shooting. The perp was pointing a handgun at a civilian. When Deputy Sams ordered him to freeze, the perp turned the handgun on him. He had no alternative." He looked at Sams. "You doing okay?"

Sams just nodded, looking at the floor. He kept jiggling his foot.

From his cell bunk, Nick said, "Deputy Sams." Everyone looked at him, Sams more slowly than the others. Nick paid attention only to Sams. "Deputy, can you hear me?"

"I . . . yes," Sams said.

"I'd like you to take your left hand and touch your right ear," Nick said.

Sams blinked, then lifted both of his hands and considered them.

"He's in shock," Nick said. "Difficulty following simple commands, jittery, disconnected."

Kettle scoffed. "Are you a doctor?"

"Actually, yes," Nick said.

Kettle's voice rose. "You've got a PhD in *history*."

"Josh," Chief Davies said, cutting Kettle off. "Let's get you some coffee. Earl, can you take Deputy Sams with you to get some coffee?"

One of the two Highlands police officers stepped forward. Sams looked at the officer, then at Chief Davies, took a deep breath, and followed the officer out of the cell area.

"Can I get my phone call now?" Nick said. "And I'd like to know why I'm being held in jail."

Kettle regained his footing. "You were involved in a public brawl that resulted in one man's death, another's hospitalization, and damage to public property."

"It was self-defense," Nick said. "And I didn't kill anyone, justifiably or otherwise. Am I being charged with anything?"

"Not at the moment," Chief Davies said. "But until such time as we talk with the DA about charges, which should be fairly soon, you are our guest."

"Then I need to make a phone call," Nick said. "Please."

Chief Davies looked at the remaining officer, who nodded and walked to a nearby desk and retrieved a cordless phone. He approached the cell door and put the phone on the floor just outside the bars. Nick stood and stepped forward, then slowly reached his hand out between the bars and picked up the phone. "Thank you," he said. He returned to his bunk with the phone and dialed the number he had called earlier that day. When the same woman as before answered, Nick said, "DDA Bhandari, please. It's Nick Anthony." This time he only waited fifteen seconds before Bhandari got on the line.

"*What?*" she said. "It's been two hours. I'm not a fucking miracle worker."

"I'm in jail at the Highlands Police Department," Nick said.

He had to hold the phone away from his ear because of the loud and profane response. After several seconds he brought the phone back to his ear to hear Bhandari say, ". . . *listen* to me about staying put, you asshole."

"Wasn't my choice," Nick said. He didn't want to go into more detail in front of the police chief and others. "Two men started a fight with me in the library. A cop shot one of them. I need your help, Rita."

There was a pause. "Pain in my ass," Bhandari said, and hung up.

Nick looked up at the men on the other side of the bars. "All done," he said.

The remaining officer stood by the bars and Nick handed him the phone, thanking him. The chief was still trying to placate the town manager, both of them heading out of the cell area. "Chief?" Nick said. Chief Davies and Kettle both stopped and turned back. "The guy in the hospital," Nick said. "Is he going to be okay?"

The chief nodded. "Got a concussion and maybe a hairline fracture in his skull, but no brain damage. He's stable, in intensive care."

"They came in a Suburban," Nick said. "There was a driver and maybe one other man. They dropped the two men off and drove out of the library parking lot and turned right. The Suburban had a Georgia tag, but I didn't get the plate number."

The chief considered him. "Sams did," he said. "We're looking for it."

Nick nodded his thanks, ignoring a glare from Kettle, then lay down on his bunk. The others left, the door swinging shut behind them. Nick heard one of the police officers turn a key, locking the door. He moved his head from side to side, stretching his neck, then sat back down on the lower bunk, wincing at the pain in his hip.

The men in the library had been professionals, of that he was sure. What he was not sure about was whether or not they had been looking specifically for him. When the two men first saw him in the library, they hadn't seemed to recognize him. It was more that they had identified him as someone of interest, or perhaps a threat. Could they have found him because of the flash drive? Those weren't traceable, as far as he knew. Perhaps when he tried to open that secured file, an alert had been sent. But how had they known exactly where to go? They must have been in the area beforehand—he hadn't been on the library computer long before they showed up. And then he understood and closed his eyes in disgust— he really was getting old. Annalise's iPhone. When he had plugged it in to recharge, it must have pinged a cell tower. That plus any alert from the secured file might have given them enough info to track him, if they had the right tech and access and skills.

So they were after Annalise. And he was stuck in here.

Briefly he wondered what information was on that flash drive that was valuable enough to send a team after it, a team willing to hurt and kill to retrieve it. Something about the Saudis and the Ghawar oil field. Halliwell Energy was wrapped up in it too. He had some ideas, but he wanted to let them fall into place without forcing them. He tried to relax and let his mind drift. His body ached from the library fight, especially his hip, but he was more immediately concerned about Annalise. She must be going stir-crazy, he thought. And she was alone, unprotected. Which was why Chitrita Bhandari had better be moving heaven and earth to get him out of here.

However, underneath all of these concerns ran a darker current, an emotional response to the violence of the struggle in the library. It was a response Nick had worked long and hard to suppress, but now it stirred within him.

It was pleasure.

CHAPTER TWENTY-SEVEN

AFTER HER UNCLE LEFT FOR THE LIBRARY, ANNALISE LAY IN BED, willing herself to go to sleep to make time pass and instead growing more and more furious, with whom she wasn't sure. Her uncle for being a typical clueless guy. Herself for having her period. Her parents for getting themselves killed. She had heard what her uncle had told her on their hike yesterday, about the dangers of walling herself off, of being angry. But it was easier to be angry with her parents, because if she stopped being angry, she was afraid of the emotions that would rush in to fill anger's place, and so she kept stoking that anger until she felt like a stock-pot of marinara on constant simmer. Maybe not the best metaphor, she thought, because she was bleeding like a slaughtered pig, and oh my *God* where was Uncle Nick with the damn tampons?

She took a quick shower and then fashioned a homemade pad out of toilet paper, wondering how women had dealt with menstruation back in the frontier days before tampons. This was the sort of thing she would happily spend a half hour researching on the internet, except, oh, yeah, Uncle Nick didn't have Wi-Fi or even a *phone*. Jesus Christ on a pogo stick, how isolated could you get?

After an hour of that, Annalise got out of bed with a groan, the wad of toilet paper in her underwear like the world's most ginormous diaper, and roamed around the house. She still felt weak and a bit light-headed, but she was on the other side of her fever and would be fine, if she didn't die of boredom or combust from emotional turmoil.

She heated up a can of chicken-and-rice soup and made more toast—God, she was getting sick of toast—and ate it all, and after cleaning the dishes, she went back into her uncle's office and looked at the old photographs of her father and uncle and grandparents, carefully examining their faces as if trying to decipher her own emotions. She opened the desk drawers to check that she hadn't missed any other photos and discovered her uncle's pistol, back in the top drawer. Had she really pointed it at Uncle Nick yesterday? And then, a more troubling question: would she have shot him if he'd said the wrong thing or tried to hurt her? She closed the drawer, putting the pistol out of her mind, and tried to distract herself by perusing the bookshelves.

Eventually she went outside onto the back porch and looked at Whiteside, the cliffs crossed by sun and shadow, then sat in a rocking chair and, for lack of anything better to do, started reading a copy of *Sir Gawain and the Green Knight* that she'd found in the office. After the first few pages, the story pulled her in. It reminded her a little of Neil Gaiman, a blend of heroism and horror written with a sense of playfulness.

She must have fallen asleep reading, because she came to with a snort. She shivered and saw that the angle of sunlight on Whiteside had changed and grown more golden. At the same time, she heard a car engine approaching. Uncle Nick, finally. The thought sent a shot of adrenaline through her heart. *Chill, girl,* she thought. She stood up, her legs a little stiff, then went back inside, changed her pad of toilet paper, and wandered into the kitchen. The digital clock on the oven said 6:47. That made her heart stutter-step for a moment. Her uncle had been gone for over eight hours. What had taken so long? She stood by the door to the carport, arms folded across her chest in what she thought was an appropriate pose of annoyance. How long did it take a man to buy tampons, for God's sake.

The engine shut off, and she heard a car door open. She unfolded her arms to quickly wipe her palms on her jeans before returning to her annoyed pose. A minute went by. Annalise tapped her foot, scowling. This was ridiculous. He had left her alone all day, with little food and nothing to do and no tampons, and now he was dicking around outside? She marched to the kitchen door and flung it open, buoyed by the dramatic moment. "Where have you—" she began, then was struck dumb by two realizations. The car, a red Jeep Renegade, was not her uncle's. And the older woman who held some sort of oven-mitt-wrapped pot or dish in both hands, standing by the open driver's door, was definitely not her Uncle Nick.

CHAPTER TWENTY-EIGHT

COLE WAS FURIOUS.

In all his years fighting in the worst places on earth, his team had rarely been hit so hard, and never by so few people. Winslow had been a necessity, true, but his death was still a loss. And now Poncho was in the hospital and Dawes was smoked. By a fucking off-duty cop, for Christ's sake.

But it wasn't the deputy Cole was upset about. It was the stranger who had beaten Poncho unconscious, the man who had the girl's phone and apparently the flash drive too. The man whose photo Cole was now staring at on his phone.

It had been a risk, staying in town once the cops came down on the library like a hammer. After dropping Dawes and Poncho off at the library entrance, Cole and Zhang had driven off and parked on the other side of the block where they had a clear view of the back of the library. Cole had handled the comms while Zhang remained on his laptop to monitor the girl's phone and his email for another alert in case someone tried to access the flash drive again. Sitting in the Suburban had tested Cole's discipline and focus, but they couldn't all go into the library at once.

Then Dawes had reported that a man had been sitting at the desktops until just a few minutes before they arrived. And then he had eyes on the man—white or possibly Latino male, midforties, green shirt and blue jeans. Dawes and Poncho moved to intercept the man, and that was when it all went to hell—thuds, cursing, a roar of static. Cole had very nearly gotten out of the Suburban, but then Dawes reported in, saying he had the man but Poncho was down.

At that point Cole heard someone else shout *Freeze* over his earpiece, followed by gunshots. Then he heard Dawes, his voice weak and clogged as if with phlegm, say *I wanted to take her to Malibu.* And that was all.

As soon as he heard that, Cole had driven away. Almost every instinct of Cole's had insisted on saving his men, but having a protracted, public firefight was the wrong call. Poncho and Dawes knew the score, had known ever since they'd joined Cole's team. Now Cole had to salvage the situation as best he could. He pulled the Suburban into a church parking lot that backed up to the library, and he put on a ball cap and walked around the block, ambling up to the library, where a small crowd had gathered in the parking lot.

A town cop was already keeping people away from the library entrance, but Cole stood in the growing crowd and watched, listening to the speculation of people around him—there had been a fistfight, a gunfight, a fire, a bomb threat. More cops arrived, two of them stringing police tape across the top end of the parking lot nearest the library entrance. Eventually a tight group of cops exited the library, surrounding a man in handcuffs. The crowd pressed forward, buzzing with excitement, two cops keeping them back. The man in handcuffs matched Dawes's earlier description—midforties or so, dark hair, green Henley shirt, jeans. Following them were three other men, two in police uniforms on either side of a third in jeans and a blue chambray shirt, his head down. He was not in handcuffs, Cole noted, and then someone in the crowd moved out of the way and Cole saw that the man in the chambray shirt was wearing a badge on a chain around his neck. He was a cop too. Off duty, maybe? But the other cops were definitely escorting him. Cole raised his phone and took a picture of the man in handcuffs, then one of the off-duty cop. Something twisted savagely in his gut. Dawes had been planning to marry that girl—Mandy. Cole had heard over the radio the very last thing Dawes said in this life, about how he'd wanted to take Mandy to Malibu, where he'd planned to propose to her. *I swear*, Cole said silently to Dawes, *I will get that man for you*. Then he backed away through the crowd and walked around the block to the Suburban, and Zhang drove through town and turned left on 106, heading back down the mountains toward Dillard.

Now Cole stared at the photo of the man in handcuffs while Zhang crossed the state line into Georgia, the road winding downhill. The photo's resolution was crisp and clear and showed the man's face in three-quarter profile, dark hair touched with silver, his expression calm.

"You going to call Jonas?" Zhang said. "He ought to be in Dillard by now."

Cole stared at his phone, memorizing the man's face. The man stirred something in his memory, a fleeting thought that vanished, like trying to grasp smoke.

"Cole?" Zhang said.

"Have to make another call first," Cole said, still staring at his phone.

Zhang shifted in his seat. "Okay, but we—"

"I'll call him when I'm goddamned ready," Cole said, looking over at Zhang. "Clear?"

Zhang kept his eyes on the road and just nodded, and Cole went back to staring at the photo. Engraving the man's face in his brain. Then he checked to see what cell reception was like and made a phone call. Two rings on the other end and then it was picked up.

"Mr. Cole," Kobayashi said.

"I'm sending you two pictures," Cole said. "I need the men in them identified. The first one is in handcuffs. The second one is between two police officers and has a blue shirt and a badge around his neck. Probably an off-duty cop."

"Of course," Kobayashi said, smooth and unruffled. "May I ask why?"

Cole stifled an urge to scream obscenities into the phone to crack the other man's calm. "The man in handcuffs is helping the girl somehow. We think he has the flash drive. Two of my men tried to stop him. The cop got involved somehow, and now both of my men are down." This last was particularly hard for Cole to say. He glanced at Zhang, who continued to keep his eyes on the road but was now clenching his jaw.

There was silence on the other end of the line. Finally Kobayashi said, "I trust you can contain this." Meaning *don't fuck this up.*

"Affirmative." *Don't fucking question me.*

"Very well," Kobayashi said. "I'll call you." He hung up.

Asshole, Cole thought. To Zhang he said, "When we get to the bottom of the mountain, turn left. There's a diner just down the road. We'll rendezvous with Jonas there."

And then, he thought, *we are going back up into those mountains to kill that motherfucker.*

CHAPTER TWENTY-NINE

"Hi," the older woman said, holding what Annalise now saw was a casserole dish wrapped in some kind of insulated carrying bag. "You must be Nick's niece. I'm Lettie."

Annalise just stared. Some part of her wondered if it was the shock of surprise or the final straw that broke her sense of caution, but she just felt done with running, done with hiding, done with poking around her uncle's cabin. A nice old lady showing up with a meal? She'd take it.

"I'm Annalise," she said.

Lettie nodded her head. "Annalise. That's a lovely name," she said. "He's not home, I take it?" Annalise shook her head. "Well," Lettie said, "I brought this for him." She held up the casserole dish. "A dinner date."

"Oh," Annalise said. She didn't know how to process that. Her uncle was kind of old, but this lady looked like a grandmother in her red sweater set and pearls, a black quilted purse slung over one shoulder.

Lettie smiled wryly. "Not that kind of date," she said.

"Oh," Annalise said again. They stood there for a moment, looking at one another, and then Annalise said, "Come in? Please?"

"Thank you," Lettie said, and Annalise backed into the kitchen to allow Lettie to enter. The older woman put the bag with the casserole dish on the counter. "I invited your uncle to dinner when he came by my store yesterday, but I knew he would just sit here and brood, so I decided to invite myself over and not give him a choice. It's pot roast. I've been letting it cook all day." Lettie eyed Annalise briefly from head to foot. "I guessed your size well enough from what your uncle could tell me. Do your clothes fit?"

"Yes," Annalise said. "Yes, ma'am," she corrected herself. "Thank you." Annalise had so many questions but was distracted by the rich, beefy smell of the pot roast. Her stomach rumbled. Then she winced as a cramp rippled through her gut.

"Honey, are you all right?" Lettie said.

"Yes," Annalise said, smiling through it.

"Oh," Lettie said. "Are you having your period?"

Annalise gawped. In her experience, women of a certain age said things like *your time of the month* or *lady business* or *moon time*. Not *period*.

Lettie laughed. "You should see your face. It's like I just walked into church and farted."

Annalise laughed at that, a single loud *ha!* followed by a second of silence, followed in turn by peals of laughter that left her breathless. Lettie just smiled and let her laugh, then reached over and patted her shoulder. "The older I get, the more I just call things as they are," she said. "Don't have time to dance around what I mean to say." She rummaged around in her purse, then pulled out a slim tube wrapped in crinkly paper and held it out to Annalise. A tampon.

Annalise reached out and took it. "Thank you," she said, and she meant it, but she hesitated. Lettie was the same age as her grandmother. Why would she—

"Yes, I'm old," Lettie said. "But I'm not dead. I have fibroids. Tumors in my uterus. They're benign, but they make me bleed, so I still use those." She nodded at the tampon in Annalise's hand. "Go on. I'm not going anywhere."

When Annalise returned from the bathroom, she found Lettie in the kitchen, peering at the oven. "Can't tell how to turn this on," she said. "It's like microwaves. Every single one is different. Ah." She pressed a button, then another, and the oven fan whined to life. "Hey presto!" Lettie said. She got the casserole dish out of its bag and stuck it in the oven. "This is just to keep it warm," she said. "Until your uncle gets home." She cocked her head to one side. "Any idea when he's coming back?"

"No," Annalise said. "But I'm sure it'll be soon. He had to go to the library." She didn't want Lettie to leave.

"Well," Lettie said, looking at the oven and then back at Annalise. "Shall we sit down? I do a lot of standing in my shop, and right now my feet could use the rest."

Annalise led the way into the great room, uncertain whether to act like a host or a guest. Lettie solved that for her by getting each of them a glass of water before taking a seat on the sofa. Annalise sat on the ottoman at the foot of her uncle's armchair.

"So," Annalise said, perhaps a bit too cheerfully, "you're, like, friends with my uncle?"

"That's right," Lettie said. "I was one of the first people in town to meet your uncle. He walked into my shop with his wife Ellie—she was such a pretty thing—and wanted to buy a map of the area. This was years ago, before they bought this place. They came back to visit every summer, renting a house or staying in a B and B." Lettie smiled. "Ellie loved it here. Loved the mountains, always asking me about hiking trails. She would drag Nick all over the place. I think they walked every path and trail within ten miles of here. Until she couldn't anymore." Lettie shook her head and took a sip of water. "Her passing was so sad. She was too young."

"Do you . . . do you know how my aunt died?" Annalise said, the words *my aunt* just as strange as the idea of asking how someone had died.

Lettie's eyebrows rose in astonishment. "You don't know?" she said. Then she closed her eyes briefly, her mouth a firm line of disappointment. "I'm sorry, Annalise. That wasn't appropriate of me to say."

Annalise shrugged. "It's all right. I never even met my uncle until a couple of nights ago."

"Well," Lettie said. "It was cancer. Pancreatic. Nothing they could really do except make Ellie as comfortable as they could. Your uncle was a saint to her. Took care of her right here in this house. He was a professor at Western Carolina then, they'd been planning to retire here, but when Ellie got sick, he took a leave of absence. She worked for the World Bank and was still trying to work from home, right up until the end." Lettie sighed and looked into her glass. "Some people are just a light, a presence that lifts others. Ellie was like that. When she died, your uncle . . ." Lettie paused, motionless, then set her water glass down. "He was devastated. Lost. He buried her at the Episcopal church just down the road, same place my husband and parents are buried, and then he shut himself up here, cut off his phone. Cut himself off from everyone. Our rector tried to reach out a few times, but Nick refused. Politely, of course, but he said he preferred to be alone. Truth to tell, I've been worried about him." Lettie let her hands fall on her knees and smiled. "But now you're visiting, and it's my guess that'll do him a world of good. Not to put any pressure on you, of course."

Pressure on her? Annalise laughed. No, no pressure. Her laughter wasn't like earlier—this was hard-edged, closer to crying. Her parents had been killed and she was essentially homeless except for the hospitality of her uncle, a virtual stranger with multiple secret identities, but what pressure? She doubled up, still laughing, her stomach hurting. Dimly she understood that if she kept laughing like this, she would end up shrieking. She could see concern in Lettie's eyes, maybe even the beginnings of fear, and she made an effort to get herself under control. "I'm sorry," she managed to say.

Lettie got up from the sofa and came to stand by Annalise, putting an arm around her shoulders. "I'm sorry, honey," Lettie said, and her kindness and empathy made Annalise cry harder, but it felt cleaner, like she was purging herself of something rather than spiraling out of control. Lettie just stood there, murmuring to her and keeping her arm around Annalise's shoulders, and eventually Annalise's grief ebbed enough that she stopped crying and could concentrate on breathing slowly, in and out. Lettie handed her a tissue and she wiped her face and blew her nose—God, how much Kleenex was she going to go through?—and just sat there, leaning against the kind older woman, breathing in her scent of powder and roses and something like carnations. She smelled like a cool grandmother. The thought almost made her laugh with embarrassment, and then she gasped. Her grandparents on Hilton Head—she had almost forgotten about them. What would they be thinking? Were they looking for her? Did they think she was dead? Or worse, that she had something to do with her parents' deaths?

She felt Lettie shift next to her, probably worried she was going to freak out again. She took a shuddering breath. "I'm okay," Annalise said. "I'm okay."

Lettie squeezed her shoulders. "In that case," she said, "we should go ahead and start on that pot roast before it dries out. Your uncle can just eat the leftovers."

CHAPTER THIRTY

Nick's memories had finally run him to ground.

After he lost Ellie, he'd been frozen in a limbo that had allowed him neither the comfort of memory nor the relief of action. The shock of Jay's death and the subsequent arrival of Annalise had thawed him, forced him to act, kept him churning forward and precluded him from stopping to think. But now, stranded alone in a jail cell with nothing but time and his own thoughts, he fell into his own past like a man falling backward, arms wide, into a deep lake.

"BOTTLECAP," BHANDARI HAD said.

They were in the US embassy in Beirut, in one of the bunker-like conference rooms below ground. Nick hated these airless rooms, felt the claustrophobic weight of the embassy above him. He'd have much preferred an outdoor café. But the embassy was routinely swept for listening devices and deemed a safer location for such meetings. And recently Hezbollah had rolled up a CIA network in Beirut, crowing on television how they had seen and identified ten CIA officers meeting with their Lebanese agents in fast-food restaurants.

Joe Martoglio snorted and rotated his thick neck, the vertebrae cracking. "Bottlecap? Christ, the names they come up with."

"I came up with it," Bhandari said. Her black hair was pulled back from her face, giving her the appearance of a hawk with kohl-rimmed eyes. "So shut your fat Italian mouth and listen for once."

Chitrita Bhandari was on a fast track to a leadership position in Analysis. All the women Nick had worked with in the Agency were outstanding professionals with spines of steel who delivered the goods quietly while some of their male counterparts postured and argued. Rita Bhandari stood out by openly challenging the Agency's old boys' network, standing toe-to-toe with senior colleagues and always producing results. Even her wardrobe was a provocation—she favored elaborate saris and upswept hairdos. Today she wore a magenta-and-gold sari that looked like stylized samurai armor.

Nick didn't know how deliberate her clothing choice was, but it was fitting. The Syrian civil war was a disaster in the making. At least sixty thousand people had died in the conflict so far. The Lebanese border was closed, but that wasn't stopping Hezbollah fighters from crossing into Syria to support President Bashar al-Assad. Syrian opposition forces couldn't agree on anything other than fighting Assad. And now rockets carrying chemical weapons had allegedly been used near Aleppo. Langley wanted intel, which was why Bhandari had flown in from a NATO intelligence summit in Brussels.

"Dr. Anthony," Bhandari said, turning those hawklike eyes on him. "How reliable is your source?"

She meant Tariq Nasser, a Syrian professor and a friend of Nick's. He was passionate about both chemistry and teaching, with a sense of humor that always livened up a seminar or conference session. When eventually Nick had made overtures to Tariq about potentially sharing intelligence on the regime, Tariq had eagerly accepted. He loathed Assad and had gleefully recounted how Assad's wife Asma apparently referred to her husband affectionately as *duck*, which had led to protestors in Damascus holding up squeaking yellow ducks.

"How reliable? I'd say fifty-fifty," Nick said. "Tariq is a good man. But he's never asked to meet like this before."

Bhandari shrugged. "Dr. Nasser is a chemistry professor who's outraged at the Assad regime for using chemical weapons against its own people. He can't meet you at a conference and pass you information, not now."

"Tariq wouldn't condone any use of chemical weapons," Nick said. "And I agree that if he had any intel, he would do his best to get it to us. But he's a teacher, not a spy."

"Says the history professor," Martoglio said, his beefy arms folded across his chest. An Agency veteran, Martoglio was the senior CIA officer in Beirut.

Nick ignored Martoglio's gibe. "A clandestine meeting at night at the Syrian border? That's not Tariq."

Bhandari raised an eyebrow. "And yet that's what he asked for."

"That's what I *received*," Nick said. "A coded message in an online forum. We can't be sure Tariq wrote it freely."

"He didn't use the duress code, right?" Martoglio said. "Look, Rita said it herself. Nasser can't meet you at a conference in Rome and hand you some documents in the men's room. And we need any intel we can get out of Syria. If Assad *is* using chemical weapons—"

"He is," Bhandari said.

"—*and* we can get proof of it, that's a game changer," Martoglio said. "We could end the war."

"Which is what everybody wants," Bhandari said. "So let's make it happen."

"Nick and I will drive up to Arsal tomorrow afternoon," Martoglio said. "That's like ten, twelve klicks from the border. Around 2100, we'll head up to the rendezvous point. With an armed escort, of course."

Bhandari quirked her mouth. "Security contractors," she said disdainfully. The CIA preferred using their own PMOOs, or paramilitary operations officers, for this kind of covert action.

Now it was Martoglio's turn to shrug. "The PMOOs in-region are already committed to other missions or injured," he said. "And you can't trust the locals. You got Hezbollah, Syrian security agents, pro-Assad militias, al-Qaeda, take your pick. I've hired a good team. Mountains are full of smuggling routes; it'll be easy to get in and out. We meet Nasser, he talks to Nick and passes along whatever he has to offer, and we leave. We'll be back here by morning."

"I'll leave the operational details to you," Bhandari said, then stood. Nick and Martoglio stood as well. Although both men were taller than Bhandari, she commanded the room. Nick realized he and Martoglio both leaned in toward her, out of deference. "Good luck, gentlemen," she said, shaking each of their hands before she left, her sari trailing gloriously behind her.

Once she was gone, Martoglio shook his head. "Analysts. 'Go do this dangerous thing and do it yesterday, but don't tell us how you're going to do it.' " He swung his arms like he was warming up to toss a football. "Get some rack time, Doc," he said. "You're gonna need it."

And Nick did, although he didn't sleep much. Ellie was gone for the week, this time to a conference in Paris. *Might as well be Iowa*, she'd told Nick. *All we see is the inside of hotel conference rooms. At least the coffee is good.* He thought about calling her, then decided not to. She would sense the tension in his voice. They had made peace with what Ellie referred to as his shadow life by not discussing it very often. Honestly, most of what he did was talk to people in cafés or at academic conferences, gathering information and then passing it along. Incidents like the one in Cairo were few and far between.

Nick liked to think he was making a difference, still standing astride two worlds like his father had said all those years ago. But he was also the son of an Afghan mother, working for an agency that had meddled in this part of the world for many decades, often with unpleasant consequences. That night, before heading to the Syrian border, Nick wondered, not for the first time, if straddling two worlds meant that eventually he would have to choose one over the other, or if he would never truly be part of either one.

THE NEXT AFTERNOON Nick and Martoglio drove to Arsal, a border town in the Bekaa Valley, where they rendezvoused with the security contractors behind a garage whose owner had been generously compensated with two hundred American dollars. The contractors arrived in pickup trucks reinforced with metal plates across the two front doors and around the engine block—armor against small-arms fire. There were four men in each truck, giving them eight armed contractors total. They were led by Duncan, tall and ropy with sun-bronzed skin and a disarming smile. His voice was pure East Texas drawl. "Gonna be headin' out by twunny-one hunnerd," he said. "You all set?"

They left Arsal in a short convoy, one pickup in the lead, one at the rear, and Nick and Martoglio's SUV in the middle. In the bed of each pickup sat a man wearing a helmet and flak jacket and holding an AK-47 across his lap. They left the lights of Arsal behind, the fields outside the town dark and empty under the moonless sky as they passed.

Stands of apricot and cherry trees lined the road for a time, and then the road climbed and the hills rose around them. The higher they went, the worse the road got. Up here, it looked as if the entire world were made of broken stone. Grit and dust floated in the beams of the SUV's headlights, the brakes on the pickup truck Nick and Martoglio were following flashing red each time they approached a turn in the road. At a rock quarry they took a hard left and switchbacked up a steep incline, the engines whining in low gear as they climbed. The temperature dropped, and Nick was thankful for the two sweat shirts he wore, as well as his gloves.

Finally they came to a stop at an abandoned house, the roof collapsed, the windows and doorway gaping holes. From here they would hike up the rest of the way to the rendezvous point, a steep-sided hollow where Nick's friend Tariq would light a fire as a signal that he was there, the walls of the hollow hiding the glow until you were almost upon it. Nick made sure his Colt 1911 pistol was secure in its holster, while Martoglio stuck a 9mm Browning in his waistband.

"Got a holster?" one of the contractors asked Martoglio. He had dirty-blond hair and carried his AK across his chest, barrel down.

"I'm okay," Martoglio said, waving him off. "I'll just stick close to you."

The man looked at the handle of the Browning in Martoglio's pants. "Just don't trip," he said. "Don't want to blow your balls off by accident."

"Y'all good?" Duncan said, AK in one hand, pointed at the sky. "Let's do this."

The hike was cold and dark, marked by the crunch of gravel and dirt beneath their boots. The blond contractor who had joked about Martoglio shooting himself in the balls took point, followed by Duncan and two others, then Nick and Martoglio, the rest bringing up the rear. No one spoke, and the contractors peered into the night, constantly scanning their surroundings. This was strictly a black op, unauthorized by the Lebanese, who would not be happy to find CIA agents operating in the countryside. If a Lebanese army unit on patrol caught them, at the very least they would be deported and cause an international incident. If the Syrians caught them, they would be thrown in prison and subjected to interrogation before most likely being shot. Hezbollah would do the same and get a propaganda video out of it. Nick didn't even want to think about what al-Qaeda would do to them.

After nearly thirty minutes, the blond contractor raised a fist and the others dropped to a crouch, weapons up. Nick and Martoglio crouched as well, Martoglio drawing his pistol. He glanced at Nick and shrugged. Nick couldn't see beyond the blond, who was maybe fifteen yards ahead of him and huddled with Duncan. Then Duncan broke off and came loping down to crouch right next to them. "The hollow is just around that spur ahead," Duncan murmured. "Somebody lit a fire. Y'all are up."

Nick and Martoglio hurried to the front with the blond point man, and the others stood and advanced cautiously. Another fifty yards and the path forked, one trail continuing uphill and another turning sharply to the left past a stone spur that extended like a short wall from the greater mass of the mountain. As they reached the spur, Nick saw the ruddy glow of firelight playing off the rocks.

The hollow was a small cul-de-sac against a narrow cliff face that rose high into the night, with lower stone ridges on either side. A small fire guttered at the base of the cliff. A tall, bearded man with a ridge of black hair fringing a bald crown walked back and forth in front of the fire, rubbing his hands to keep them warm. He looked up and came to a stop when he saw Nick and Martoglio approaching. The contractors spread out, hands on their weapons, their eyes on the ridgelines.

Nick raised a hand in greeting to Tariq. "As-salaam alaykum," he said. *Peace be upon you.*

"Wa alaykum as-salaam," Tariq murmured, barely above a whisper. *And also with you.*

Nick lowered his hand. Tariq had not moved toward him. The fire flickered, casting shadows over Tariq's face, but then Nick saw something gleam on his friend's cheeks. Tariq was crying.

"Something's wrong," Nick said to Martoglio.

"Samehni, sadiqi," Tariq whispered. *Forgive me, my friend.*

There was an explosive *whoosh* as if a large can of spray paint had been punctured, followed immediately by a screeching *hiss*. Nick dropped to the ground just as the rocket-propelled grenade shot down into the cul-de-sac from the stone ridges above. It struck the ground at Tariq's feet and exploded. Immediately Nick's hearing cut out, as if someone had turned the volume all the way down. All he could hear was a muffled, high-pitched ringing. From his prone position on the ground, he lifted his head. A canteen lay on the ground right in front of him, water gurgling out into the dirt. He stared at it, uncomprehending. A hand, severed at the wrist, lay in the dirt next to the canteen. He blinked, his ears and brain stuffed with cotton. Where Tariq had been standing there was now a blackened spot on the ground. The firelight showed a dark stain thrown on the cliff wall. From the ridges above, lights winked in the dark. Muzzle flashes.

A hand grabbed the back of his shirt between his shoulder blades, and he was yanked up and then half dragged out of the cul-de-sac. It was Martoglio, his Browning in his fist and pointed up at the ridgeline. He was shouting something to Nick—*Go.* Nick now heard sounds as if he were underwater. *Go*, Martoglio shouted, and with his free hand he shoved Nick back the way they had entered.

Nick began to run. Now he could hear the roar of the AKs, see two of the contractors ahead of him, crouched and firing up at the ridgeline behind Nick. The muzzle flash from each was like a tongue of flame. Then Nick was past them, running for the stone spur just a few yards ahead. Something ricocheted off a rock to his right. The air was dry and dusty in his throat as he lunged for the spur, scrambling around it. He drew his .45, but there was no shot, uphill at night against an unseen enemy. Still, he peered around the spur, the .45 in a two-handed grip. Two men were trying to drag a third out of the cul-de-sac, all of them backlit by the fire that still burned. Whoever was on the ridgeline was firing down at the men. Nick braced his .45 on top of the spur and fired three shots at the ridgeline, then ducked a second before bullets whined overhead, one striking stone two feet from Nick's head and skimming off into the dark.

Someone grabbed Nick and hauled him back, away from the spur. He spun around, trying to break the grip and bring his pistol to bear, but then he saw it was the blond contractor. "Get the fuck out of here," the man snarled. He put his AK to his shoulder and fired a long burst into the cul-de-sac.

There was another *whoosh* and a screeching *hiss*, and this time Nick covered his ears before dropping to the ground. When the grenade exploded against the stone spur, the blast was loud and concussive, but Nick didn't lose his hearing. He looked up and saw the blond contractor writhing on the ground, a bloody hand clapped to one ear. Nick crawled to the man, who was grunting in pain but still trying to get to his feet. The man had managed to get an emergency bandage out of a pocket, and Nick took the bandage out of his hand, opened it, and began wrapping it around the man's head and ear, careful not to cover his eyes with the gauze.

More gunfire roared from the cul-de-sac, and then Duncan and another contractor hurried around the spur, panting as they carried a slumped figure between them. It was Martoglio. They laid him on the ground behind the spur, then began firing back into the cul-de-sac. "We are leaving right quick!" Duncan shouted at Nick. He yanked out a magazine and shoved another one in, then continued firing. More of the contractors backed out of the cul-de-sac, dragging or carrying wounded while Duncan provided cover fire.

Nick reached for Martoglio. He appeared to be napping, his chin on his chest, but when Nick touched the man's shoulder, he could feel the wet blood even through his gloves. Martoglio's eyes were half-open, staring at nothing.

Nick still couldn't fully recall how they made it down the mountainside in the pitch dark. He and Duncan carried Martoglio's body. Three other contractors each carried a dead comrade. That left one contractor, the blond with the injured ear, to protect their rear. It was a nightmare of corpse-carrying and sliding down the stony incline, short bursts of gunfire occasionally chasing them. The contractor with the ear wound vanished for a time, then reappeared, limping slightly. After that, no more gunfire followed them.

They found their vehicles safely parked where they had left them, loaded the dead into the pickups' beds and covered them with tarps, then drove down the mountain, grim and too exhausted for anger.

THAT ANGER SURFACED later. The station chief in Beirut exploded at Nick, even as he sat bruised and stained with Martoglio's blood. Syria had released a statement about an incursion at the border and threatened retaliation. The Lebanese government had countered by accusing Syria of violating their border, and then for good measure summoned the US ambassador for a dressing-down. The security contractors had vanished. Langley demanded to know who had fucked this up and sent Chitrita Bhandari to clean up the mess. She arrived in a midnight-blue sari trimmed in silver that managed to be both somber and fabulous.

"They're going to hang it on Martoglio," Bhandari told Nick in the same bunker-like room where they had first discussed Bottlecap.

"Convenient, seeing as he's dead," Nick said.

"They thought about blaming you," Bhandari retorted. "But Martoglio was in charge. And he's the one who hired the fucking mercenaries who walked you into a firefight."

"If it hadn't been for the fucking mercenaries, we'd both be dead."

"That would be even more convenient."

"Fuck you, Rita."

Bhandari raised her eyebrows. "Don't play shocked with me. We live in the real world. You know how easily this could escalate. Do you want us to start another war in the Middle East?"

"We seem to be pretty good at starting those."

Bhandari shook her head. "Are you getting jaded now?"

Nick wished he smoked just so he could do something with his hands, maybe childishly blow smoke in Bhandari's face. Instead, he grimaced and threw his hands up in disgust. "Tariq lured us there," he said. "The Syrians must have turned him. But they didn't send regular army."

"How do you know that?"

"They fired RPGs at us. Who fires an antitank weapon at ground troops, at night? Not well-trained soldiers. It was probably a militia. Pro-Assad thugs with guns. This way Assad can disavow the whole thing."

Bhandari gave him a thin smile. "Dr. Anthony gets a gold star."

"So I'm not fired." Nick posed it as a statement, not a question, but they both knew what he meant.

"You are a valuable officer who has been of great service," Bhandari said.

"But?"

"But nothing. Get back to work."

Nick frowned—he'd been certain there would be retaliation for Bottlecap going to hell. Then he understood. "They're going to ask me to retire when this blows over, aren't they?"

Bhandari gathered her files and then stood. "Do you see yourself jockeying to become station chief somewhere? Or riding a desk at Langley?"

Nick couldn't help himself. "No, that's more your speed."

She looked disappointed. "I'm a woman who is busting balls and crossing names off lists," she said. "I'm an ambitious bitch and I make no apologies for it. And you, you are a very good intelligence officer who doesn't give a shit about advancing up some ladder." She put her hand on the doorknob, then paused. "Too many people like you end up dead. Joe Martoglio died in service to his country. He'll get a star on the wall at Langley, and Bottlecap will be buried with him. And you'll get to grow old with your wife."

NOW, IN THE Highlands jail, Nick stretched out on his bunk, staring up at the bunk above him. The mattress lay on top of a solid sheet of metal—no springs or wire mesh that prisoners could use to fashion a weapon, or kill themselves.

He had to get out of this cell. Rita Bhandari had to come through. She owed him that much, at least. He only hoped she would see it that way as well.

CHAPTER THIRTY-ONE

ZHANG DROVE TO THE DINER IN DILLARD THAT COLE HAD mentioned, and they went inside to eat while they waited for Jonas. They said next to nothing, Cole feeling his anger and frustration tightening in a coil while Zhang, sensing Cole's building outrage, kept his attention fixed on his food. They had already finished eating and paid, sipping their waters as the waitress hovered, when a gray Chevy Tahoe pulled up and parked in front of the diner and Waco got out. Cole slid out of the booth and walked out the door into the parking lot, Zhang following. Waco saw them and smiled. "Hey, boss," he said. "You—"

"Where the fuck have you been?" Cole said. "Been sitting here for a half hour."

Waco glanced at Zhang, who gave him a brief shake of the head. "Sorry, boss," Waco said. "We were checking in at the motel, and Jonas—"

"Where is he? Where's Hicks?"

Waco blinked. "They're back at the motel. They said you—"

"Forget it," Cole said. He stepped around Waco and headed for the Suburban. "We'll follow you there."

Waco looked at Zhang, who just shook his head again.

They followed Waco in their Suburban further down Highway 23 to a single-story motel that had last been redecorated when Reagan was president, with a cracked parking lot and a faux-stone facing. Cole parked the Suburban and got out as Waco pulled up next to them. As soon as Waco opened his door, Cole asked, "Which room?"

"Twenty-four," Waco said. "He got three—"

Cole walked across the lot toward the door to number 24. Before he reached the door, it opened and Hicks poked his head out. "Boss," he said by way of greeting, then glanced over at the Suburban. "Where's Poncho and Dawes?"

Cole could already smell Hicks's goddamn dip. "Move," he said, still walking toward the doorway. Hicks hesitated, then stepped back quickly as Cole bore down on him. Cole passed through the doorway. Across the room, Jonas stood in front of the sink, brushing his teeth. He watched Cole in the mirror, then leaned forward and spat into the sink. "You okay?" his reflection asked Cole.

"No," Cole said. "I'm not goddamn okay."

Jonas rinsed off his toothbrush and laid it on the counter, then turned to face Cole. "Hicks, go give Zhang a hand with the gear," he said. Hicks took the cue and left the room, shutting the door behind him.

Jonas leaned back against the counter, hands resting against the counter top edge. "What happened?"

"Why'd you send Waco to pick us up?" Cole said. "I told all of you to come."

Jonas looked at him for a moment before replying. "This place has got about as much diversity as a Klan rally. I stick out. Figured we wanted to keep a low profile, so I sent Waco. We barely fit the three of us and all our gear in the Tahoe."

"Well, while you were calculating cargo space," Cole said, anger sizzling like grease jumping from a frying pan, "Poncho and Dawes got taken out by a civilian and a cop."

"Taken out?"

"Poncho's in the hospital and Dawes is dead," Cole said. He refrained from snatching up a lamp and throwing it at the wall, although it would have felt good for a moment to break something.

Jonas's eyes widened with shock, but in an even tone, as if he were asking the time, he said, "So what are we going to do?"

Cole grinned mirthlessly at Jonas, lips curling back from his teeth. "We are going back up there, and we are going to find the girl, and get that flash drive, and kill the motherfucker who took two of our men off the board."

Jonas frowned. "Who? The cop?"

"The *civilian*," Cole said. "He's helping the girl. I got his photo and sent it to Kobayashi to get an ID." He took a deep breath through his nose and exhaled loudly. "We resupplied. Get all the gear loaded. Soon as I learn where he lives, we head out."

Jonas was about to say something when Cole's phone rang. Cole looked at the screen—Kobayashi—and smiled. "Synchronicity," he said to Jonas, then answered the phone. "Tell me you have good news," he said.

"That depends," Kobayashi replied on the other end.

"I don't like riddles."

"The man in the second picture is Joshua Sams, a sheriff's deputy in Jackson County, North Carolina. He was in the Army, served as a military policeman, and then returned to North Carolina, where he has been a deputy for seven years."

"What about the other one?"

"Ah," Kobayashi said. "The other one. His name is Nicholas Anthony. He was a professor of medieval literature at Western Carolina University until nineteen months ago, when he went on extended leave to take care of his wife. She died of pancreatic cancer a few months later."

"How touching," Cole said. "So why would he be helping the girl? Is he a Boy Scout?"

Kobayashi barely paused. "I do not understand your reference."

"A do-gooder," Cole said. "Helps old ladies across the street, protects orphans. Is that it?"

"I cannot speak to his altruism, but I believe his motive is more personal," Kobayashi said. "It appears that Dr. Anthony is the brother of Jay Bashir. He is Annalise Bashir's uncle."

Cole gripped the phone tightly. "Now that *is* interesting," he said in a soft voice that made Jonas turn to look at him, eyes alert and wary. "Especially considering that you never mentioned an uncle. Would've been helpful to know when we started looking for the girl."

"An error that has been corrected," Kobayashi said smoothly.

Fuck you, Cole thought. If they had known about an uncle, then Poncho and Dawes might be okay right now. Cole swallowed his anger—he could ream Kobayashi later. "You have an address for this professor-uncle?" he said.

"He lives outside of the town of Cashiers. I will send you the address." Kobayashi paused, the silence stretching.

"You make me nervous when you're quiet," Cole said.

"We have reason to believe Dr. Anthony is more than a professor," Kobayashi said. "He served in the US Marine Corps before getting a PhD in medieval studies from Notre Dame. He then taught for many years at several universities in Europe and the Middle East before returning to the United States."

"Okay, so he was a Marine," Cole said. "We'll be careful."

"Dr. Anthony's mother emigrated to the US from Afghanistan just before he was born," Kobayashi continued. "He is fluent in Dari and Arabic and, of course, English, and he reportedly has a working knowledge of several other languages. His career has taken him to places that are of great strategic interest to the United States, especially in the Middle East. When he was not teaching, he often traveled in the region to do research."

"Skip to the end," Cole said.

"We believe with a high degree of probability that Dr. Anthony was an intelligence officer," Kobayashi said. "Perhaps military, but most likely CIA."

Cole had always thought the metaphor of a thought appearing in your brain like a lightbulb turning on was a stupid cliché, but now he felt like someone had flipped on a set of stadium lights in his memory, illuminating his earlier, half-realized thought about his picture of the professor in handcuffs. He *had* recognized the man. Cole felt a grin stretch across his face.

"Mr. Cole?" Kobayashi said.

"I'm here," Cole said, still grinning. "It's not a problem."

"Dr. Anthony was trained by your government as both a soldier and an intelligence officer," Kobayashi said. "His skill sets would make him rather more dangerous than a mere professor of literature."

"Nothing we can't handle," Cole said. "But this changes things somewhat. Makes for a higher risk factor."

Kobayashi's voice grew fractionally cooler. "Meaning?"

"Meaning we need to renegotiate our contract," Cole said. "An extra ten thousand. Each. For that we'll bring you the flash drive and take care of the girl."

"And Dr. Anthony, I presume."

"I'll personally deliver you the man's head on a spike."

There was more than a hint of amused contempt in Kobayashi's voice. "The picture you sent me showed him in handcuffs. Would he not currently be in jail?"

"If he hasn't already been released," Cole said. "But he could be in fucking Saskatchewan and I would get to him."

Kobayashi was quiet for a moment. "There is an old saying," he said finally. "A man who desires revenge should dig two graves."

Now Cole smiled like a man appreciating a dogfight. "If you know the enemy and you know yourself," he said, "you need not fear the result of a hundred battles."

Silence at the other end of the line. Cole waited the man out, letting the silence build.

"Very well," Kobayashi said finally. "Each remaining man of your team shall receive ten thousand dollars upon successful completion of your mission."

"Pleasure doing business with you," Cole said. "Soon as you send us that address, we will be on our merry way." He disconnected before Kobayashi could, then smiled at Jonas. "Easy money," he said. Then he laughed.

"You said something about a spy?" Jonas said.

Cole tapped at his phone, then held it up to show Jonas the photo of Nick. "He's one of the cousins," he said. "And I *know* the motherfucker." He laughed again and started pacing around the room. "God, karma is a cast-iron *bitch*."

Jonas frowned. "What are you talking about, Cole?"

Cole stopped pacing. "That job I took in Lebanon before I formed this team? When my ear got all chewed to shit? We were hired by the cousins. It was a fucking shit show. They sent two spooks with us. The one in charge died." Cole stabbed his finger at the photo of Nick on his phone. "And he was the other one."

HICKS HAD TAKEN the Georgia plates off the Suburban and replaced them with a Florida plate he had lifted from a car in a strip mall outside Tampa. Now the two SUVs headed up into the mountains, Hicks driving the Suburban with Cole and Zhang, Waco and Jonas following in the Tahoe. At their backs the sun had fallen behind the tree-lined ridges, burning golden for a few moments before slowly fading to a sullen red, smearing the horizon and backlighting the ridges so they turned solid black as the red light faded, and then the ridges were swallowed up in the oncoming night.

It took them less than half an hour to return to Highlands, and both Hicks and Waco drove carefully, obeying the speed limit. The streetlights were on and small knots of people were strolling the sidewalks, enjoying the cooler evening or maybe heading to a late dinner. Cole knew it was a risk driving the Suburban back up here, but they hadn't had time to find a replacement, and they couldn't all fit in the Tahoe. Plus, so many tourists drove large SUVs that he hoped theirs would blend in, along with whatever camouflage the Florida plate provided.

The two vehicles crawled through the streets. No one took any notice, least of all the police. Cole wished they could confirm whether or not the professor was still in jail, but they didn't have time. Once through town, they stayed east on Horse Cove Road rather than turning north onto 64 for Cashiers. Buildings gave way to trees, and the road rose up onto the back of a low ridge and then doglegged to the right and began a series of switchbacks down the other side of the ridge. A single car passed them in the opposite direction, and then they were alone for nearly a mile, everything silky darkness past the range of their headlights as they wound through the trees. They came out onto the floor of a valley that ran due east. Fields opened on the left, along with a few homes, their lights yellow and dim in the dark. They left those houses behind and plunged back into the woods, the road turning one way, then another, before it finally curved north toward Whiteside Cove, the valley where the professor lived.

Cole sat in the front passenger seat of the Tahoe, looking out the windshield but seeing instead the face of the man they had come up here to find. He continued to burn with a fury he'd thought he'd become too callous to feel. The rush of anger felt good, righteous—cleansing. It clarified things. This professor-spy had hurt him, kicked him right in the balls. Winslow had fucked up, but Dawes had been a good man, their communications specialist, steady under fire. He had an ailing father wasting away in a VA somewhere—Kentucky, maybe. Cole would make sure Dawes's father was taken care of. And Mandy in LA. And he would take care of Poncho too. Poncho was alive, granted, but he was in the hospital, no doubt under heavy police guard. No way to extract him without a firefight. Better to take care of the girl and this professor now, and then they could see about springing Poncho.

"Field coming up in five," Zhang said from the back seat.

"Copy that," Hicks said, his hands on the wheel.

On their left, Whiteside Mountain rose into the night, a high central granite face with lower cliffs to either side, like a collapsed layer cake. They passed a turnoff for a lodge on a low rise to the right, where Cole could see the flickering light of a bonfire maybe a hundred meters through the trees. Then the road curved and the firelight vanished behind them. It would be dark as the inside of a boot in a few short minutes. Perfect.

Out of the gloaming appeared a small house with a dirt driveway and an American flag on a pole, and then it disappeared as they drove into a darkened tunnel of trees. Then the trees fell away, and on their left they saw a red log cabin and another house, behind which a broad field rose up the base of Whiteside for a couple hundred meters before reaching the tree line. The road continued straight past the two houses, then curved left, marking the far end of the field.

They took the left curve and then, just before the road hooked back to the right and tunneled into the trees again, Hicks turned left onto a dirt road that led into the back of the field. After a few yards Hicks braked to a stop, and five seconds later the Tahoe pulled up next to them. The five men got out of the vehicles, Cole, Hicks, and Waco with their pistols drawn, Zhang and Jonas taking out duffel bags and gun cases from the back of the Suburban.

There was an outdoor floodlight shining from the corner of the nearest house, a cold white star in the dark. Cole kept an eye on the house while Hicks watched the road. No one came out of the house; no voice called to them. The others pulled on black tactical overalls from one of the duffel bags, then stood guard as Cole and Hicks did the same. Jonas opened the other duffel bag and the hard cases and passed out their gear. Each man already had a pistol and a knife, and to that Jonas added an MP5 submachine gun with a suppressor and extra magazines. Jonas made sure every man's comms were working. Waco passed out sticks of face paint, which they applied to each other's faces for camouflage. Less than ten minutes after they had parked, they were ready to go. Zhang checked his weapon's suppressor, and Jonas kept his eyes on the surroundings, but Cole felt the men standing there, suspended, waiting for him.

Cole kept his voice low. "We cross the road and head due east through the trees about one klick. I'll take point. The target is at the southern end of the lake there. We'll stop fifty meters out and assess. All we want is the flash drive. Once we secure that, the girl and her uncle are both expendable."

They each nodded, Hicks adding a quiet, affirmative grunt. Cole paused. He could feel the men ready to go, feel their blood surging like his own. They wanted to find the man who had hurt them, wanted it as badly as he did. Cole felt something in his chest tighten so hard that it was both painful and beautiful. Goddamn, to be with these men, hunting with them under the stars at the foot of this mountain. This was what they had been born to do, right here, at this moment.

"Let's go," Cole said, and he walked toward the road, MP5 in both hands, and his men followed.

CHAPTER THIRTY-TWO

THE DOOR TO THE CELL BLOCK WAS UNLOCKED AND SWUNG OPEN. Nick sat up, nearly hitting his head on the bunk above him. Chief Davies and another police officer walked into the cell block and looked at Nick through the bars.

"Time to go," Chief Davies said.

"Go where?" Nick said.

The police officer unlocked the cell door and opened it wide.

"Home," the chief said. His expression was pleasant enough, but something in his eyes made Nick think he wasn't altogether happy. Rita must have pulled some strings.

"The DA isn't pressing charges?" Nick said. He was still sitting on the bunk.

"Not at this time," Chief Davies said, his mouth drawn a little tighter than before.

Nick almost felt sorry for the chief. He wouldn't be happy in his position either. He wanted to say something, apologize somehow, but instead he just stood and walked out of the cell, the other two men escorting him. Time to get home and check on Annalise. And then he and his niece would leave these mountains.

NICK DROVE OUT of Highlands, nearly taking out a mailbox on a particularly tight curve. It was a quarter moon, but Nick could barely see anything beyond his headlights. Peering through the windshield, he drove with one hand and with the other dialed Bhandari, then put his phone on speaker. After two rings, there was a click. "Duty officer, DDA," a male voice said.

"DDA Bhandari, please," Nick said.

"The DDA is not available—"

"Tell her it's Nick Anthony. Tell her *Bottlecap*."

"The DDA is not available," the man said.

There would be an operational code, Nick knew, some magic phrase that would get him access to Rita. "Look," he said, "this is—"

A red Mercedes coupe slowly pulled out onto the road ahead of him, either not seeing Nick or misjudging the distance. He yanked the wheel, swerving to the left to avoid rear-ending the Mercedes. The Honda's suspension protested loudly. He sped around the Mercedes, which honked at him, and then found himself driving straight toward a van coming around the curve up ahead. "Shit!" Nick shouted, pulling back into the right-hand lane with a squeal of tires. The van blew past, missing him by inches.

"Sir?" the man on the phone said.

"Anthony, Nicholas, EIN 428165312," Nick said, hands gripping the wheel. "I have a priority message for DDA Bhandari."

"The DDA is not—"

"I was talking to her earlier today. Put her on the damn phone. I have a—"

A series of clicks, then a dial tone.

Furious, Nick reached for the phone, but his headlights picked out a sharp turn to the right just ahead, and he hit the brakes and hauled the wheel to the right. The Honda left skid marks as it crossed the center line but stayed on the road. Once out of the turn, Nick veered back into the right-hand lane, the SUV rocking slightly. At this rate, he would run into a tree or another car. Nick ignored his phone and kept his hands on the wheel. He had to make it down the sharp switchbacks here on Horse Cove Road, and once down in the valley he could pick up speed and make it home.

You have to hurry, Ellie said. *She's alone.*

Nick clenched his jaw and said nothing. When Ellie had been dying at home, Nick had rarely left her side, paying locals to deliver groceries and prescriptions and medical supplies. He had bought a hospital bed for her and put it in the living room so she could look out the windows at the lake and the mountain. He had brewed teas for her and tried to make her laugh and only cried when she was asleep, going into their shared closet and letting out half-choked sobs. One day, when Nick had been rubbing lotion onto her feet, Ellie said, her voice weak but clear, "I don't want to leave you alone."

Nick didn't stop rubbing her feet, although something in him shuddered at her words. "I'm fine," he said, and he even looked up at her and smiled.

She looked so small in the bed, almost swallowed by her pillows and quilt, but her eyes burned fiercely in her pale face. "I hear you at night, you know," she said. "In the closet."

Now he did stop rubbing her feet. "Ellie."

"Shh," she said. "I'm dying. I get to talk."

He stood and began pacing around the living room, as if by moving he could erase what was happening.

"Nicholas," she said, and at the word he stopped, although he gazed at her quilt and not her.

"I'm going to die, Nick," she said. A nerve twitched in his jaw. "And when I do," she continued, "you'll be alone."

Still not looking at her, Nick said, "Because we didn't have kids."

Ellie said nothing for so long that Nick finally dragged his gaze from the quilt to her face. His breath left him at the sight of Ellie weeping. "Oh God," he said, hurrying forward. "Oh, El. I'm sorry. I didn't—"

"That wasn't what I was thinking," she said. "And even if I was, I wouldn't *say* that to you, Nick. That's not fair."

Fair. Nick wanted to laugh, except he knew it would come out like a bellow. None of this was fair. God, fate, the universe, whatever, had fucked him in the ass and was taking Ellie from him. But he swallowed his anger and instead got a tissue and gently wiped Ellie's tears away. "I'm sorry," he said. "I'm sorry I said it. And I'm sorry I never wanted . . . that I was too scared to—" He couldn't finish, couldn't say *I was too scared that any kid I had would go insane like my mother.* Ellie already knew, but still he couldn't say the words aloud.

"Shut it," Ellie said. "We're grown-ups. We made our choice, together."

Nick realized he was crying, but he made no effort to hide it, just smiled through his tears. "I wish I'd made a different choice."

Ellie reached out a thumb, wiped a tear from Nick's cheek. "Well," she said, "might not be too late." When Nick stared at her, Ellie raised one eyebrow. "You think I'm too sick to jump you right here?"

Nick did laugh then, a burst of mirth that didn't dissolve his tears. He wiped his arm across his eyes and shook his head. "You're terrible," he said.

"I'm sexy and adorable," she said. "The whole package. Now shut up and kiss me."

Now, driving down into the dark valley, Nick felt tears at the backs of his eyes but willed them away for now. Ellie was gone. Now he had to get home to Annalise. She was only sixteen, no mother, no father, no siblings. No one except for one set of grandparents three hundred miles away, and him.

And she was the only family he had left.

He could not fail her like he had failed Ellie.

Nick drove faster into the night.

CHAPTER THIRTY-THREE

Lettie's pot roast was delicious and filling and the exact kind of comfort food Annalise didn't realize she needed until she started eating. She scarfed down one plate and most of another before sitting back from the table with a sigh. Across the table, Lettie smiled. "Looks like you needed a good meal," she said.

Annalise smiled back. "That was awesome," she said. "Thank you."

"You're welcome," Lettie said. "It's all in the meat and how you tenderize it. Hank loved my pot roast."

"Hank?"

"My husband," Lettie said. "He's been gone, oh, eleven years now. Stroke. He was a good man. Followed me up here after college in Virginia." She put her hands on the table and pushed herself to her feet. "I think there's still enough pot roast left for Nick, if he ever comes back."

"I'm sorry about that," Annalise said. "I'm sure he'll be here any minute. Oh," she added, standing. "Let me help, please."

They rinsed their plates and put them in the dishwasher and covered the remaining pot roast with tinfoil, then adjourned to the living room. Lettie built a fire, and soon the stack of logs was aflame, putting out heat and light and a comforting crackling. Annalise sat on the couch next to Lettie, legs tucked up beneath her as she stared at the fire.

"So you've lived here a long time?" Annalise asked.

Lettie nodded. "Daddy moved us up here fresh out of the Navy after World War Two. I was born in Asheville while he was fighting in the Pacific. When he came back, I was two years old and didn't know who he was. Daddy was the picture on Mother's nightstand, not this man standing in our kitchen. I hid behind my mother's skirts. But Daddy just smiled and was patient with me. We came up here for a picnic and I let Daddy put a flower in my hair, and he turned to my mother and said, 'We're moving here.' They built a house and sold things out of their living room. Built a second house next door and turned the first one into a full-time shop. First real shop in Cashiers. They ran it for almost fifty years." Lettie smiled. "Now I run it."

"So you're really from here."

Lettie laughed at that. "That's what your aunt and uncle said when they first met me. I told them that's a tricky thing to judge. Daddy served on the parish vestry and helped get a volunteer fire department in Cashiers, hired girls from local families to work in the shop. But Daddy was also a Yankee from Pennsylvania, and it took a while for the mountain people to accept him."

"How long?"

"After I got married and moved back here with Hank, my mother broke her foot. Dropped a box of dinner plates on it in the storeroom. She couldn't stand and work in the shop with her foot in a cast, and getting up from a chair was a struggle. A week after she came home from the hospital, one of the locals knocked on our front door. He'd made a wooden stool for Mother, by hand. Perfect height for her, easy to get on and off. 'Thought Mrs. Lambert might need it,' is all he said. Refused any payment. That's when Daddy said he knew he'd been accepted."

Annalise thought about how her family had moved every few years, her father always chasing something new, how she'd had to leave schools and friends behind. She tried to imagine living in the same place for five decades. She'd thought Tampa might be more permanent than the other places she'd lived. Then she closed a door on that thought. She had no desire to start bawling again.

"What can you tell me about my uncle?" she asked.

Lettie looked puzzled. "What do you mean?"

"I just . . . I don't really know him."

"Well, he was a history professor. And he loves the Middle Ages." Lettie waved her hand at a stack of books on a side table. "Although I suppose that's obvious from his reading material."

Annalise shrugged. "Yeah, I looked through his books for something to read earlier. He's pretty into the medieval stuff." She shifted on the couch. "But he carries himself differently, you know? Not like a professor."

Lettie smiled. "Not all professors wear tweed jackets and smoke pipes."

"No, I know. But . . ."

Lettie glanced at Annalise, one eyebrow raised, but said nothing.

Annalise thought about how to frame her question. *He said he was a spy,* she thought. *He owns a gun and has a bag full of fake passports. And he killed a rattlesnake with a machete. He didn't talk to my father for twenty years. What kind of person does that describe?* Annalise threw her hands up. "I don't know," she mumbled.

A log in the fire popped.

"He was a Marine," Lettie said. "At least, I think he was."

"Really?" Annalise knew this from what her uncle had told her earlier when they drove to Charlotte. But she wanted to hear what Lettie knew.

Lettie nodded, looking at the fire. "It was a couple of years ago, before Ellie died. We were all at church, and I was sitting in the choir, and our rector had invited one of the locals, Dick Jennings, to give the sermon. Dick told us about serving in Korea, what he learned about sacrifice and duty. To be honest, he rambled a bit, but he's almost ninety, so I suppose he's earned the right. Anyway, when he finally finished, he closed by saying, 'Semper fi,' the Marine Corps motto. Always faithful. And sitting up there in the choir, I could see everyone in the pews, and when Dick Jennings said, 'Semper fi,' I saw your uncle say it too, like a response, only he sort of mouthed the words rather than saying them aloud. The look on Nick's face when he said it . . . it was like he felt pride and pain at the same time." Lettie paused, sifting her memories. "Your uncle is still grieving Ellie," she said. "I think he probably always will. But he's not a sad or angry person by nature. He's a good man. Any pain or darkness that he's carrying around, it won't define him." She smiled. "And he's very loyal. He might hole up in his house here and act like he wants you to leave him alone and snap at you if you don't, but if you need him he'll be there for you, sure as sunrise."

They sat quietly then, watching the fire, Annalise turning Lettie's words over in her mind. So much about her life depended on her uncle now, a man she had known for three days. *He's very loyal*, Lettie had said. He'd saved her from the rattlesnake, taken her to Lapidus to learn what they could about her father. And he had bought her gas station candy.

Her thoughts were interrupted by a sound. She turned her head, listening—yes. There it was. The faint whine of an approaching car. "About time," she muttered.

CHAPTER THIRTY-FOUR

Cole led his men through the trees, his eyes scanning the darkness, MP5 up and ready. Twice he raised a clenched fist and they all stepped behind tree trunks or crouched behind a screen of rhododendron. The first time it was a screen door slamming from the cottages almost half a klick north. After a minute of silence there was no further noise, and Cole resumed walking. The second time they stopped, Cole felt rather than saw something. Then an owl, its wings wide and breast pale, glided ghostlike through the trees not ten feet over their heads. It swept into the dark without a sound.

They continued due east. Soon the ground beneath Cole's feet began to slope downhill and he knew they had crested the ridge between the road and their target. Cole held his arm out behind him, palm facing his men: *Stop.* There was the faintest glow at the bottom of the hill, about a hundred meters away. He raised his binoculars to his eyes and the world became a shimmering green, the cabin suddenly leaping to what seemed like an arm's reach away. The professor's cabin sat at the end of a dark lake, light shining from windows on the back porch. He couldn't see through the windows, but he saw smoke rising from the chimney. Someone was home. Cole let the binoculars hang from a lanyard around his neck and waited a few moments for his eyes to readjust to the darkness, then grasped his MP5 and waved his men forward. He began slowly picking his way down the hill toward the cabin, keeping his eyes on the faint glow from the windows.

He was more than halfway down the hill when he heard the car engine, and he held up a clenched fist and knew without looking that his men had again stopped and taken cover. He crouched behind a fallen tree. It was hard to tell in this narrow little lake valley, but he thought the car was approaching from the far side of the cabin. Just as he grasped the binoculars around his neck, he saw the tiny headlights of a vehicle making its way down the far ridge.

CHAPTER THIRTY-FIVE

THE PHONE ALMOST KILLED HIM.

Nick had turned into Whiteside Cove, barreling over low rises and taking turns as sharply as he dared. His line of sight was reduced to the twin cones of his headlights, dark trees whipping past on either side, the road unfurling before him, twisting and turning through the dark.

His phone lit up and rang.

Nick glanced down at the phone lying on the passenger seat: NO CALLER ID. Rita. He grabbed the phone and glanced back up just in time to see, through the windshield, an enormous black shape reared up on two legs. It was in the center of the road not twenty yards away. The phone dropped from Nick's hand just before he wrenched the wheel to the left. The tires squealed as his Honda fought a skid. Nick passed the behemoth, barely missing it. He shouted, adrenaline slamming through his heart. Then his left front tire went off the road and the front fender clipped a mailbox in a squall of metal and wood. Nick hauled the wheel to the right, the back fender smacking what was left of the mailbox. The SUV began to lift up on its two right wheels. Nick yanked the wheel once again to the left, and the car dropped with a sickening jolt onto all four tires. Nick finally stomped on the brake pedal and the SUV smoked to a lurching stop. His hands gripped the steering wheel as if he were hanging from the edge of a cliff. He gulped air, his eyes wide and startled. He turned to look behind him. The road was empty. The black shape was gone.

A bear, he thought, his heart thudding against his breastbone. *Had to be.* He had missed it by a foot.

A faint glow lit the inside of the SUV at the same time he heard a ring. His phone. He threw the gear selector into park and groped around in the footwell until he found the phone. It was still ringing. He answered and put it on speaker. "Rita?"

Her voice, as always, was a rasp of barely contained outrage. "Where the fuck are you?"

Nick looked in the rearview mirror, half expecting to see a gigantic grizzly behind his car. The road was still empty.

"Nick, goddammit," Rita barked.

"I'm driving back to my house."

"Stay there. There's a unit from Fort Bragg flying in by helicopter. You—"

"Who's after me, Rita?"

"How should I know?"

"You're sending Green Berets from Bragg. You know."

Bhandari paused. Nick listened to the sigh of his air conditioner, the engine's low rumbling. He rolled the dice. "If it's about Ghawar, it's either the Saudis or an oil company," he said. "Who did my brother piss off?"

When Bhandari spoke, her voice was disturbingly calm. "Somebody gave your brother information that wasn't theirs to give, along with a large amount of money. We think the money was payment for Jay to take that information and act as a courier. Instead, he tried to sell it. And someone hired a team of mercenaries to retrieve it."

Jesus. Fucking Jay. Nick closed his eyes briefly. When he opened them, he saw something at the edge of the illumination from his headlights, to the left in a field just before the road curved back to the right.

Rita was saying something, but Nick put the car into drive and rolled his window down and drove slowly forward, looking at the field. The night air flowed over him, cooling his blood. And then out of the dark there emerged a gray SUV. It was parked in the field, about twenty yards away from the road. And next to it Nick saw another vehicle, this one black. He saw no one in either vehicle or in the field.

"Nick?" Rita said on the phone. "Are you listening to a goddamn thing I'm saying?"

Nick turned into the field, the Honda jouncing as it struggled over a few ruts. Then the twin beams of his headlights revealed both SUVs— a gray Chevy Tahoe and a black Suburban. The men at the library in Highlands had arrived in a black Suburban. Nick checked the license plate on the Suburban, saw that it was Florida, not Georgia. They could have switched the plates, though.

Rita's voice issued angrily from the phone. It reminded Nick of the rattlesnake. "Rita," he said, cutting across her voice. "They're already here."

"Who?"

Nick stopped just behind the SUVs. "The men looking for my niece," he said. He took his phone off speaker and held it up to his ear as he got out of his car. "Just found their vehicles half a mile from my house." Whiteside Mountain rose straight before him, the cliffs a pale gray.

"Don't you go and play fucking Rambo in the woods."

"Tell me the boys from Bragg are ten minutes out." Nick peered in the back of the Suburban. The glass was tinted and too dark to see through.

"More like sixty," Rita said.

The Tahoe's glass was not tinted, and when he looked through the rear windshield, he saw two large cases lying in the back cargo area. He knew what cases like that held. He turned and looked east, away from the mountain. Toward his cabin.

"Nick?" Rita was saying.

He walked to his car. "That flash drive I told you about," he said. "I left it with the Highlands police chief. If something happens to me, you can get it from him. And look at Halliwell Energy. There's a PI in Charlotte named Lapidus; he can fill you in." He opened his passenger door and rummaged in the glove compartment.

"What are you doing?" she said.

He took a Swiss Army knife out of his glove compartment and walked back to the Tahoe. "Tell the team from Bragg to hurry," he said. "And tell them that there's a friendly on the ground."

"Goddammit, Nick—"

Nick hung up, then put his phone on silent and wedged it into his back pocket. The SatSleeve made the phone chunky but there was nothing he could do about that. He unclasped the Swiss Army knife, wondering if the two-inch blade would work. It sank into the sidewall of the Tahoe's tires well enough. He had to apply more pressure to stick the blade into the Suburban's sidewalls, but soon he had put holes into all eight tires. His phone vibrated two separate times in his pocket. He ignored it.

He returned to his Honda one more time, opened the back hatch, and grabbed an old black fleece and pulled it on, zipping it up over his green Henley. Then he lifted up the floor of the rear cargo compartment to reveal the spare tire and jack. He took the tire iron out of the jack, dropped the cargo compartment floor back down, and closed the hatch. After a moment's thought he took his phone out of his back pocket, powered it off, and put it into a pocket in his fleece and zipped it close.

Across the road from the field, the trees stood dark and silent, watchful sentinels. He knew them like he knew the inside of his cabin. He and Ellie had walked every trail in these woods and made a few of their own. They had moved here because Ellie loved the trees, how the landscape was so different, the green mountains a stark contrast to the hammering heat of the desert sun that shone on the places where they had lived for over a decade, in Beirut and Cairo and Jerusalem and Istanbul, their moves from city to city partially due to his changing teaching positions.

You were a good teacher, Ellie said.

Her comment surprised him, but not as much as his reply. *I miss it. More than the other thing?*

That left him cold, as if his marrow had turned to ice. He had stepped away from that life, with fewer regrets than he had felt later upon leaving academia to care for Ellie. But there had been moments, when he had been in his office grading papers or sitting in a faculty meeting or even when watching Ellie sleep, that he had found himself bored and restless, longing for something, that old shot of adrenaline that sent the pulse racing, the senses on high alert. The gap of danger—the unknown that lay waiting just beyond your perception. It was absurd to feel that way, even repulsive.

You were good at that too, Ellie said.

No.

Yes, Ellie said.

I didn't want to be. I don't *want to be.*

You were pretty good at taking care of the guy in the library with the knife, Ellie said.

And I let the other one catch me off guard. Nick was surprised at his own bitterness. *I'm too old for this. My hip is killing me.*

Well, I'm dead, Ellie said. *So you're better off than I am.*

Nick pressed the palms of his hands against his eyes. He felt wrung out like an old washcloth. His hip ached. He was frightened for Annalise. And he was not up for an argument with his dead wife, even if she was just an imaginary phantom. He could have avoided this, could simply have walked away from the library once he'd seen those two men step inside. He could have turned Annalise's phone off and vanished from their radar, taken Annalise and gone somewhere else, maybe to her grandparents, and that would have been an end to that. But even as he thought it, he knew that was wrong. Whoever those men were, they hadn't been alone. The others were here, advancing on his home right now, and they wouldn't just go away from wishful thinking. The confrontation with the two in the library had made Nick draw on skills he had learned and honed in his other life. And now he had to draw on them again, and he dreaded the cost.

Stop thinking about it and go, Ellie said. *Annalise needs you.*

He took a breath, let it out, and strode across the road toward the woods. When he stepped off the asphalt, he knelt by a creek, runoff from the culvert under the road, and scooped up a patch of dark soil and rubbed it over his face and neck and the backs of his hands. Then he stood, the tire iron in his hand, and stepped into the trees.

CHAPTER THIRTY-SIX

ANNALISE COULD HEAR A CAR COMING DOWN THE GRAVEL ROAD AND driving out of the trees into the front yard. Thank God. She hoped whatever her uncle had found out at the library had been worth the wait. She walked into the foyer and looked out the sidelight, and her heart dropped. "It's someone in a blue pickup," she said to Lettie.

"It's not Nick?" Lettie asked from the living room.

The blue pickup's engine cut off, the headlights winking out, and then the cab door opened and a man stepped out. "No," Annalise said, her voice lower, as if the man outside could hear her. Where the hell was her uncle? There was a man in the yard, tall, with big hands. Hands that could easily wrap around your neck. *Chill*, Annalise told herself, and she took a deep breath and let it out, trying to calm herself.

"Who is it?" Lettie asked, suddenly right behind her, causing Annalise to jump. God, the old lady had crept right up on top of her. "Where's the light? I can't see a thing."

"No!" Annalise said, nearly batting Lettie's hands away from a table lamp in the foyer. The older woman's look of shock and hurt nearly made Annalise quail, but she reached out and grasped Lettie's hands. "I'm sorry, but I'm scared. I . . . someone is looking for me."

Lettie looked at Annalise. "Well," she said. "In that case, we shall leave the light off." She squeezed Annalise's hands, once, then let go and moved to the sidelight, bending forward to peer out the window. Annalise heard her take in a short, sharp breath. "He's coming up to the door," Lettie said.

Annalise turned and hurried through the great room to the library, pulled the pistol out from the desk drawer, and went back to the foyer. Lettie was still looking out the sidelight.

"Oh," Lettie said, and straightened up. At the same time, there was a rapping at the door. Annalise held the pistol in one hand behind her leg as Lettie turned and smiled at her. "It's Joshua Sams," she said. "He's a deputy. He's good people."

Annalise hesitated. After hiding from the police for a few days, at this point she would welcome them. Maybe he knew where Uncle Nick was.

Lettie opened the door. "Hello, Josh," she said.

"Lettie," the man said, nodding. He clasped his hands together as if trying to still his fingers. "Saw your Jeep in the carport. Is the professor home?"

"No," Lettie said. "We've been waiting for him."

Sams leaned slightly to look around Lettie and see Annalise, standing farther back in the foyer, still holding the pistol behind her leg. "You must be Annalise," he said, and gave her a smile. It seemed genuine but it looked sickly, somehow, as if the man had forgotten how to smile and was doing a bad job remembering. "Y'all know where he is?" Sams said.

Lettie glanced at Annalise, then back to Sams. "We were hoping you'd know," she said. "Do you want to come in and—"

"I just—" Sams said, then swallowed. Annalise saw his clasped hands twitch and fidget. "I just need to talk to him. He . . . I shot someone, today." Lettie held a hand to her mouth. Annalise stared. Sams kept talking, not really to them. "I shot someone," he said. "In the library." At that, Annalise gasped. Sams continued, oblivious. "I've never shot anyone before. Not in the Army, not as a deputy."

In a low, calm voice, Lettie said, "Who did you shoot, Josh?"

"Man holding a gun on the professor," Sams said. "I told him to freeze, and he tried to shoot me. I shot him first." He seemed to recover himself slightly and looked at Annalise. "Your uncle's okay," he said, "he's fine," and Annalise nearly buckled at the knees with relief, but she was able to keep standing. "He saw—he saw me, afterward," Sams continued. "I was in shock, and he knew. He knew what I was . . . thinking. I thought maybe if I could talk to him, he could help me."

Annalise saw Lettie shiver, either from the cool night air or from the deputy's story. "Help you what, Josh?" Lettie said.

"Help me stop seeing it," Sams said, and his eyes looked haunted— that was the only word Annalise could think of, haunted. "I keep seeing myself pull my thirty-eight out of my holster and shouting, 'Freeze!' and the man whips around, trying to point his pistol at me. I shot him, twice. It was so loud, my ears still . . . he wouldn't freeze and I shot him twice and he fell to the floor and died, and then it happens all over again, like a film loop, and I—" Sams took a deep breath and let it out in a shuddering exhale. "I—I'm sorry." He took a step back.

"Where are you going?" Lettie said.

"Sorry to bother y'all," Sams said. He started to turn to the truck.

"Joshua Sams," Lettie said, and Sams stopped and turned back. "You aren't going anywhere but inside this house. We have a nice fire going, and you can meet Nick's niece and we'll wait for the professor to come home."

Sams hesitated, clasping and unclasping his hands. "I don't want to be any trouble," he said, glancing at Annalise.

"Oh, Josh," Lettie said, and she stepped forward, opening her arms.

CHAPTER THIRTY-SEVEN

Fʀᴏᴍ ᴛʜᴇ ʜɪʟʟsɪᴅᴇ, Cᴏʟᴇ sᴛᴀʀᴇᴅ ᴛʜʀᴏᴜɢʜ ʜɪs ʙɪɴᴏᴄᴜʟᴀʀs, unbelieving. It was the deputy from the library. Cole watched the man pause at the front door of the cabin before raising a hand to knock. How civilized. Cole gripped his binoculars so that his knuckles ached. That man down there had shot Dawes. And now his showing up at the cabin royally screwed up their mission.

"Cole, all good? Copy." That was Jonas in his ear, like the proverbial angel on his shoulder keeping him on track.

"Got eyes on target," Cole murmured.

"The professor?"

"Negative," Cole murmured. Quickly he scanned the deputy's truck—maybe the professor had gotten a ride home. The truck looked empty. He swung the binoculars back to the deputy just in time to see the front door open, but whoever had answered the door did not step outside into Cole's view. Cole lowered his binoculars, blinked rapidly, and peered at the deputy. He was in clear profile to Cole, maybe forty meters away, slightly downhill from Cole's position behind the fallen tree. Cole raised the binoculars again. The deputy was talking to someone. The man looked like shit, Cole thought.

"Cole," Jonas said in his ear. "Do you have eyes on the professor?"

"Negative," Cole murmured. "Stand by."

The deputy kept talking, fidgeting with his hands. Whoever was inside the house still hadn't stepped outside, and Cole couldn't see who it was without breaking cover and moving. Again he swept the front yard with his binoculars. Nothing—the deputy was alone.

The deputy took a step back from the door. He looked like he was about to turn and go back to his truck. Cole dropped the binoculars to let them hang from his neck and raised his MP5 to his shoulder. They didn't need someone else to worry about.

This is for you, Dawes, Cole thought. *You and Mandy.* His sights tracked on the man's chest, then up to his head.

The old woman ruined the shot.

Cole was far enough away at forty meters that he selected single-shot mode for better accuracy. Just before he squeezed the trigger, the deputy's head clear in his sights, an old woman came out of the doorway with her arms open, apparently to give him a hug. The deputy leaned slightly forward toward the woman, whose head moved in front of the deputy's.

Cole fired, the shot a single, hard *pop*—the people down at the cabin probably didn't even hear it. The bullet struck the old woman at an angle in the very back of the head, probably creasing her skull like a stone skipping off a pond. Cole saw her sag against the deputy. Blood flowed down the back of her head. From inside the cabin, someone started screaming—a high voice, a woman. The girl.

Shit.

"Cole, we heard a shot," Jonas said in his ear. "What's your status?"

Cole flipped the selector switch to three-round burst and fired, *rap-ap-ap*, just as the deputy lunged toward the doorway, the old woman in his arms. The doorframe magically splintered, and the deputy jerked as if his arm had spasmed. Then the deputy and the old woman were inside the house and out of his line of sight.

CHAPTER THIRTY-EIGHT

ONE MOMENT LETTIE WAS MOVING TO HUG THE DEPUTY—SAMS, SHE
had called him—and the next moment she fell forward into Sams's arms,
not dramatically but almost leaning in to him, like someone who'd had
too many drinks at a party. Annalise saw the skin at the back of Lettie's
head split open as if an invisible knife had sliced across her scalp. Her
blue-gray hair bloomed dark red.

Annalise screamed. That seemed to galvanize Sams into action. He
lowered his shoulders and plowed into the house, carrying Lettie. As he
did so, part of the doorframe burst jaggedly apart, and Sams grunted.
Then he was stumbling in the foyer, trying to keep his feet and not drop
Lettie.

Annalise let the pistol she was holding fall to the floor and reached
out to take Lettie. "Oh my God," she said. Blood was flowing down the
back of Lettie's head. Annalise struggled to hold her up. "Oh my God,"
she said again, and she lowered Lettie as gently as she could to the floor,
squatting and then sitting on the floor as she did so. She hesitated for just
an instant before laying the older woman's head in her lap. She could feel
Lettie's warm blood soak through her jeans and onto her thighs.

Sams kicked the front door shut behind him, and Annalise looked up and saw with horror that the sleeve of his left arm was wet with blood.

"Got shot," Sams said strangely, as if his tongue were thick in his mouth, and then he sat down heavily on the floor. "Going to need a . . . bandage."

Annalise stared at Sams, then down at Lettie, her head still bleeding into Annalise's lap. Lettie's eyes were open and wet, and her lips moved as if she were whispering, but no sound came out. *Oh fuck*, Annalise thought.

CHAPTER THIRTY-NINE

COLE MOVED DOWN THE HILLSIDE, HIS WEAPON UP AND TRACKING the front door. It had slammed shut after the deputy ran inside, but Cole was pretty sure he'd hit the man at least once. "Jonas," he said into his mic, "I'm at the bottom of the hill, five meters from the cabin. One, possibly two targets hit. Need to breach the house."

"Copy that," Jonas said. "Coming in on your six. Zhang, Hicks, you're with me."

"What about me?" Waco asked in his ear. *Jesus,* Cole thought, *the kid earned a place on my team and he still sounds like a whiny bitch.*

"You watch our backs," Jonas said in a do-not-disappoint-me voice. Then they said nothing more.

Cole crouched behind the rhododendron that bordered the lawn, eyes never leaving the front door. Within sixty seconds Jonas crept up beside him. "Still no professor?" Jonas murmured.

Cole shook his head. "I shot the deputy who took out Dawes. Some old woman from the house stepped into my line of fire—tapped her in the back of the head."

"Dead?"

"The deputy was still on his feet and got the old woman into the house. Don't know about him. But the old woman's a goner. Where are the others?"

"Hicks and Zhang are going around the back, Waco's up in the trees."

Cole nodded. "Then you and I go in the front."

CHAPTER FORTY

Nɪᴄᴋ ᴍᴏᴠᴇᴅ ᴛʜʀᴏᴜɢʜ ᴛʜᴇ ᴛʀᴇᴇs, ᴄʀᴏᴜᴄʜɪɴɢ ᴀs ʟᴏᴡ ᴀs ʜᴇ ᴄᴏᴜʟᴅ without sacrificing speed. He remembered his instructor at Quantico making them run through the woods again and again. *You have five minutes to reach the objective without being detected*, he would say, and Nick and his squad would have to cover two hundred yards of forest and get to a tree with an orange ribbon tied around the trunk, all without being spotted. He'd been wearing full combat gear then, which had weighed him down. He'd also been fully camouflaged and almost thirty years younger. Nick ignored the memory and advanced from tree to tree, eyes peering into the darkness. He knew the terrain, knew where the men were going. He just needed to surprise them.

He was cresting the top of the hill above his house when he heard the *rap* of a single shot—even suppressed, there was no mistaking the sound—and froze. Then a muted shriek, followed by the *rap-ap-ap* of a burst. Every instinct screamed at him to sprint downhill to save Annalise. Instead, he crept even more quietly, keeping low, zigzagging rather than advancing in a straight line, eyes scanning ahead, looking for the outline of a head, a shoulder, an arm.

There. Next to a lightning-blasted oak, not halfway down the hill. A thin slice of exposed flesh, like a white grin in the dark. The back of a man's neck.

Nick froze again, then slowly reached out and moved his free hand over the forest floor, careful not to brush against any dead leaves or brush, searching for a loose rock or a pine knot. Nothing. The man below him began slowly moving downhill. Nick could see his profile, the stubby automatic weapon in his hands. Nick passed the tire iron to his left hand and, with his right, carefully unzipped his fleece pocket and withdrew his cell phone. Then he took two steps forward and hurled it several yards to the man's right.

The phone in its chunky SatSleeve thumped onto the forest floor, crunching dead leaves. The man whirled, his weapon up. Slowly he took a step toward the phone, then another. Then he was moving more rapidly, searching for the source of the noise, Nick padding downhill after him.

The man had reached the area where the phone had landed and was scanning the woods when something deep inside him—instinct, maybe, or his lizard brain firing on high alert—made him turn just as Nick leapt at him from behind a tree, arm raised. Before the man could even lift his weapon, Nick swung his arm down, the tire iron connecting with the top of the man's head. The man fell to the ground as if poleaxed.

Nick dropped the tire iron and crouched next to the man, feeling for his carotid artery. He was alive, although his pulse was thready. The tire iron had left a gash in the top of his skull. Nick saw that the man was young, not much older than Annalise. This registered as mere fact— Nick had no time for regret. That would come later. The man wore a black jumpsuit and his face was covered with camo paint. But his collar hadn't been fastened correctly, which was how Nick had seen the back of his neck. It was a break Nick knew he probably wouldn't get again.

Nick hesitated as he stood over the man, looked at his MP5 lying on the ground, at the knife and pistol on his belt. He knew it would be safer to kill him. Instead, he picked up the MP5, the pistol, and the knife, found two spare magazines for the MP5 in the man's jumpsuit and shoved them into his own pockets, and then vanished into the trees like a wraith.

CHAPTER FORTY-ONE

"DEPUTY SAMS," ANNALISE SAID, CRADLING LETTIE'S BLEEDING HEAD in her lap. "Deputy Sams?"

Sams sat slumped on the foyer floor, but when Annalise spoke, he lifted his head to look at her.

"I need you to get me towels," Annalise said, taking a slight bit of comfort in the fact that her voice barely trembled. "Dish towels. From the kitchen. As many as you can find, okay? Please?"

Sams's face was pale and glistened with sweat, but he nodded, and then with a grimace, holding his left arm stiff and close to his body, he got to his feet. Once there, he leaned against the foyer wall as if to catch his breath. "Dish towels," he said, looking at Annalise as if for confirmation. Annalise nodded, and wearily Sams nodded back and then stepped into the dining room, from where Annalise knew he could walk into the kitchen. Sams left a bright smear of red on the arch leading into the dining room, at shoulder height.

"Annalise," Lettie said weakly, and with a shock Annalise looked down at Lettie. My God, there was so much blood. So much.

"Hey," Annalise said with a smile, batting away tears with the back of her hand. "The deputy is getting me some towels. It's going to be okay."

Lettie blinked. Annalise realized how suddenly old Lettie looked, the wrinkles in her face like deep trenches. Lettie wet her lips with her tongue. "My head feels like . . . someone hit me with a . . . cast-iron skillet."

"Don't try to move," Annalise said, hoping desperately that she wouldn't keep crying. "Just lie still. Towels are coming."

"Why? Is somebody . . . wet?"

Annalise let out a hiccup of laughter. Looking up at her, Lettie smiled. The smile transformed her. Her face was radiant, joyful. "Gotcha," she said.

A heavy *thud* sounded against the door, and Annalise jerked her head up to stare at it. Fear lit up her spinal cord, but she was unable to move. Another *thud*, and there was a dull crack. Just as she registered that someone was trying to kick the door down, there was a third *thud* punctuated by another, louder crack, and the door burst open. Without thinking, Annalise picked the pistol off the floor and raised it. A man dressed in black stood in the doorway. Annalise pointed the pistol at him.

CHAPTER FORTY-TWO

COLE STARED AT THE TEENAGE GIRL AND THE OLD WOMAN ON THE floor. There was a lot of blood on the girl's jeans and, Cole could see, in the old woman's hair. That must have been where he'd shot her. But where was the deputy?

In that moment of hesitation, the girl raised a pistol and aimed it at his chest. Cole stared at the open end of the gun barrel. He was dead.

The girl squeezed the trigger. Nothing happened. Confusion and anger ran across her face. She squeezed the trigger again, and Cole stepped forward and smacked the pistol out of her hand. It skittered across the floor into the dining room, where it disappeared under a sideboard.

"What—" the girl managed.

"Safety was on," Cole said. He raised his MP5, holding it across his chest.

Behind him, Jonas stepped through the ruined front door. "Cole," he said.

Cole spared him a quick glance and saw Jonas was holding his MP5 to his shoulder, aiming it at the dining room. Cole followed Jonas's sight line and saw, on the arched entrance into the dining room, a smear of blood against the white paint.

257

"Check it out," Cole said, returning his attention to the girl and the old woman. Jonas walked into the dining room and out of Cole's sight.

"You were there," the girl said to Cole. Her eyes were swollen from crying and she looked exhausted, but she was also furious. "At my house."

Cole tilted his head slightly, saying nothing.

"You killed my parents," the girl said.

"Where's your uncle?" Cole said.

The girl shook her head, her dark hair swirling around her face.

Cole fired a single shot. In the enclosed space, even suppressed, it made a loud *pap*. A vase on the hall table next to the girl's head shattered. The girl cried out.

"The next one goes in the old woman's leg," Cole said. "Then her arm. And when she's dead, I'll start shooting you." He paused to let the words sink in. She was tough, he'd give her that—aside from that one cry, she was holding it together, but her eyes were wide with fear. "Where is your uncle?"

"He's not here," she said.

Cole stared at her briefly, then nodded. "Then we'll wait for him."

At that moment the lights cut out, plunging the cabin into darkness.

Cole immediately stepped to his right, away from the girl and into the dining room, his weapon up. "Sound off," he said into his mic.

"Number two, copy," Jonas said in his ear. "In the kitchen."

"Number four, copy," Zhang said.

Cole stood in the darkened dining room, waiting. He could hear the girl and the old woman in the foyer whispering. "Hicks, Waco, sound off," he said. "Zhang, where are you? Do you have eyes on Hicks or Waco?"

Zhang said, "I'm behind the house, by the—"

A burst of gunfire came over the comms, followed by another.

"Zhang, report!" Cole barked. "Hicks! Waco!"

Two sharp gunshots rang out, this time from inside the house, the sound deafening and accompanied by muzzle flashes like a strobe light.

CHAPTER FORTY-THREE

When the lights went out, Annalise froze. Even if she'd wanted to try to run from the man with the gun, she was still holding Lettie's head in her lap, and her legs were numb from sitting in the foyer for so long. She heard the man with the gun—Cole, the other soldier guy had called him—say something that sounded like *sound off* and realized after a second's confusion that he must be talking to someone else, but then Lettie said something and Annalise bent her head closer to her, Cole forgotten for the moment. "What?" Annalise said.

Lettie's voice was weak but steady. "Why is it dark?" she said.

"The lights went out," Annalise said. "I don't know why."

"It's your uncle," Lettie said.

"What?" Annalise wished she could see Lettie's face.

Lettie's voice was calm, a benediction in the dark. "Take care of him," she said.

Take care of her uncle? They were captured by gunmen and Lettie was bleeding from her head and Annalise was beginning to realize she was probably going to die here, but Lettie wanted her to take care of her uncle. "I don't—" she began.

There was some sort of muffled sound from outside. To Annalise it almost sounded like the *put-put* of a lawnmower, but much briefer. The man with the gun had taken a step or two away and was muttering something, but Annalise heard his sharp intake of breath. Then came two explosions from the kitchen like a pair of cherry bombs, flashes of light in the dark. Gunshots. Annalise cried out, startled, clapping her hands over her ears. She just wanted this to stop, to get out of this house, to go far away.

A hand grabbed her arm. "Get up," Cole said.

"Wait!" Annalise said, but Cole was pulling her up and Lettie was already sliding off her lap. Lettie's head struck the carpet with a thump that made Annalise's heart leap to her throat. "She's hurt! I have to—"

"She's dead," Cole said, yanking her to her feet. "Let's go."

"No!" Annalise cried out. "I'm not—"

He slapped Annalise across the face, the bright shock of it cutting through everything. "I said, let's go," Cole snarled, and then he was pushing Annalise into the kitchen. A flashlight beam snapped on from behind Annalise and scanned the kitchen counters, the floor, and then Annalise nearly cried out again as the light found a man facedown on the floor at the opening to the library. It was the other man who had come in the front door, and there were two bloody wounds on his back. The flashlight pivoted back toward the great room and caught another man on the floor, slumped against the back of the love seat. It was the deputy, Sams, his eyes closed, blood drenching his left arm and side, his face pale as paper. A revolver lay on the floor by the deputy's unmoving hand.

The flashlight snapped off, and a hand spun Annalise and pushed her toward the kitchen door that led to the carport. "You do what I tell you," Cole said in her ear, "or you'll be as dead as them."

CHAPTER FORTY-FOUR

Nick limped across his backyard, his hip on fire and a slice of pain across his thigh where a bullet had grazed him. That had been the last man getting off a burst before Nick brought him down. The one before him had required knife work so Nick could get to the cabin and the outside shutoff at the meter on the back wall. Cutting off the power was a temporary diversion, but it was the best he could come up with if he was going to get into the house and save Annalise and Lettie—he had seen Lettie's car parked under the carport. She'd probably brought him a pie or something. Her goddamn insistence on being his friend was going to get her killed. He had to get into the house without being shot. His limp was a problem, but his leg was barely bleeding, so that was something.

Two gunshots erupted inside the house, each punctuated by a flash from the windows. Nick flinched. *Shit. No, no, no.* He ran as best he could to the side porch and crouched behind a low stack of firewood. Those had sounded like pistol shots, not an MP5. He peered over the firewood and saw the truck parked near the front door. Sams's truck. Nick's heart lurched in his chest. Had that been Sams firing his pistol? Nick had heard someone fire a short burst earlier, but he'd assumed they had been shooting the front door down—had they been shooting at Sams instead?

Ignoring the pain in his leg, Nick ran in a crouch to the truck, putting it between him and the cabin. He saw his front door was cracked and splintered. All was silent. Dread began to build in Nick's chest, along with another, sharper emotion—rage. He drew a deep breath through his nose and exhaled through his mouth, then did it again, trying to calm himself. His eyes remained open and flicked back and forth between the front door, the carport, and the side yard.

A door opened and closed. Nick peered around the rear bumper and brought his MP5 up, aiming the muzzle in the direction of the carport. After a moment, someone stepped out from the shadows of the carport, hands raised. Nick sighted on the figure. The person took two more steps forward and Nick's stomach dropped. It was Annalise.

"Professor!" someone shouted, and a man stepped out from the carport, holding an MP5 of his own and pointing it at Annalise. "I know you're here. Come on out."

Nick stayed where he was, trying to draw a bead on the man. Annalise was between them. And even if she took a step to one side, the man was too close to her. One burst from his MP5 would cut her in half.

The man fired a single shot, dirt kicking up around Annalise's feet. She screamed and nearly fell but managed to stay on her feet.

"I'm not fucking around," Cole called out. "Let's go."

"You've got nowhere to go," Nick called back. "There are men coming—"

Cole fired again. Annalise spun and this time did fall to the ground, facedown. Nick throttled back a scream and heard Annalise scream instead, followed by sobs. Cole stepped forward so he was standing directly over her and lowered his barrel to point it at her head.

"Shot her in the ass, Professor," Cole said. "Cute ass, too. Won't be so nice the next time. So step the fuck out."

Nick squeezed his eyes shut, opened them. He stood up slowly from behind the truck, hands slightly raised, the MP5 still in his right hand but pointed up to the sky. "Okay," he said. "I'm here."

"Step out from the truck," Cole said.

Nick took two side steps away from the truck, still holding the MP5.

"Drop it," Cole said.

"I—"

Cole fired, another single shot, right next to Annalise's head.

Nick held the MP5 further out from his body, then, very slowly, bent and lowered it to the ground and just as slowly stood back up, both hands raised. "Okay," he said again.

"No, it's not," Cole said, and then he raised his weapon and fired a burst at Nick. The rounds knocked him back and down, the ground coming up too fast, too hard.

COLE WALKED FORWARD, ejecting the magazine from his MP5 and slapping another one in before reaching Nick. He stood over the man, watched him gasping on the ground. He'd hit him at least twice, blood blooming on his torso. From the sound of the professor's breathing, one of the shots had perforated a lung.

Cole knelt beside Nick. "That was a good try, Dr. Anthony," he said. "You were really kicking my ass there for a little bit." He leaned closer. "Do you recognize me? Remember Lebanon, up in the mountains? You and your fat-ass partner who got shot?" He watched Nick gaze up at him, trying to place him, and then inevitably Nick looked at his ear. Cole saw it in his eyes then, and he grinned. "This is what I call karma," he said. He slung his weapon over his back and started patting Nick's pockets. "Do you know Sun Tzu? 'The clever combatant imposes his will upon the enemy, but does not allow the enemy's will to be imposed upon him.' I'll let you figure out which one of us is the clever one." He continued patting Nick's pockets and legs, but now he frowned slightly.

"Don't have it," Nick managed to say. He coughed, weakly.

Cole looked disappointed. "Your brother was stubborn too. Wouldn't tell us where his baby girl was, not even when we worked on his wife. Pain in the ass."

Cole had to give it to the man—even shot and bleeding into the dirt, his voice barely louder than a breath, the professor looked calm, almost comfortable. "Fuck you," Nick said.

Cole drew his pistol and placed the muzzle on Nick's cheek, next to his nose. "Where is it?"

Nick smiled up at Cole. There was blood on his teeth. "You'd be doing me a favor," he said.

Cole's voice was tight with frustration. "Then I'll take it out on your niece. One bloody piece at a time."

Nick looked past Cole toward the cabin, then rolled his eyes back toward Cole. "He who hesitates is lost," he said.

Cole whirled around. The girl was gone.

"Mother*fucker!*" he said, straightening up. He holstered his pistol and swung his MP5 off his shoulder. She couldn't have gone far. He looked to the tree line, to the cabin, back to the tree line. His men were down and he had to assume someone had heard at least the deputy's shots and called the local cops. He had to evac now. But he couldn't leave without the flash drive, which the professor had fucking hidden somewhere. And the girl was his one hold on the professor. Cole hadn't heard a door open, so the girl wasn't in the house. Which meant she was hiding outside somewhere.

He glanced down at the professor, who was staring up at the stars, blinking slowly. He wasn't going anywhere. Cole stalked back to the carport, his boots crunching on the gravel, weapon up and scanning. He looked through the windows of the Jeep—empty. The door to the house was shut tight. From the woods he heard an owl hoot like a question, but there was no other sound. But he could smell her. A faint scent of soap and the iron tang of blood. Where was she?

The quarter moon came out from behind a cloud, and Cole saw someone lying in the yard beyond the carport. She had fallen to the ground. Cole switched his MP5 to his left hand and, with his right, unsheathed his knife. He came out from the cover of the carport and was about to place the muzzle of his weapon against the back of the girl's head when he realized it wasn't the girl—it was Hicks, his body cold, his blood on the grass black in the weak moonlight. His throat had been sliced open.

The sight made Cole want to sob with rage. Every one of his men, gone. He felt as alone and exposed as if he were standing in some vast desert. He wasn't afraid of Kobayashi or whoever was pulling his strings. It was the weight of failure, the shame, that threatened to crush him. It was fucking Winslow's fault. Winslow hadn't done his job, and so everything had fallen apart. He'd had to put Winslow down, show his men how wrong Winslow had been, how careless. It wasn't his fault. It wasn't—

Cole's thoughts distracted him so that he almost didn't see the girl. As it was, he started to turn away from Hicks's body and saw the girl running at him, a snarl on her face as she lifted something—a sword?—over her head like an avenging angel.

CHAPTER FORTY-FIVE

ANNALISE BROUGHT THE MACHETE DOWN, THE BLADE EMBEDDING itself into the crown of Cole's head above his left eye. The impact jarred Annalise's arms so that her hands flew open, letting go of the machete's hilt. Cole took a single step backward, mouth in a surprised O, the machete a bizarre, horrible piece of headgear jutting out from the top of his skull. Blood ran like paint down his face. Then he fell backward, landing with an ungainly thump, his feet twitching convulsively before they, too, were stilled.

Annalise dropped to her knees, adrenaline thrumming through her body, her mind spinning like a carousel. She felt sick. She allowed herself to close her eyes and tried to calm herself. Pain lanced through her left buttock where Cole had shot her, the bullet scoring her flesh without doing serious damage. She concentrated on the pain, a sharp, bright light in the dark. When her breathing slowed and she opened her eyes, she saw Cole was still lying there, the machete sticking up out of his head. Not far away lay another man who was also dead. Her uncle must have done that.

Oh God. Her uncle.

Annalise got to her feet, swaying a bit before putting out a hand for balance and resting it on the hood of Lettie's Jeep. Somewhere at the back of her mind she cried for Lettie, but she hurried through the carport and back into the front yard. There, next to the deputy's pickup truck, Uncle Nick lay on the ground, unmoving. "No," she said, and she ran toward him as best she could. "No, no, no." Just before she reached him, she tripped and fell on all fours, nearly collapsing on top of him.

"Easy," her uncle said, and Annalise raised her head to see him looking back at her, his face gray in the moonlight. He had blood on his shirt front. She reached out her hands and pressed them on top of the bloody parts of his chest and stomach. He groaned.

"Okay," she said, blowing her hair out of her face as she applied pressure to his wounds. "You're going to live, okay? You can't die on me too."

So faintly that she almost missed it, he said, "I'm tired."

"Doesn't matter," she said. "She said I have to take care of you. Lettie did. So you can't fucking die."

"Don't want—" he started, then coughed weakly. "Don't want to piss Lettie off," he said.

"Or me," Annalise said, still applying pressure. Her hands were wet with blood, but so were her legs. She didn't think her uncle was bleeding anymore. She didn't know if that was good or bad.

"Or you," he whispered. "Sorry . . . this is how we met."

"You have to tell me about my dad," Annalise said. She tasted something salty. Tears. When had she started crying? "You have to stay alive and tell me about my dad. And my aunt. Ellie. Okay? You have to do that."

She sat there, hands pressing down on her uncle's bleeding torso, as she heard a distant sound that soon became the chop of an approaching helicopter, like the long-delayed cavalry finally approaching over the horizon.

CHAPTER FORTY-SIX

ANNALISE OPENED HER EYES BEFORE DAWN AS USUAL, A GRAY WASH OF light coming through the window. The light here was different than at home, or in the mountains, but she had gotten used to it, just like she no longer felt confused and scared when she first woke up. She sat up in bed and stretched, then pulled on a pair of sweat pants and padded downstairs. She smelled coffee and cinnamon and sugar.

"Good morning," her grandmother said. She was in the kitchen, wearing a flowered bathrobe and house slippers, and she smiled warmly at Annalise.

"Morning," Annalise said, yawning. "Are you making cinnamon buns?"

"Monkey bread," Grandma said. She bent down to peek in the oven. "Almost ready. Did you sleep okay?"

Annalise nodded. "Is Granddad going fishing today?"

"After church, if I can get him out of bed," Grandma said. She shook her head. "The older he gets, the more he wants to sleep."

Annalise got two mugs with travel lids and poured coffee into them, adding milk and sugar to one and sipping it to confirm it was acceptable. She looked at her grandmother and raised an eyebrow.

Grandma nodded. "He's out there." She walked through the living room to the sliding glass door and opened it for Annalise. Annalise stepped outside onto the deck. "Thanks," she said, and Grandma smiled and nodded and closed the door behind her.

Outside it was already muggy, but a steady breeze off the dunes felt good on her skin. Annalise carried the two mugs across the wooden deck and down the rickety stairs to the beach path, her bare feet welcoming the cool sand. She knew that by noon the sand would be unbearably hot, but for now it was pleasant to wiggle her toes in it.

A short hike up between two dunes, sea oats waving in the breeze like feathered grasses, and then the beach opened before her, a wide stretch of sand that sloped gently down to the surf. The tide was out, leaving behind tidal pools like a strand of silver lakes. Down by the water a man jogged past with a golden retriever trotting behind, but otherwise the early-morning beach was empty, save for a man sitting in a beach chair halfway between the dunes and the surf, gazing out at the ocean. There was an empty chair next to him.

Annalise made her way down to the chairs. "Coffee," she said.

Uncle Nick turned his head and smiled up at her. "Thanks," he said. He took the mug of black coffee. Annalise sat in the empty chair. The few clouds on the horizon had started to glow, but the sun had not yet risen, and the western sky behind Nick and Annalise was still a dull, shadowed blue.

"How'd you sleep?" she asked.

"Better," Nick said.

"Define better."

"Three hours in a row without waking up. Only needed one pain pill."

"You walk this morning?"

"Two miles."

"Don't push yourself too hard."

"Yes, doctor."

They sat in comfortable silence. Far out on the water, a cargo ship inched its way toward Savannah.

"School starts tomorrow," Nick said.

"Hmm," Annalise said, sipping her coffee.

"I liked the principal. She seemed competent."

"You mean the headmaster?"

"There's a difference?"

"It's a private school. She's the headmaster."

"Duly noted." Nick looked at Annalise. "You excited about school?"

Annalise shrugged. "It's school. It'll be good to get back into a routine. Meet new people."

"You talk to some of your friends from Tampa last night?"

"Yeah, we FaceTimed last night. It's just . . ."

Nick waited. He'd learned, after a lot of trial and error, mostly error, that waiting was the best way with Annalise.

Annalise pulled her legs up and hugged her knees. "It was fine, they were really nice and everything. But it's not the same. I miss them. And . . . I miss Eric."

Nick nodded. She had cried when he told her that her boyfriend was dead.

Annalise took a breath, then blew it out. "I miss Eric, and Mom and Dad, and . . . it's like I'm afraid I'm going to forget them, like I'll *really* lose them, you know?"

Nick looked out at the water, the waves rolling endlessly forward and spilling on the sand. "Yeah," he said. "I know. But you won't."

Annalise glanced at her uncle. He looked calm enough, but she knew he still missed Aunt Ellie, that he always would. That was one side of Uncle Nick. But now, after the mountains, she knew another side of him, knew what kind of violence he was capable of. It had scared her, and he must have sensed it, because he'd been very careful to treat her gently since. She knew now that he would never hurt her, but he had parts inside that he kept closed and locked away from her, maybe even from himself.

She leaned against him, and she felt him stiffen in surprise. But after a moment he lifted his arm and put it around her shoulders, and they sat that way, waiting for the sunrise.

FOR THE FIRST time in months, Nick thought about the future.

Annalise's grandparents, Nora and Ed, had welcomed both of them into their home in Hilton Head without hesitation. Of course they would take in their granddaughter, but Nick was surprised by how they had welcomed him, a virtual stranger, the brother of their dead son-in-law. It was a good thing they had. He couldn't stay in Cashiers, not even if he wanted to. While he had somewhat recovered from his injuries, living alone in a cabin in the mountains before he was fully healed wasn't wise. And he didn't want to think about Lettie every time he walked through his foyer, or be reminded constantly of the men he had been forced to kill in his own yard. It was time to let go, in more ways than one. And the look of relief on Annalise's face when her grandparents had offered to take them both in had gone straight to his heart. She had wanted him to go with her. Nick had said he would find his own apartment, but Nora and Ed had insisted he move into their other guest room. Nick suspected they were also happy to have someone else to help with Annalise—if their lives were going to be disrupted by the sudden arrival of a teenager, what was one more person, especially a mostly functioning adult?

His chest itched, but he resisted the urge to scratch. The bullet wounds were scarring nicely. He didn't remember the soldiers from Bragg arriving the night he'd been shot, or his evac to the Highlands hospital. According to Nick's surgeon, he had nearly coded twice, but barring pneumonia or some other infection, the surgeon had predicted Nick would make a full recovery.

He had been in his hospital bed in Highlands when Joshua Sams came to visit, pushed in a wheelchair by an orderly. Sams's left arm was in a sling. The orderly had wheeled Sams to the foot of Nick's bed and engaged the brake, then left.

"You look terrible," Sams said, his voice weak but firm.

Nick glanced down at himself, wired and tubed like a half-built cyborg. His own voice was a rasp. "I'm fucking fantastic."

"No doubt." Sams managed a smile. He was pale and his hair was greasy and he needed a shave, but Nick found his smile a welcome sight.

"Arm okay?" Nick asked.

Sams nodded. "Lost a lot of blood, but I'll live. They don't think there's any permanent nerve damage or anything." He looked around the room, as if trying to find what he'd come to talk about.

"I'm sorry I lied to you," Nick said. "About Annalise."

Sams shrugged with his good shoulder. "She's your family," he said. "And looks like she's innocent, anyway." He took a breath, blew it out. He looked exhausted. "I'm sorry I couldn't help her more. Sorry I couldn't help Lettie."

Nick closed his eyes, grief forming a hard, cold ball in his stomach. He made himself open his eyes and look at Sams. "You did fine," he said.

"I don't feel fine," Sams said.

"You shot and killed two people. If you weren't bothered by it, that would be worse. Trust me."

"Are you bothered by it?"

The words surprised both of them. Sams looked on the verge of apologizing when Nick cut him off. "Yes," he said.

Sams shook his head slowly. "How—" he began, then cleared his throat. "How do you live with it?"

Nick felt a heavy weariness settle over him, everything starting to fade. The pain meds had kicked in. "Talk to someone about it," he said. "Don't keep it all inside. Then go jogging or play basketball. Climb a mountain. Something physical."

Sams looked at him, eyes both haunted and hopeful. "And then?"

Nick struggled to finish before he passed out. "Then you make a place for it. And you leave it there."

THE NEXT DAY it was Chitrita Bhandari's turn to visit. First two men in suits and earpieces appeared in Nick's room over the protests of a nurse, and then Nick heard her heels clicking down the tiled hallway. She barged into the room in a swirl of golden orange sari and dark hair and indignation. "You have royally fucked the pooch, do you know that?" she said.

"Why do all your insults have to do with fucking?"

"I want to make sure you understand them." Bhandari looked down at him in his hospital bed. "You look like shit."

"You sound disappointed."

"I sound annoyed. Nine people dead, one sheriff's deputy seriously wounded, and every law enforcement agency in western North Carolina asking what a heavily armed team of mercenaries wants with a retired professor of medieval studies."

"They didn't ask about the Green Berets? Who came late, by the way."

She snorted. "And the Highlands police chief wanted to get up my ass about the flash drive you left with him. I practically had to get the Supreme Court to demand he turn it over."

"You probably had to make a single phone call." Nick shifted in his bed, wincing. Gunshots to the chest and abdomen were no joke. "You said nine dead?"

"Your brother and his wife, your niece's boyfriend, a local store owner, and five mercenaries, including the one your deputy friend shot in the library."

"Should be six."

"What six?"

"Dead mercs."

"You mean the one you hit over the head with a fire extinguisher? He's alive and in custody. Singing like a parakeet or a blue jay or whatever the fuck kind of bird sings."

"You mean canary. What about the one I left in the woods? Young kid. I hit him with a tire iron."

Bhandari stared at him. "They found the tire iron. And your phone. But there was no mercenary left in the woods."

Nick stared up at the ceiling, then shook his head. One loose end to worry about later. "So what's wrong with the Ghawar oil field? That's what's on the flash drive, isn't it?"

Bhandari looked at the two men in suits and jerked her head in the direction of the hallway. Both men left the room, closing the door behind them. Bhandari took a step closer to Nick and lowered her voice. "Saudi Aramco depends on the Ghawar oil field, which means the Kingdom of Saudi Arabia depends on the Ghawar oil field. And Ghawar has the largest conventional reservoir of oil in the world."

"According to the Saudis."

Bhandari lifted an eyebrow. "Who have been very secretive about any information having to do with their oil production. Until a couple of years ago when they released a bond prospectus describing their production capacity, among other things. It confirmed what the Saudis have been saying forever—Ghawar can pump out oil for the next three and a half decades."

"I don't—"

"Unless someone lied," Bhandari said.

The statement hung overhead like smoke.

"So the prospectus was false?" Nick asked.

"I didn't say that," Bhandari said. "I said Ghawar is exactly what the Saudis have been saying all along, *unless* someone lied. And just the suggestion of that could mean billions in stock market losses and more volatility in the Saudi kingdom and in the region in general." She brushed lint off the sleeve of her sari. "There are Saudi technocrats who would like that to happen. They want the kingdom to change, to become more democratic. Reforms aren't enough for them, so they want to burn it all down. They would make Iraq look like fucking

Disneyland. Your brother had a reputation as a private contractor willing to take risks. Someone sent him information about Ghawar on a flash drive. They paid him half a million dollars to get it to the US government."

Nick shook his head. "And instead Jay tried to sell it to the highest bidder."

Bhandari said nothing.

Nick licked his lips. He was so damn thirsty. "Have you been able to get the info off the flash drive yet?"

"We're working on it."

"It's going to have something to do with Halliwell Energy and production levels at Ghawar."

"What makes you say that?"

"Because I'm good at figuring shit out, Rita. Halliwell's got a billion-dollar contract with the Saudis. If anything on that flash drive could upset that, somebody at Halliwell would get mighty upset."

"Why not the Saudis?"

Nick shook his head. "The Saudis would have just outbid everyone to get the flash drive back. Then my brother would have met with an unfortunate accident. My guess is some Halliwell executive went rogue, panicking about the thought of all those billions vanishing overnight. Look at how the mercs were paid. I want to know—"

"You want to know fuck all," Bhandari said. "You're out of it now. Stay that way. Heal. Go relax on a beach. Spend some time with your niece."

Nick slowly grinned. "I'm right, aren't I? You already know."

Bhandari scowled. "If you ask me a single thing about a certain deputy director of operations at Halliwell being taken in for questioning by the FBI, I'll say 'no comment' and think even more poorly of you than I do right now."

Nick held the grin for a few more moments, and then it slid off his face. "Doesn't matter," he said flatly. "Doesn't help Jay any."

Bhandari's fierce scowl relaxed. "I'm sorry about your brother," she said. "The best way to honor him is to take care of his daughter." She nodded once, then turned for the door.

"Rita?" Nick said.

She paused and looked back over her shoulder.

"Do you have kids?" Nick asked.

Bhandari scowled again. "Two," she said. "A son and a daughter."

Nick struggled to formulate his question. Finally he said, "How do you raise a teenage girl?"

Bhandari's laughter followed her out the door and down the hall.

NOW, SITTING ON the beach with his arm around Annalise, Nick took in a lungful of air. He smelled the salt air, the deeper organic tang of dead fish, the coconut scent of suntan lotion. He took another breath. It smelled different from the mountains or the desert. The clouds on the horizon were beginning to blush, the sky shifting to blue.

Beneath his arm, Annalise stirred. "Can I ask you something about Aunt Ellie?" she said.

Nick kept his eyes on the waves rolling in. "Sure," he said.

"Was she okay with you being a spy?"

Nick blinked. He hadn't expected that question. "Not at first," he said.

Annalise glanced up at him. "What did she do when she found out?"

Looking out over the waves at the coming dawn, Nick told her about that early morning in Cairo, when Ellie had caught him sneaking home at dawn. Annalise didn't interrupt to ask questions. When he finished telling the story, Annalise thought about it for a few moments.

"So she stayed," she said.

Nick nodded. "She stayed."

"She really loved you."

The words sliced cleanly through Nick's heart. For a moment he couldn't speak. "Yes," he finally managed. "She really loved me."

Under his arm, Annalise sighed. "Good," she said, and then fell silent.

The clouds on the horizon now looked like they had been forged out of gold. A breeze blew off the sea, causing Nick's eyes to water. Or maybe they were actual tears. But they weren't from grief, not exactly. More from gratitude for having been loved by a woman he had not deserved. Perhaps all love was like that, an astonishment at one's extraordinary fortune in finding someone who, despite all your failures, loved you anyway.

A month ago, such thoughts might have led him to throw himself off the top of Whiteside Mountain. Now he was sitting on a beach with his newfound niece and merely weeping. He was getting better.

You are, aren't you? Ellie said.

Uh-huh, he said.

Don't get shot again.

Not planning on it.

He could almost feel Ellie pause, sense her slow grin. *We finally have our kid*, she said.

Beneath his arm, Annalise shifted to get more comfortable, her head against his chest. He left his arm around her shoulders, not yet ready to let go.

A cloud of gulls wheeled overhead, one of them giving a sharp cry, and with that the earth turned and the sunlight rolled over the ocean, bright and almost painfully beautiful, the start of a new day.

ACKNOWLEDGMENTS

THANKS TO MY AGENT, PETER STEINBERG AT FLETCHER & COMPANY, for his advice and encouragement.

Thanks to my editor, Jenny Chen, for making me a better writer. Thanks also to Madeline Rathle, Melissa Rechter, Rachel Keith, and the rest of the great team at Crooked Lane Books.

Thanks to Henry and Dorothy Conkle for being my grandparents, and for letting me work summers in the real Carolina Mountain Shop.

Thanks to my mother, Nancy Swann, for answering my random questions about Cashiers, Highlands, Whiteside Mountain, and the surrounding area. Love you, Mom.

Thanks to the Hudson Library in Highlands, North Carolina, for supporting me and other authors. I took a few liberties with the layout of the library for dramatic purposes.

Thanks to Holy Innocents' Episcopal School for continuing to support my writing habit.

Thanks to my neighbor Mark, retired U.S. Marine, for answering my questions about the Marines and mercenaries.

Thanks to Brian Panowich for his friendship and unflagging support, and for being a great audience when I shared the idea for this book over dinner at the Dallas Bouchercon in 2019.

Thanks to my readers for making it possible for me to keep writing books.

And as always, thanks to my wife, Kathy Ferrell-Swann, for helping to make my dreams come true. I love you.